MOTHER OF PEARL

KELLIE COATES GILBERT

Mother of Pearl

This book is dedicated to my husband, Allen, who provided the wings for me to fly toward my dream.

ISBN-978-0-9985238-7-3

Published by Amnos Media Group
www.kelliecoatesgilbert.com

Cover design by the Killion Group

The persons and events portrayed in this work of fiction are the creations of the author, and any resemblance to persons living or dead is purely coincidental. Library of Congress Cataloging-in-Publication Data
[TO COME]
Printed in the United States of America

1 2 3 4 5 6 7 8 9 10 / 17 16 15 14 13 12

1

"Where's Graeber?"

I freeze. Guess it was only a matter of time before Coach Warren came gunning for me. I toss my coffee in the sink, listening while Bill Miller, the pudgy biology teacher who always smells of formaldehyde, rats me out. "Barrie? I just saw her heading for the teachers' lounge."

"Graeber," the coach barks as he storms through the doorway. "What's the deal with you pulling Dennis Cutler off the team right before our big game?"

Okay, here goes. I muster everything I've been taught about effective communication and look Coach Warren directly in those deep blue eyes. No way is he going to bully me. "I did not pull the Cutler boy. I simply asked Sharon to enforce what we all agreed upon last spring. His academic improvement plan requires him to attend the special tutoring sessions I put in place. As it stands now, he's not going to pass his core subjects and graduate. I already went to bat for him once, based on a promise he'd work hard this year."

Coach Warren shakes his head. "But—"

"But nothing. Sleeping through his classes and skipping

tutoring sessions is not acceptable. I'm sorry, I really am. But we both know if Dennis is not on target to graduate, he's ineligible to play. Simple as that."

When I tell people I'm a school guidance counselor, they think it means I spend hours helping students fill out college application and FAFSA forms. And that's true. But my job is so much more. I'm here to advocate for my students, to look out for their best interests. Sometimes that means protecting them from a coach who has yet to understand that the one with the most trophies can still wind up a loser.

Don't get me wrong. I have nothing against a good football game. But why must education always take a back seat to sports? Truth is, in this town football reigns. Academics are often abandoned and left to drift to shore while the athletic program leans back, clipping along like a Kennedy on a sailboat.

Warren pulls his arms tighter across the chest of a jacket that reads *Sawtooth High Cougars.* "So, let me get this straight. You're going to let down a whole team, the entire town of Falcon, Idaho for that matter . . . what, so you can make a point?"

I huff. "That is the point. When Dennis failed to do his part and study, he's the one who let his team down." I feel myself gaining emotional steam. "And what does it say if we let Dennis flunk out? Will that prepare him for his future?" Satisfied I'd made my point, I smugly climb down from my imaginary soapbox.

Coach Warren unfolds his arms and leans forward. With a lowered voice he speaks, pausing between each word for emphasis. "I don't give a rat's tail about how nice little Dennis's future is. That's your job. Mine is to win football games."

Before I can respond, several teachers enter the lounge. Coach Warren instantly plants a smile on his face and works the room like a politician, assuring everyone that yes indeed, the Cougars will put the Vikings back on the bus after the game this afternoon with their heads hanging low. He glances back at me. Those striking blue eyes narrow to drive his point home.

"Count on it," he says.

NOBODY WANTS TO ADMIT THIS, but often adults don't understand how hard life is for teenagers these days. In this pressure-cooker life, young people need someone they can trust, someone who will encourage them to work hard so they can accomplish their dreams.

That's where I come in.

I head for my counseling office, a tight little room lined with bookshelves filled with college catalogs and FAFSA publications. Sliding into the chair behind my badly marred walnut desk, I pull a scheduling book from the drawer and assess what the rest of my morning holds.

A knock at the door alerts me to my first appointment—Cade Walton, a kid whose single mom is working two jobs so he can attend college next fall. I motion him in and have him take a seat. Then, lifting his file from the stack on my desk, I begin my work for the day.

By four o'clock, I've finished my student interviews and move to grab my coat and gloves. Today is the only afternoon football game of the season and I'm anxious to join the cheering crowd I hear outside my window.

Moving quickly I juggle my purse and coat while trying to lock my office door.

"Mrs. Graeber?"

I turn to find Emily Jorgensen, a rather high-strung girl who comes from a family of known achievers.

"Hey, Emily. What can I do for you?"

Emily bursts into tears.

I muffle a sigh, unlock my door and invite her into my office. I hand the distraught girl a tissue and she plops down in the chair at the side of my desk, apparently oblivious to the fact nearly every other student from Sawtooth High School is currently out at the football field.

My eyes glance at the wall clock. Pearl's dance team is performing during halftime, and I don't want to miss seeing my daughter execute the moves she's been practicing all week.

"Okay, sweetie, why the tears?"

"It's just that Mr. Baxter won't relent on my grade in English comp, and if I don't score at least a ninety-seven, my chance to get accepted to Harvard will be ruined."

I lean closer, slightly amused at her melodrama but silently wishing all students I counsel cared this much about their academic careers. "Emily, I know you worry." I look her directly in the eye to make sure she feels validated. "But, you are an excellent student. A single grade on one paper this early in your senior year won't impact your university plans. I promise. Besides, a ninety-five is still impressive."

The plain looking girl, who has yet to come out of her shell and even wear makeup, looks unconvinced.

After sneaking another look at the clock, I opt for a different approach. "But tell you what, I'll talk to Mr. Baxter and see what extra credit opportunities he'll be offering this semester." Mindful of the no touching rule imposed on educators these days, I still stand and give her a brief hug. "In the meantime, focus on doing your best. That's really all you can do."

The teary-eyed girl nods and moves for the door. "Thanks, Mrs. Graeber. I really appreciate it." She gives me a little wave as she leaves.

After cramming her file in my drawer, I gather my things for a second time and head out to the big game.

Stepping into crisp fall air, I hurry past lines of parked cars toward the sound of band drums and referee whistles. Slowing, I flash my staff badge at the tired looking security guard at the gate before continuing toward the stands. My eyes pan the crowd until I finally locate Joe and Connie Anderson and my son, Aaron. I wave and make my way up the bleachers.

"Where've you been?" Connie scoots over, making room for me.

I roll my eyes. "Don't ask."

Connie's expression turns sympathetic. "Well, we're about to finish second quarter."

My son greets me without pulling his gaze from the field. "Hey, Mom."

"Hi, sweetheart." Glancing around to see if I can spot Pearl, I move to give my son a hug before I remember my eleven-year-old hates any public display of affection.

I turn to Connie's husband. "Hey there, Joe."

Joe Anderson is one of Steve's closest buddies. They go way back, football teammates from when they attended Sawtooth years ago.

No one loves football more than Joe. Despite his respected position on the school board, he's been known to yell like a banshee when the Cougars' score falls behind. I dip my hand in his container of popcorn, painfully aware I should never have skipped lunch today. "Where's Steve?"

Joe nervously scans the field. "No sign of him yet."

"I'm not surprised," I eye his popcorn but decide it'd be rude to grab another handful. Instead, I check my phone for messages. "My husband is always running late these days. If he doesn't quit burning the candle at both ends, he's going to wind up with a heart attack before he turns forty."

The scoreboard at the south end of the field flashes twenty-one to twenty. Too close for comfort. Barely in our favor. Joe tells me we'd run the ball well so far, but the Vikings' place kicker had been hot. Now, with just a minute left in the second quarter, they'd punched up the grass into field goal range. Lowering my gaze to the forty-yard line, I breeze past the action to the sidelines.

"Oh look, there's Pearl." Beaming, I pull up my cell phone and shoot a photo. I watch as she waves at number thirty-two as he jogs back to the sidelines from the line of scrimmage.

Pearl has been going out with Craig Ellison, the team's quarterback, for a little over a year. Together, they look like the Ken and Barbie dolls I played with growing up. At times, I worry they might be getting a bit too close. She has a whole lifetime ahead of her, and I certainly don't want her duplicating my mistakes.

I'd worry a lot more if she wasn't with a boy like Craig. He's a polite kid from a good family. When Pearl was in junior high, I co-chaired a school carnival with his mom.

Back at the field's edge, Coach Warren and his assistant huddle with the defense, barking out orders. With a slap on the back of number forty-two, he launches the players out on the field.

"C'mon! Hold the line!" Aaron screams.

I join the rest of the crowd already on their feet when the Vikings' quarterback takes the snap and drops into the pocket. He scans for an open receiver as he pats the ball once. Twice. Then he whips the ball past his ear and a perfect spiral soars forty yards into the straining hands of the Vikings' tight end. He cradles the ball tight and sprints for the goal line.

"STOP HIM!" the diminutive woman in front of us belches out, causing more than a few of us to look at her in surprise.

The crowd across the field explodes into cheers. I snap my head back to the action just in time to watch the Viking receiver cross the goal line and slam the ball on the end zone grass. A routine extra point a minute later cements their lead at halftime.

Joe curses and I reach for my phone, thinking I'll text Steve to see if he's going to make it in time for Pearl's halftime show.

"Mom, can I have some money for popcorn?" Aaron holds his hand outstretched.

"What happened to the twenty I gave you yesterday?"

He explains in detail, reminding me buying his vintage Joe Namath card cleaned him out. I hand him my wallet. "Put it back in my purse. And only take a twenty."

He follows my directions, then starts down the bleachers. "And get me some," I add.

Connie gives me a nudge. "Barrie, the dance team's taking the field. Hey, there's Pearl." She points.

I let my cell phone drop back into my purse and crane my neck around the tall guy in front of me. Nobody gets between me and the half-time show.

My daughter takes her place in the formation with the rest of the group at the edge of the field. She's been practicing for this routine every night this week, working hard to master the complicated moves.

On the field, girls in gold-colored glittery tops and short black skirts march in precision formations to the Star Wars theme song. My daughter snaps her head left in unison with twenty other girls from her spot, third from the end.

When the dance team finishes their final number, uniformed band members follow the girls off the field, playing the last strains of a snappy march. I am applauding with the rest of the crowd, when Steve juggles his way past the Andersons and moves in next to me on the bleachers. "Sorry I'm late." He kisses my cheek. "What'd I miss?"

Joe shakes his head. "The Vikings just crept ahead. I hate to say this, but I hope Coach cleans clock at halftime. That Baker kid especially."

"Honey—" Connie looks at her husband with disbelief.

"How can you say that? You know Vince Baker's mother is battling cancer. Cut the poor kid some slack."

Brushing his hand across his shaved head, Joe continues looking out at the field. "Well, another wrong move and we won't even have a chance at playoffs."

Connie rolls her eyes, leans over and says in a low voice, "I swear, he'd sell his grandmother to win a football game." Steve's eyes lock with mine and we share a smile.

Aaron climbs back up in the stands, his hands juggling a hotdog, two bags of popcorn and cola. "Hey, Dad." He hands one of the popcorns to me.

"Hi, Scoot." Steve ruffles our son's hair. A flicker of guilt crosses my husband's face as he leans over to me. "So, did I miss Pearl's halftime routine?"

"Afraid so, honey." I smile and offer him some popcorn. "But don't worry, she'll understand. I almost missed her routine myself because of a meeting with a student."

"I thought you didn't have any afternoon appointments?"

I lean toward him and lower my voice. "A student showed up in tears."

Steve nods. "Ahh."

I stretch my hand out toward Aaron. "Hey, where's my change?"

My son grins and juggles his drink while he reaches in his back pocket. I relent and tell him he can keep the money if he'll help me rake the leaves tomorrow His face brightens. "Sure!"

Minutes later the players take the field and the third quarter begins.

A sense of palpable excitement throbs in the bleachers as the Vikings kick off to the Cougars' line of receivers. I find myself holding my breath as the Cutler kid lines himself up with the soaring ball. Wait—?

I shade my eyes for a better look. "Steve, is that Dennis Cutler out there?"

"Yeah, why?"

A wave of frustration hits me like a tsunami. Looks like Mr. GQ Coach got his way after all. No telling what strings he'd pulled this time.

I shake my head. "Long story." Miffed, I tell myself that Michael Warren may have won for now, but I'll make sure this issue is revisited.

On the field, Dennis catches the ball and races down the field, advancing thirty yards before a Viking slips past one of our blockers and tackles him to the ground. Joe and Steve high-five each other. The ref blows his whistle and Pearl's boyfriend, Craig, jogs out to the field and gathers the team in a huddle. Seconds later, they break and move to the line of scrimmage.

My attention diverts to our daughter, gathered with her friends on the edge of the field. Her laughter fills my heart with joy.

It's true. A mother loves all her children the same. But I have to admit I feel especially connected to my firstborn. Maybe because for the first four years of her life, it was just the two of us.

Steve leans over and whispers in my ear—"Where're you at?"—which is his way of telling me he notices I've been deep in thought and not plugged in to the game. I smile and weave my fingers in his, enjoying the feel of his calloused palms against my own.

Just before the game ends, our receiver sprints into the end zone. The extra point a minute later hands us our victory.

Joe lets out a whoop followed by a rather colorful expletive. Connie slaps his arm. "Watch it," she nods toward Aaron. "We have young ears nearby."

"That Craig sure has an arm," Steve says, his face beaming as if Pearl's boyfriend were his own son. And he might as well be, for the amount of time he spends in our home.

After a few parents in the stands mutter, "*great game*," and "*knew Coach Warren would pull off another one*," I gather my things and trundle down the bleachers with the Andersons and Steve. Aaron trails close behind.

We make our way out to the parking lot before Joe turns to Steve. "The Kiwanis are holding a reception for the coach Tuesday night. You guys going?" Holding my breath, I wait for Steve's reply.

"Naw, can't. Got a meeting with my new business partner and it'll likely run into the evening."

At least I've been spared *that* misery. The last thing I want to do is join a mob of Coach Warren worshipers.

We wave our goodbyes to the Andersons, agreeing to try to get together for dinner soon, when Pearl rushes up, breathless. "Hey, Mom. Craig isn't going to be able to take me home. Something about a team meeting with the Coach. He said he'd pick me up later, so can I catch a ride with you?" Without waiting for a reply, she turns to Steve, looping her arm in his. "So Dad, what did you think of my routine?"

Coming to Steve's rescue, I jump into the conversation. "We're both very proud of how you did, sweetie." Pearl grins and says she'll gather her things and meet me at the car.

"I owe you one," Steve tells me as soon as Aaron is several steps ahead and out of earshot.

"Only one?" I tease. "Oh, and you'll need to pick up chicken on the way home because I don't have anything thawed."

"Again?" A grin crosses his face and his hand playfully slaps my behind. Laughing, he hurries to catch up with Aaron. He places his arm around our son's shoulder and I listen to their fading discussion about which team the Cougs will be matched up with in the playoffs.

Pearl joins me at the car a few minutes later. She's changed out of her dance uniform into a cute pair of jeans and a light yellow sweater that sets off her blue eyes. No longer pulled back in a ponytail, her lengthy blonde curls fall over her shoulders. I look at her and wonder if she has any idea how beautiful she is.

She smiles. "What are you looking at, Mom?"

"You, sweetheart."

She waves me off. "What did you think of the routine?"

Before I can respond, she goes on to tell me she thinks she missed a step, in the third set of ten count, but hopes no one noticed. I assure her she looked perfect out there.

"Dad didn't get there in time, did he?"

The question catches me a bit off guard. "Well, no honey. But he wanted to. Traffic just held him up." I watch her face in order to gauge her thoughts, something that is progressively more difficult as she gets older.

She shrugs and smiles. "Oh, I know. I'm not making a big deal of it, I just kinda need you to understand you don't have to treat me like I'm gonna break over something like that."

I open my mouth to interrupt, but she goes on.

"Mom, I think I found the perfect shoes to match the dress we bought for homecoming."

"Oh? How much?"

"I know the dress cost a lot, but these shoes are perfect. So, I've already arranged to babysit for Mrs. Emberly next weekend.

I nod, wondering when my daughter became so responsible. I'm tempted to give myself a pat on the back, but raising kids is a day-to-day task. One I wouldn't trade for the world.

We chat while I drive. She tells me about her trig class and about the upcoming play she might try out for in drama, about the low-lights she'd like to have in her hair and says she's out of nail polish remover, could I pick her up some tomorrow.

"Mom, Callie heard that Craig and I have a good chance of being voted King and Queen at the Homecoming Dance."

"Honey, that's wonderful." I smile and check the rearview mirror, before changing lanes.

Pearl grabs a tissue from the compartment on the dash and spits her gum into it, wadding the Kleenex into a tight ball. "And the decorations are really going to be over the top. Our committee agreed nothing cutesy this year. So, Coach suggested we go with a casino theme."

"The coach? What's he doing advising the Homecoming Dance committee?"

"He offered. Besides, he has the *best* ideas. Way better than Mrs. Franklin's. Last year she pushed for that awful hoedown theme. No one wants to sit on a bale of straw while dressed in a gown."

I frown. "But, I'm not sure a Vegas-like theme is appropriate for—"

Suddenly, her head darts to the window. "Mom, slow down."

"What?"

"Turn around, quick." "Pearl—"

"Mom, please—" she pleads. "Just turn around. Hurry."

I grip the wheel and check my mirrors. Finding the way clear, I whip my Acura around then glance back in Pearl's direction. "What's going on?"

She points at a pickup parked near the back of the Texas Roadhouse restaurant. "There."

I slow the car and my eyes follow where she points to a guy letting a girl out of his truck. *Craig's* truck. He bends and kisses —Callie.

My eyes dart back to Pearl. She sees as well. With tears pooling, she barks, "Go! Don't let them see us."

I nod and quickly pull away. "Oh, honey . . ."

She holds her hand up. "Mom, stop. Don't say anything. Not now."

I watch helplessly while my daughter's face crumbles and tears roll down her cheeks. I take a frail breath, wanting desperately to find the right words.

When she was little and fell off her bike, I knew how to bandage a scraped knee. And as her heart filled with disappointment in junior high when the principal awarded the coveted science fair prize to someone else, I knew how to salve her hurt feelings. But this time, a still voice deep inside my head warns me to do as she asked and remain quiet. At least for now.

Moms are supposed to run interference for their children, protect them from the hard things in life. Perhaps for the first time, I understand mothers can't fix all things.

I press my foot on the accelerator and focus on the road ahead, silently driving my daughter and her broken heart home.

2

As soon as we arrive at our house, Pearl races inside and up the stairs without saying a word.

Steve and Aaron wander out from the kitchen, Steve wiping his hands with a towel. “Was that Pearl?”

Before I can answer, a door slams and we both glance up in the direction of the sound. My husband frowns. “What’s going on?”

“Oh, Steve,” I toss my purse on the hall table. “It was awful.” I slump onto our sofa and fill him in on the details of what we’d seen.

“Are you sure it was Craig and Callie?” he asks. I nod. “There’s no mistake.”

Aaron leans against the stair railing, his eyes wide. “Boy, sounds like trouble.”

Steve flings the towel over his shoulder. “Scoot, why don’t you give me and your mother a few minutes.”

Aaron scowls and slaps the side of his leg. “Man, I miss all the good stuff.” He turns and trudges through the kitchen and for the garage, our yellow lab trailing close behind. “C’mon Omelette. Let’s get you some dinner.”

I can tell the news has caught Steve off guard. He moves to the fireplace. "This is crazy."

I kick off my shoes and pull my feet up onto the cushions. "I know. Steve, I don't understand. That boy has spent more time around our dinner table lately than even you have. How could he do that to her? And just before Homecoming."

Steve nods in agreement. "Aaron's going to take this almost as hard. He adores Craig."

"His success out on the football field simply went to his head, that's all." I punch a pillow and shove it behind my back. "And he doesn't even have the decency to break it off with Pearl before he takes up with—" I groan. "Oh, Steve. And it had to be Callie. I mean, really."

Steve's face darkens. "Yeah, pretty cheap on both their parts."

I scramble from the couch. "Perhaps I'd better get up there and check on her."

"Don't push, Barrie. She might need some space."

The comment rubs. "Steve, I know that. I'm her mother." Upstairs, I make my way to her bedroom. "Pearl?" I gently slide the door open. She's sitting on her bed with crossed legs.

My daughter acknowledges my presence by closing her eyes and rocking gently to the music filtering from her iPad. I join her on the bed and place my hand on her knee, waiting.

After a few moments, she relents and pulls the ear buds from her ears. "What?"

Despite her brisk tone, I notice a slight tremble in her chin. "Oh, honey." I move to hug her, but she quickly pulls back. Maybe Steve's right. Perhaps it's still too early. "Pearl, honey. I'm here when you're ready to talk."

"I'm over it already, Mom. Those two aren't worth it."

I hear her words, but something in her eyes tells me there might be a tiny fault line running beneath the surface of her conviction. I've always been able to read Pearl by searching those beautiful blue eyes.

I remind her it's okay to feel pain when someone we're close to betrays our trust.

"I said—I'm over it." The words sound as brittle as the dried leaves in our back yard. She crams the ear buds back in place and her eyes grow dark as a tomb.

My breath catches, unaccustomed to this side of Pearl. I want to tell her she'll feel better tomorrow, but think better of it, knowing I can't make that promise. Instead, I lightly brush her cheek with my thumb, and decide to leave her alone. As much as I want to protect my daughter, I can't.

Sometimes life hurts.

BY SUNDAY AFTERNOON, I feel like something inside our family is slowly going bad, like a tomato left on the vine too long. We've all been in a foul mood throughout the weekend, and today is no different. I even snap at Steve on the way to Mother's for dinner.

"Do you need to have the radio so loud?" I lean toward the dash and lower the volume, creating enough drama for a Lifetime Movie on television.

Steve reaches across the seat and folds my hand in his, an unspoken signal he's had enough of my bad temper. I glance across the seat at him, allowing a weak smile that expresses my apology. People who've been married thirteen years don't always need words.

We head east about ten miles before making our way onto Mother's street. Harrison Boulevard is lined with stately homes nestled among lampposts and a median filled with pumpkins and colorful gourds accenting lush fall-colored mums. A sign at the entrance boasts the area is listed on the National

Register of Historic Places, a fact that fills my mother with pride.

Steve pulls up to the curb and cuts the engine. Aaron grabs his handheld game player and exits the car, following Steve and me through the wrought-iron gate and up the brick sidewalk to the steps leading to Mother's front door.

Before we reach the front portico, the door opens. "Where's Pearl?" Mother cranes her neck, looking out at the street.

I exchange glances with Steve. "Uh, she's not feeling well." Mother straightens the jacket on her favorite silk suit—the one she'd worn to Daddy's funeral two years ago, lets out a *hnmpf* sound and demands to know what's going on.

"Nothing is going on, Mother. She's simply a bit under the weather." I look to Steve for support. His mouth draws into a weak smile, but he offers nothing.

Aaron, however, pipes up like a news reporter. "Her boyfriend dumped her."

I throw my son a scowl.

Mother raises her brows, steps back and invites us inside, while I rush to explain. "It's nothing really. She just feels a little sad, so we let her stay at home today."

"All day?"

"She's seventeen, Mother." I shake my head, trying to pass off my growing frustration that instead of feeling concerned, my mother is jumping up on her judgment seat—the exact reason I elect to share as little as possible with her about so many things.

For example, I don't tell her that Pearl has not come out of her room in two days, not eaten, and that I laid awake last night, helplessly listening to her cry. I don't tell Mother no matter what I do or say, nothing seems to help my baby catch her breath on this one. And I certainly don't divulge the details of how she's been betrayed by two people she deeply cared about. People she trusted.

My mother tilts her perfectly coifed head, lifts her chin and warns we'd best get a handle on the situation. She looks pointedly at me. "You know the trouble that can develop for young girls when boys are involved."

No matter how much armor I build around my heart, I'm amazed how much it hurts when one of her little darts pokes through. Daddy, God rest his soul, served as a buffer when he was alive. Now that he's gone, I simply have to remember to brace myself in every conversation.

Perhaps lack of sleep is the real culprit, but I'm not in the mood for another reminder of how my own actions shamed the family. "Mother, please. Not today."

I might as well have slapped her, for the shock that crosses her face. Both Steve and Aaron look toward the door, as if calculating how quickly they can bolt if this conversation escalates further. Feeling immediate guilt, I break the awkward silence that follows with a quick apology, and mumble something about how good dinner smells.

Trailing my mother to the kitchen, I offer to help carry the salad plates to the table, again remarking on how good everything looks. Regardless, her countenance shifts and it's as if she were a downtown boutique with the doors locked and the shades drawn.

Finally, we take our places at the table, bow our heads and Mother blesses our food.

Fishing for small talk, I comment on her favorite topic—politics. She's known throughout her party as a major financial contributor. Consequently, her reputation provides a level of respect she relishes. "I see Jack Simpson has thrown his hat into the race for lieutenant governor."

She takes the bait. "He doesn't have a chance. No candidate from the eighteenth precinct has won a successful bid in the last thirty years," she says, her voice still tinged with a slightly curt tone.

Across the table, Steve weighs in. "Mmnnn. . . . I don't know about that. He might have a chance with all the liberals moving into Blaine County."

Mother, a staunch conservative, blasts the idea. "Well, we'll just see if the ranchers in the southern part of Idaho will tolerate his ideas on expanding the wolf introduction program. Cattlemen and sheep ranchers won't have any part of that."

The thought crosses my mind how much Pearl would love to be included in this conversation with my mother. Their shared love for politics and all things newsworthy form a bond I'd never been able to create with my mother.

My mind wanders to the comment Pearl made on our way home from Mother's last weekend. "Too bad Grams wasn't born a generation later, huh Mom? She'd have given Hillary a run for her money." Like Pearl, I find it easy to picture my mother on Capitol Hill, perhaps her missed destiny. With her family connections, Daddy could've been elected to a congressional seat, but as Mother often reminds us, sadly he'd settled for state auditor.

Mother gathers the empty salad dishes. "Steve, I hear you've found a business partner?" She turns for the kitchen. "Excuse me, will you? I'll be right back with our entrees."

I offer to help, but she waves me off. "No, stay put. Won't take me a minute." She glances at Aaron. "Sit up, dear."

He obliges, looking completely bored.

Frowning, I butter a roll. My third.

Mother enters the dining room with a large platter of roast beef garnished with parsnips and butternut squash. The entrée looks like a centerfold plucked right out of a Better Homes and Gardens magazine. She sets the dish proudly in the center of the table, nestled among candle votives placed so as to look scattered at random. Then Mother takes her seat, settling her napkin across her lap. "So, did I hear correctly?"

Steve clears his throat. "Well, sort of. Before we go forward with anything, I'll need to talk with an attorney and make sure we draw up papers and such."

Mother frowns at Aaron. "Honey, don't kick your chair." Then she turns to Steve and tells him she'll place a call to Walter, her own attorney. I suspect the generous offer is her way to keep tabs on what Steve is doing. Attorney client privilege doesn't exist in Elaine Taylor's rules of procedure.

My husband rubs at his chin, looking uncomfortable. I attempt a rescue by explaining we have our own counsel, the same guy who drew up Pearl's adoption papers when I married Steve.

She shrugs. "Have it your way. But, there is no one better than Walter Mack. You might know construction Steve, but business dealings can become intricate and I'm not sure you—"

She stops mid-sentence when I give her one of my looks.

The only thing worse for my mother than *being* controlling is being seen as controlling. She raises her chin and asks who wants pumpkin mousse.

I hate it when Mother makes my husband feel small. In the back of my mind, I know she believes I married beneath myself. But that's not true.

I let my mind wander back to nearly fourteen years ago. The meat department manager had just asked me how many slices of bacon I needed when the loudspeaker at my local Albertson's blared "Attention shoppers. We have a little girl at the front office who seems to have lost her mommy."

My eyes flashed to the empty space next to me and my heart lurched.

I raced for the front of the store, leaving my cart behind. At the service counter stood a man in jeans and a button-down shirt, his hand tucked securely around my little daughter's.

"This yours?" he asked, smiling.

Pearl teases she went looking for a new daddy that day. Truth is, Steve's grin sent a clear message as he stared at me holding a package of hickory-smoked bacon: I was the one he'd been hoping to find.

Mother serves dessert, reminding me she's used a low sugar recipe because she knows I worry about my weight.

I eat two helpings, out of spite.

When the meal is finally over, I help clear the table. We hug at the door, and I promise to call with updates about Pearl.

On the drive home, I only half listen to Steve and Aaron argue over which game they'll watch tonight. My attention is directed outside the car window, where it's that soft gray time when day has retired but night has yet to take over. Missing is the soft orange glow of the setting sun, instead masked by a layer of darkening clouds sandwiched between the hills to the north and the Owyhee mountains bordering to the south.

"Looks like thunder might be rolling in," I mumble, calling Steve and Aaron's attention to the blackening horizon, and the storm that lay just ahead.

3

A familiar blue Honda Civic is parked in front of our house.

Inside sits Callie Pratt.

"Looks like we've got company," Steve remarks, pulling into the driveway. He reaches for the button on the visor. The garage door grinds its way up, and Steve eases the car forward.

A slightly unsettled feeling gnaws at my gut as Aaron lets out a low whistle. "Looks like trouble."

I agree, but refrain from saying so. "Aaron honey, you go inside with your dad."

"Do you think Sis knows she's here?" He climbs out of the car.

"I—I don't know." I grab my purse. "I'd better go see what's up."

Steve nods before placing his hand on our son's shoulder. They head inside with Omelette close on their heels, tail wagging. "C'mon Scoot. I think we'll let Mom take care of this one."

Smiling weakly in return, I draw a deep breath and walk

toward Callie's car, wondering how many neighbors would see if I grab the girl and snatch her bald.

Callie opens her car door and steps out, swollen eyes and puffy red blotches on her face hard to miss. She hangs her head. "Hi, Mrs. Graeber." She sniffles and brushes her damp bangs off her forehead. Under different circumstances, I might laugh at the piece of red hair sticking straight up, giving her the appearance of a unicorn. But today, I feel like doing anything but laughing.

Instead, I try to conjure some level of compassion for the girl standing in front of me, especially given the close friendship she's had with my daughter since they were in second grade. The task is nearly impossible, and I choke out a single word. "Callie."

She lifts her head, eyes filled with tear-pooled despair. "I need to talk to Pearl. I've tried to call her. I've sent text messages and she won't respond. Now she won't answer the door." Callie rubs her hands against the front of her tight black jeans. "I've done something awful, and I need to talk to her," she pleads.

Taking a deep breath, my mind races for an appropriate response. I'm a high school guidance counselor, for goodness sakes. This shouldn't be so difficult.

The pain on my daughter's face when she discovered Callie and Craig kissing runs through my mind. The mother bear in me wants to slam this girl to the ground in a full pin, but my mental referee whistles and I refrain from revealing the full extent of my anger.

"Callie, what you did was a huge betrayal. Do you realize that?"

She nods, fresh tears rolling down her cheeks. Callie runs her arm across her face. "I—I only went for a ride with him to talk. He said he needed to sort some things out, about—about Pearl." She hiccoughs. "I did it for her."

Leaning forward, I look at her with astonishment. "For her?"

"Yes, I mean—at first that's what I meant to do. It's just, one thing led to another and pretty soon I realized Craig and Pearl would soon be over anyway. So, the way I figured, it wouldn't really make any difference in the long run." She looks up, as if to emphasize her point. "He said he was going to break it off with her . . ."

Rubbing my forehead, I try to take in how this girl could possibly justify her actions—even for a moment. "Callie, listen to me. True friends are very hard to find."

The young girl's shoulders slump, as the truth of my words sink in.

"Actions have consequences." Something inside me sparks a glimmer of compassion toward this girl who truly doesn't get it. "You trampled on something—someone you should have valued, but didn't."

"But I'm sorry."

I hesitate, wondering how to make Callie understand being sorry doesn't fix everything. I take a different tact. "Look, say you take a needle and poke out your eye. Afterward, you might be sorry—but unfortunately you'd still be blinded by your actions."

Callie flinches and tears pool in her eyes. "But what do I do now?" she asks, her voice quivering.

I step close and lay my hand at the place above her heart. "You learn from this. Before you dive in and do something that will hurt someone you care about, or anyone for that matter; stop and remember." I pause, letting my words sink in.

"You alone determine the kind of woman you want to grow into, Callie—and whether or not you aspire to be the kind of friend someone can trust." I let my hand drop, studying her face, hoping she'll understand what I'm trying to teach her.

"But what should I do about Pearl?"

I shrug, and divert my gaze to Pearl's darkened window. "I don't know." Shaking my head, I respond with the only words I know to say. "Maybe in time she'll feel differently, but I can't make that promise."

Callie thrusts her hands in the back pockets of her jeans and steps back. "Well, guess I better go. But, would you tell Pearl I stopped by? Tell her I want to talk, okay?"

I wait for her to get in her car, then I gently press the door closed hoping something I've said will penetrate and reshape her moral compass. Feeling chilled, I wrap my arms around myself and watch as she drives away, then I turn and head for the front door.

Inside, I toss my purse on the table in the foyer, kick off my shoes and move to the den where my men are watching Sunday Night Football.

Steve looks up, concern written on his face. "Hey Honey, how'd it go?"

I shrug. "I'm not certain she really understands the gravity of the situation, or the pain she's inflicted on Pearl." My hand reaches and releases my hair clip. I shake the long strands loose, ruffling through the curls with my fingers. "Speaking of our daughter, I think I'll go check on her."

Steve focuses his attention back on the television. "She's not up there."

I scowl. "What do you mean?"

Steve lowers the volume on the remote. "She's not in her room. I'm guessing she went out. I tried to text, but she doesn't answer."

"But she has school tomorrow." I glance out the window. How could we have missed her car not in the driveway? I grab for my phone. "Did she leave a note?"

Steve shakes his head. "I don't think there's anything to worry about, Barrie. At least she's out of her room for the first time since Friday. That's got to be good, right?"

"Yeah, I suppose," I admit, rubbing my neck. "I'm calling her anyway. I know she's hurting, but that's no excuse for not letting us know where she is."

When Pearl fails to answer, I leave a message. "Pearl, you need to call home and tell us where you are. You know the house rules."

I click my phone off, deciding not to get too anxious. Pearl's normally good about checking in, and she probably just forgot this time. What, with all that's been going on.

I move for the refrigerator. "Anybody else want something to drink?"

Steve holds up his can of diet soda and shakes his head. Turning back to the game, he raises the volume and nestles deep inside his leather recliner.

Aaron watches from the sofa. "Mom, Dad said I could stay up and finish watching the game. The Chargers are smearing the Packers, huh Dad?"

"Yeah, sure. But then it's right to bed."

I grab the stack of mail at the end of the counter and sort through the rather large pile of bills and advertisements until I reach the last item, a Coldwater Creek catalog. Opening the glossy cover, I pan photos of classy wardrobe items, all color coordinated with matching accessories, something a fashion-challenged woman can appreciate.

I'm in the middle of calculating how many times I'd have to feed my family beans next month to afford the teal sweater on page fifty-two, when the phone rings. It's Sharon Manicke, my school principal.

I've been a fan of Sharon Manicke for years. Early in my career, when budgets were extremely tight, she advocated for my hire. She runs a tight ship, and isn't afraid to battle school board members when necessary. And even though often her hands are tied, I believe she tries her best to be fair.

"I hope I didn't interrupt anything, especially on a Sunday

night, but I have good news," she says. "And I didn't want to wait until morning to tell you."

"Oh?"

"I just received an email announcing you're the recipient of the Idaho School Counselor Association's award."

My hand goes to my chest. "What? Who nominated me?"

"Yours truly. And Leigh Barton at Channel Seven wants to interview you after the ceremony. The awards banquet will be held in mid-November."

I look over at Steve, a smile beaming across my face and my heart beating wildly. Words can't begin to describe how excited I am. "I can't believe it, Sharon. How can I thank you? I mean, this news comes as a huge surprise."

She congratulates me again, and when the call concludes, I relay the news to Steve, my voice brimming with pride.

"That's wonderful, Barrie." He joins me in the kitchen and gives me a congratulatory hug.

Aaron chimes in. "Way to go, Mom."

I grab the catalog and rip page fifty-two from the binding. When Steve gives me a funny look, I hurry to explain. "I'll need a new outfit." With a huge grin, I add, "Especially if I'm going to be on television."

"Hey, somebody's here." Aaron bounds off the sofa. Headlights flash through the living room window and snap off as Aaron heads that way. Pulling back the curtains, he peers into the dark.

"Honey, that's not polite. They'll see you," I warn, trying not to be conspicuous as I glance out the window. In the muted outdoor lighting, I see a steel-gray Jeep parked in our driveway.

"Who is it?" Steve calls from the den.

Before I can respond, the doorbell rings and Aaron rushes to the door, opening it wide. I watch him take a step back at the same time I hear a deep voice say "Hey."

Aaron giggles.

Standing on the front porch is a young man with more piercings than a clove-studded ham.

Taking in his appearance, I step forward and place my hand on Aaron's shoulder. Unsure which is darker, the visitor's clothes or the long black shock of hair hanging over his left eye, I finally realize I'm being rude and speak up. "Can I help you?"

Looking a bit uncomfortable, he introduces himself. "I'm Troy. I . . . ah, I know Pearl from—"

"You're friends with Pearl?" I find it hard to believe my daughter and this boy are connected in any way. "I don't recognize you from school?" Staring at his nose-ring, I explain I'm the guidance counselor at Sawtooth.

Ham-man shifts his weight and crams his hands in his jean pockets. "Uh—just moved here." When I give him a puzzled look, he quickly adds, "Pearl is in the car."

My head jerks up. "Pearl? I peer around him at the vehicle in our driveway. "But where's her Toyota?"

"We left it over at—uh, at the party."

Alarmed, I tell Aaron to get his dad before I brush past this kid and make my way to the Jeep. I yank the passenger door open. "Pearl?"

"Mom—mee!" My daughter giggles, then lets out a belch that would put a trucker to shame. The smell of liquor immediately hits my nostrils.

"Barrie, what's up?" Steve comes up behind me, concern evident in his voice.

I step back, feeling like someone just pulled the concrete out from under my feet. Fearing Steve might not hear me over the beating of my heart, I choke out my reply.

"It's Pearl—she's drunk."

4

I carefully fold a pair of True Religion jeans and lay them over the end of my sleeping daughter's bed.

From the time she was an infant, I loved watching Pearl as she slept. When she was tiny, I cradled her for hours, gazing at the sweet expression on her little slumbering face wondering if she'd ever know how fiercely I cherished everything about her.

With a heavy heart, I reach out and lightly brush her cheek with the back of my hand, trying to ignore her skin is the color of uncooked chicken. I turn off her lamp to the sound of deep breathing, tinged with a ruffling light snore. Is she really sleeping, or simply passed out? Deciding it doesn't really matter, so long as she's safe, I move down the hall toward my own room.

Exhausted, I remove my own clothes and get ready for bed, then climb under the covers beside Steve. "You get Aaron in bed okay?"

"Um-hum," he says, his arm flung over his eyes. "Did you remember to let Omelette out?"

"Yup."

I reach over and turn off my bedside lamp, as if today had

been like any other day and I didn't have an intoxicated minor down the hall. I nestle down into the pillow and close my eyes, determined to settle the thoughts that whirl in my head, threatening to rob me of sleep.

Ham-Man. A gray Jeep. Pearl's bobbing head as Steve guided her to our front door. The scenes are dizzying, making me feel a little like Dorothy in the tornado. I can almost hear the music that played when the wicked witch flew by.

I sit up. "Steve?" He doesn't move, so I give him a slight poke. "Steve, you awake?"

He sighs. "Barrie, I know you're upset. But there's not much more we can do about all this tonight. I've got a big meeting tomorrow and I need some sleep. I'm just as concerned as you are about what Pearl did, but can we talk in the morning?" He pats me and rolls over.

Despite my desperate need to talk this thing out, I follow Steve's example and roll over, pulling the covers up tight against my chin. I close my eyes and will myself to sleep, knowing just like Dorothy Gale, my Pearl has dropped into a foreign land, and somehow I am going to have to come up with a way to get her home.

THE FOLLOWING MORNING, I meet Pearl in her bathroom with a bottle of Tylenol in my hand. From the pain-filled look etched in her eyes, I know my mother's instinct has been right on.

Or, perhaps the gesture really isn't intuition, but a faded memory of a particular morning following my own stupid decision to sneak into my dad's liquor cabinet. I don't remember which made me feel worse, the pounding in my head or Mother's voice drifting from behind their closed bedroom door where she warned my father she wasn't going to live with two drinkers.

I can still hear his reply. "Now, Elaine—Barrie's a good girl. She was only experimenting."

My mother responded with silence. A silence that lasted the rest of my father's life, if I remember correctly.

I line up the child-proof cap with the little arrow on the bottle and pop the top open. Shaking a couple of white caplets into my hand, I offer them to her.

Pearl pulls her long blonde hair back into a knot, then scoops the pills from my palm. "Thanks, Mom." After dropping them in her mouth, she reaches for the cup on the counter as if it's her lifeline, and swallows the medication down.

Finally she raises her head and looks at me.

"Want to tell me what last night was all about?" I say, knowing the important thing is not to push too hard, but to open the door for her to talk with me.

"It's nothing," she replies, slamming that door shut.

I take a deep breath and work to ease it back open. "Honey, it's important we—"

Pearl shuts her eyes and shakes her head. "Mom, please . . . can't you just this once leave things alone?"

This time, the door shuts on my ego. "What do you mean? I'm your mother and—"

"Mother, back off *please!*"

"You listen to me, Pearl. I've watched you get hurt, then respond by staying in your room for days, never eating or showering." My voice escalates. "Then you take off without asking permission, or leaving a note. Some strange boy, who by the way looks like he just stepped from the depths of the dark place, shows up on our doorstep announcing he has you in his car—and there you are. *Drunk!*"

I straighten my shoulders, place one hand on the bathroom counter and lean forward, pointing my finger in her direction like a weapon. "I am most certainly not going to leave this one alone."

Immediately I realize I've broken the golden rule of communication by raising my voice and letting my emotions get the better of me. I take a deep breath, opting for a more reasoned approach. "Pearl, honey. I'm worried about you. Can't you see that?"

Guilt clouds the resignation in her eyes. "Look, Mom. I already know what I did was stupid. It'll never happen again."

Despite her immediate contrition, I have questions. I want to know how she knows Ham-Man—or Troy-whatever-his-name-really-is. And why was my daughter at a party where alcohol was involved? I know my Pearl. She's a responsible girl. None of this makes any sense.

A picture of my own mother, the drill sergeant, pops into my head and I refrain from shooting my long list of inquiries at her. Instead, I take a deep breath and swallow the inquisition poised on the tip of my tongue.

Pearl swipes her hand across her forehead. "Mom, can I stay home from school?" She gives me a pleading look.

I believe my daughter when she says she knows what she did was wrong. Still, I don't want to shield her from the consequences of her actions. I shake my head. "Sorry. Hangovers are no excuse to miss classes."

A look I've never seen from Pearl flashes across her features, a look much stronger than the times I've had to discipline her and she's been angry.

No, this is different. She looks as if she hates me, and the force of her rejection leaves me stunned.

Her expression tells me she knows I've caught her emotional grenade. She turns and marches down the hall to her room, slamming the door behind her without saying another word.

Mothering is not for cowards.

5

Some people define politics in terms of liberal or conservative viewpoints. Those people have never worked in the Sawtooth High School education system.

"Barrie, I understand your concerns. I do. But you know my hands are tied." Sharon Manicke leans back in her chair, fingers steepled. "I simply have to pick my battles. And the truth is, the team needs Dennis Cutler as we head into playoffs. Officially, he could still graduate. If he works hard."

"But this kid isn't taking his grades seriously. Perhaps if we give him a bit of a scare, he'd—"

"The whole town would have my hide if I consent to that. And I don't need to remind you donations from the Rotary Club renovated the library last year."

I release a heavy sigh. "I don't envy your job, Sharon. Truly." Lifting the caramel macchiato I'd picked up at Starbucks on my way in this morning, I drain the cup. On mornings like these, I wish they made their caffeinated drinks in an IV bag.

"Sorry I couldn't support you on this one."

I stand and hand her my empty cup. My principal tosses it in her trash. "Yeah. But, I had to try."

She smiles weakly. “I know.”

I make a beeline for the teacher’s lounge in desperate need of more coffee. With only fifteen minutes until the first bell, I have to bump and maneuver my way past banks of lockers, barely visible for the moving students.

“Hey, you two.” I tap the shoulder of a young guy tangled with his girlfriend. “Careful you don’t swallow each other’s tongues, huh?”

The students move apart, looking sheepish.

I step into the teacher’s lounge and greet the history teacher, a man with curly red hair who wears plain black reading glasses on the end of his nose and no less than three pens in his shirt pocket at all times. “Morning, Don.”

He looks up from where he’s tearing into a pink packet of sweetener. “Hey, Barrie.” He empties the powder into his cup. Taking a stirring stick from a basket next to the coffee pot, he swirls the dark liquid. “So, I hear congratulations are in order.”

Francis Webber and Sandy Martinusen look up from where they sit on the worn sofa against the wall. “Guess we have a celebrity amongst us,” Francis says with a wide smile.

Sandy stops writing in her notebook. “What an honor. Heard you’ll be on television. That Leigh Barton is such a nice anchor lady, don’t you think?”

Francis’ eyes grow wide. “Television? Are you nervous? What are you going to wear?”

A man’s voice interrupts. “Nothing to be nervous about.”

I whip my head around. Michael Warren slips past me and pulls two cups from the wall dispenser. The coach fills the first one and hands it to me, before filling his own.

“This your first appearance on the tube?” he asks, a hint of condescension in his voice.

Without waiting for my response, he sits at Don’s table and explains the key to working with the media is to look them in the eye and make sure you maintain control of the interview.

"Don't just answer the question," he says to what used to be my fan club on the sofa.

"Your objective must always be to communicate your key messages." He unzips his team jacket and turns in my direction. "Use the questions as an opportunity to make your points. In other words, answer the question, but then add one of your key messages or key issues outlined in your game plan."

When the self-appointed publicity director finally comes up for breath, I mutter thanks and make a point of looking at the wall clock to the right of the vending machine. "I'd better get going."

"Say—" Coach Warren eyes take on a glint. "—word has it there was a little party last night. A lot of drinking. And just so you know, I can assure you I've asked around and none of my players were involved."

A sly grin forms on his face. "However, I'm told there were other students out there whose actions might need some of those consequences you take a shine to."

WARM AUTUMN SUNSHINE and a blustery breeze fight to dominate the late afternoon, as I make my way across the school parking lot to my car, the coach's remark still ringing in my ears.

Some Mondays never end soon enough.

When my cell phone rings, it's Steve.

"You did what?" I open the car door and throw my briefcase in the passenger seat before climbing inside.

"We finalized the papers and closed the deal today at the bank," Steve answers. "A celebration is in order. So, I invited the Hohmans for dinner."

"Tonight?" I shake my head and sigh. "It's nearly four

o'clock now. What do you expect me to cook for company this late?"

"I'll help."

"That's not my point. You're lucky I'm even getting home on time tonight." I sit in my car, mentally planning how to murder my husband and where I will hide the body parts. "It's a week night. I've had a bad day, and we're still dealing with Pearl's situation. The kids have homework. The laundry's piled up." I mentally paw through our freezer. "I don't have anything to *feed* them."

"Okay. I get it. But I already invited them," Steve reasons. "Jackie offered to bring a lemon meringue pie."

"I'm sure she did." I jab my keys into the ignition, yank the car in gear, then back out.

I've heard all about Jackie Hohman. With my luck, she'll probably bake the pie herself—from scratch. Women like her actually use the kitchen appliances their husbands give them for Christmas.

"C'mon, Barrie. The kids and I will help."

Realizing I am fighting a losing battle, I concede. "Well, you're going to have to vacuum, upstairs and down. Start the dishwasher and sweep the kitchen floor. Oh, and make sure the kids pick up their stuff. Nothing will be out of place when I get home," I warn, not caring that I sound like a drill sergeant. "And Steve . . . ?"

"Yeah?"

"Wipe down the bathroom sinks. And clean the toilets." With that, I slap my cell phone shut, toss it in my purse, and stomp on the accelerator.

Now where is the nearest grocery store?

I LEAN over the pot of simmering spaghetti sauce and toss in chopped fresh basil and garlic cloves. Satisfied, I smugly toss six empty store-bought sauce jars into the trash, then gather up the bag and take it out to the garage to hide the evidence.

When I step back into the kitchen, Steve is leaning with his back against the counter, a sheepish grin on his face. "Need any more help?"

"No thanks. You've helped quite enough." In an effort to punctuate my statement, I march to the sink, pick up the wet dishcloth and wipe the counter with all the indignation I can muster.

Steve moves next to me and rubs my shoulders. "Still mad?"

"What do you think?" I stop wiping and lean into Steve's hands, feeling my conviction fade with each stroke of his thumbs.

A smile finally makes its way to my face and I turn to face my repentant husband. Steve never fights fair. I press my face against his chest and feel him kiss the top of my head.

Aaron bounds into the kitchen. Omelette slides in close behind. "What's for dinner?"

"Dog out." I point to the back yard. "I don't want her in here while we have company."

"But, Mom . . ."

I direct a pointed look at Steve, filled with a message even a blind man could plainly see.

"Let's go, buddy. Your mom's right. Omelette needs some air." Steve puts his hand on Aaron's shoulder and leads him to the back door.

Aaron glances back over his shoulder at his canine companion. "C'mon, girl."

I grab the sourdough bread off the counter and take it out of its wrapper. Once I finish slathering on the garlic butter spread, just the way Steve loves it, I wrap the loaf in foil and slide it into the warm oven. After a quick peek at the wall clock, I head for Pearl's room.

Upstairs, I knock lightly and open the door. "Sweetheart?"

Pearl is stretched out on her bed, poring over the latest fashion magazine. "Yeah?" she says without looking up.

"The Hohmans will be here soon."

Pearl slowly flips a page, then another.

"We're having spaghetti. With meatballs. C'mon, I could use your help."

"I already helped," she complains. "Dad made me clean the bathrooms. And, Mom—you've got to talk with Aaron about his aim. His bathroom is gross."

I scowl. "Oh, Pearl . . ."

"Well, it is."

I ponder momentarily whether to acknowledge I agree with her, when the doorbell rings.

"I'll get it," Aaron yells from downstairs.

I spin and glance at my reflection in Pearl's mirror. Why is it the furrows between my brows grow deeper by the week? No wonder some women poke poison into their wrinkles. I shake my head and follow Pearl down to greet our guests.

We all have insecurities. Often feelings of inadequacy piggyback on a cultural epidemic I fight nearly every day with the young girls I counsel. So the wave of emotional instability I experience when the stunning woman I spot at the bottom of the stairs leaves me a bit unsettled.

Steve takes a pie from Jackie Hohman's extended hands. And I am not talking just any pie. This thing is crowned with fluffy white meringue, each peak toasted to a perfect light caramel brown. Obviously homemade.

Jackie's shoulder-length blonde hair sweeps the shoulders of her deep sapphire blue silk top. Heels the exact same shade of blue peek from below her fashion jeans. The epitome of shabby chic—and as elegant as a well-cut jewel.

Next to her, I feel like a middle-aged matron in my denim and sensible loafers, a brown wren next to a peacock.

After brief introductions, I remove the pie from Steve's hands before he drools on it. "This looks wonderful, Jackie." I force a smile. "I'm so glad to finally meet you two. Steve talks about you all the time."

I stand holding the pie, waiting while Steve takes Paul's coat.

Paul looks exactly like my husband described him. Warm and friendly. His wide smile frames eyes the color of avocados, a startling contrast to his tan skin and dark receding hair.

He too is dressed like he stepped out of a magazine. He's not much older than Steve and it appears he may be going for a rugged look, except that his black cashmere sweater, which he wears with the sleeves pushed up, ruins the attempt. His boots are nice though. Some kind of exotic skin that looks expensive.

Paul extends his hand. "Barrie, both Jackie and I have been looking forward to meeting you as well."

When Steve introduces Pearl, she tells the Hohmans she knows their son.

Jackie cocks her head and smiles. "You know Troy?"

Troy? My mind flashes back to the black-haired kid who delivered Pearl to our door last night.

Ham-Man is the Hohman's son? I glance at Steve. The look on his face tells me he is as shocked as I am.

My mind races in the awkward silence that follows. Do they know about Pearl's indiscretion?

Jackie places her hand on Pearl's back as we all move into the living room together. "Troy couldn't make it tonight." Turning to me, she explains. "He's in a band at church."

I smile weakly and tell them I'm sorry their son couldn't join us, while trying to reconcile the image I saw standing on my doorstep with this new revelation. First appearances can be deceiving.

Pearl turns to Jackie. "By the way, I love your shoes."

"Oh?" Jackie lifts her foot, turning her heeled pump this way and that. "They're Via Spiga."

"Get out!" Pearl leans down for a better look. "They're gorgeous!"

"Bought them in Italy last spring," our beautiful guest adds.

I follow everyone to the dining room, glancing down at my own footwear. Aerosoles from J.C. Penneys.

Paul rubs his hands together, and peers over Steve's shoulder toward the kitchen. "Something sure smells good."

"We're having spaghetti and meatballs." Aaron announces.

"Oh?" Jackie follows me into the kitchen. "I wished I'd known we were doing Italian. I'd have made tiramisu."

I sigh. Of course she would have.

"I JUST DON'T UNDERSTAND where they get all their money. And if Paul Hohman is so well off, why would he risk going into business with you?" I lean over from where I sit on the edge of the bed to remove my socks.

Steve raises his brow. "Thanks a lot."

"Oh, I don't mean it that way. It's just I really don't understand. They take trips to Italy, drive cars we'll never be able to afford in a lifetime, and . . ."

"Maybe they have investments, Barrie. You don't know."
"But, Paul's your business partner," I argue. "Surely you've seen his balance sheet or something."

Steve pulls his shirt off and reaches for a hanger from the closet. "Barrie, what's gotten into you? I don't look at that stuff. It goes to the banker."

"I suppose you're right." I change my angle so I can face him. "But even if they have all the money in China, you'd better never invite them over again without clearing it with me first—and not a few hours before either."

"I know, honey." Steve tosses me a contrite smile. "I'm sorry. Really, I am." He winks and heads for his side of the bed.

That's the way we always argue. Steve does something, I get mad, and then he somehow charms me into forgiving him. Hoping this time I've made my point, I lean over and turn the lamp off, punch my pillow and get in beside Steve, my back to him.

I draw a deep breath, letting the air escape my nostrils slowly as I snuggle deep into our down comforter. I feel Steve's hand on my thigh and playfully slap it away.

"Nuh-uh. Don't even think about it."

6

Steve places his arm around my waist and we make our way from the covered parking garage into the lobby of the Grove Hotel.

Mother is already there with Aaron, waiting near a table filled with a floral arrangement that had to have cost hundreds of dollars.

We're greeted by one of the awards officials and immediately escorted into the grand ballroom and to a linen-draped table. In the center stands a large placard with my name.

Steve's tone is playful as he pulls out my chair. "Nervous?"

I don't bother to pull my attention from the crowded banquet room. "Maybe, just a little."

I'm not the only one being honored this evening. In addition to my award, there will be honorary citations bestowed upon recipients from organizations like the National Science Teachers' Association and the prestigious Governor's Teacher of the Year committee.

I remind Aaron to quit fidgeting, before glancing towards the door to see if I can catch any sight of Pearl.

As if reading my mind, Steve reaches over and clasps my hand in his own, giving me a reassuring smile. "She'll be here."

Mother, on the other hand, voices what I'm thinking. "Where could Pearl be? The program's scheduled to start any minute."

I look up as Michael Warren's wife appears at the door across from us. She stands several seconds, scanning the room. Finally, she moves to an open table and takes a seat, saving the chair next to hers by draping a napkin over the back.

My fingers nervously play with the gold hoop hanging from my right ear, as I pull my attention back to our table. "Do you suppose Pearl got held up in traffic?" Even as the words leave my mouth, I question how many cars could be out on the road on a snowy Friday night in November.

Earlier that evening, Pearl had stood at my bedroom door. "You look great, Mom." She plopped down on the bed and watched me slip my heels on. "Are you nervous?"

"Maybe a little," I'd told her. "Not about the presentation, but I've never been interviewed for television before."

"You'll do just fine," she assured me. "And I'll be there cheering you on."

I cupped her chin with my hand. "So, you'll meet us at the banquet then?"

"Of course, Mom. I'll see you there."

That assurance makes her absence tonight all the more glaring.

In the recesses of my mind, I hear my name called. I look up, realizing too late I hadn't been paying attention and everyone is staring at me.

Steve leans over and kisses my cheek and I take the stage, stopping to shake hands with Sharon Manicke.

After reading my prepared speech, I thank everyone and carry my plaque backstage where Leigh Barton is interviewing the recipients for the ten o'clock news broadcast.

When it's my turn to sit in the overstuffed chair next to my favorite television anchor, my stomach feels like it's filled with grasshoppers.

Leigh smiles at me. "So tell me, Barrie—what does winning this award mean to you tonight?"

I take a deep breath.

Surprised, I hear Coach Warren's advice ringing in my ears. *Use the questions as an opportunity to make your points.*

I lean forward slightly, remembering to speak slowly and clearly. Looking Leigh in the eyes, I smile and begin. "One of the elements of my profession I most enjoy is the fact school guidance counselors work with educators and community resources to provide early identification and intervention for potential dropouts and other students who may be considered at-risk through a comprehensive, developmental counseling program. I'm proud of what the American School Counselor Association stands for, and I'm delighted to receive this award this evening."

Leigh looks directly in the camera and a smile teases at the corners of her mouth. "Perhaps you can give me some counsel on how to motivate my own teenagers?"

I relax, feeling my confidence swell. "Well, it's true what they say, guiding teenagers is a little like herding rabbits . . ." I pause while she laughs. "But the key is communication. Kids aren't terribly impressed with what adults have to say until we're willing to first listen." My gaze is drawn to the woman sitting across from me. Her warm smile makes me feel at ease.

"The second most important thing is trust. Most young people will rise to the occasion when support is communicated. Knowing the door is always open will help them choose to do the right thing."

Leigh Barton praises my wise words and wraps up the segment. The camera man gives a signal with his arm and the bright light dims.

I follow the anchor's lead and stand, expressing my own gratitude for the time with her. We shake hands and before I can get up the nerve to ask for her autograph, she's already gone.

On the drive home, Aaron pummels me with questions. "What was it like, Mom? Were you scared?"

"A little. But truthfully, once I started talking, it wasn't so bad."

I lean against the headrest and close my eyes, suddenly exhausted. "Now I understand why Leigh Barton is so good at what she does. In some ways, I felt like I was talking with a friend. After a few minutes, I nearly forgot we were on television."

The satisfaction with my television debut is tempered by the fact Pearl never showed up. I reach in my bag to check my phone for messages. Seeing none, my finger presses her number again.

Suddenly, I feel the car turn. Aaron pipes up, "Hey, where we going?"

I lift my head. "Steve?"

He eases along the curb in front of Jackson's Drugstore on Main. It isn't until my husband turns the engine off that I notice why we've pulled over.

There in front of us is Pearl's silver Toyota . . . empty.

I GAZE out the kitchen window the following morning, as the sun breaks over the horizon slowly revealing bare trees that have forfeited their leaves to the changing seasons. A slight breeze catches a solitary crimson leaf hanging from a branch in our backyard, lifting it up in the air. The leaf jumps as if buffeted by a cold, strange wind, circling slowly above the garden where a light blanket of snow covers the withered remains of plants I nurtured through the summer.

"What's this I'm hearing from Aaron?"

I turn and watch as Mother sips her tea from the delicate teacup I use when she visits, a family heirloom. Mother believes fine china is a sign of good breeding.

From somewhere deep inside, I steel myself and invite the judgment I know is coming. "Please, Mother. Quit circling around and just say what is on your mind."

She puffs up like a Budgie bird, feathers ruffled. "You don't need to take that tone with me." She picks up a spoon, like the effort wears her out. Of course, a lot of work is involved in guarding the morals of our family.

"I'm sorry," I quickly apologize, knowing I'm a bit testy this morning.

"So, you believe her story?" Mother slowly stirs her tea, not caring to hide the scorn from her voice.

I lift my chin, slowly exhaling the breath I'd been holding. "Pearl has never given us a reason to mistrust what she says."

"Oh?" She raises her eyebrows. "What about that incident a while back?"

Bracing myself, I try to defend my daughter. "True, she made a mistake. But she didn't lie about it. If Pearl says she ran out of gas, I believe her."

"But then she fell asleep at a friend's house? Barrie, what sense does that make?"

I admit, it might be easy to question the validity of what she told us. At first, I didn't understand why Pearl didn't call or text us, but she says she forgot to charge her phone.

I can't very well call her a liar. Not until I learn otherwise.

Mother reminds me the politicians who garner the most success not only assess what's said, but listen carefully to the words left unspoken. "The same goes for good parenting," she says. "I understand you want to allow Pearl the benefit of the doubt, but don't give my granddaughter too much rope. Pearl has a bright future at stake. I don't want her harming that potential."

My mother's words feel like fingernails scratching a chalkboard, a grating reminder of the disappointment my own choices had heaped upon the family.

I want to remind her Pearl is no longer the six-year-old I caught hiding under the dining room table eating jelly beans I'd stashed in the pantry out of her reach.

My daughter is seventeen. Teenagers are supposed to begin withdrawing from their parents at this age. It's all part of the march of independence that will move her away from home and eventually into a life of her own—separate from me.

I admit I'm not ready. I find myself wishing I could grab the drumsticks and toss them aside, silencing the beat that is drawing her away. Especially lately.

Months have passed since the Craig and Callie incident. Mostly, Pearl is back to herself.

But sometimes she still seems preoccupied with the unexpected turn of events. In some ways she's like a kite that caught a downdraft and slammed to the ground. After careful prodding, she's ventured back into the sky but has yet to soar with the same abandon.

Which is why I fiercely choose to believe my daughter—despite the look in her eyes.

7

This afternoon's pre-game celebration marks the fact our town's end-of-the-season football frenzy has begun. Nearly everyone in town lines the sidewalks waiting for the cannon blast that will signal the start of the parade.

Bunting in our school colors drapes the awnings on Main street, creating a festive atmosphere.

Connie turns to me. "What time is the Rotary dinner tonight?"

My answer is drowned by a loud sweeping melody of trumpets, drums and clashing cymbals. I crane my neck, knowing the dance team typically follows the school band in the procession.

I feel a pull on my sweater. "Mom, can I video Pearl?"

Leaning down, I hand my son the camera. "Sure, baby," I yell over the noise. "Make sure to get some good shots of her, okay?"

"Hey, Barrie."

I turn in the direction of a voice straining to be heard over the pounding beat. Paul stands smiling.

Next to him is Jackie, looking like she could step inside the pages of Vogue magazine. Her shell pink sweater sets off the slight blush of her cheeks. She looks—healthy.

Even though a bit out of place in his khakis, button-down shirt and business loafers, Paul appears to be genuinely having a good time. "Boy, when Steve told me this was a football town, he wasn't kidding."

I like Paul. With each encounter, my fondness grows.

Rumors are going around he donates a small fortune each year to a well building program in Africa and flies there annually to check on the program's progress.

Jackie is nice as well. But something about her still makes me a tiny bit jealous.

I know how silly that sounds, given she's been nothing but kind to me. Maybe it's the way she shows up at my door with a meatloaf warm out of the oven, wrapped in aluminum foil and a bow. When I thank her—she says I'm more than welcome. She knows how hard I work and hopes we'll enjoy her recipe. Then she informs me the color of the ribbon is called "tangerine in paradise."

Who even knows things like that, other than my mother?

And, why does Jackie think it's necessary to deliver a meatloaf to my door? Never mind she interrupted my frantic search for the pizza coupons I'd cut out of Sunday's paper.

Remembering my manners, I make introductions.

Connie pulls her attention from the parade and exchanges hellos, but not before looking Paul and Jackie over.

I forget how difficult it is to be a newcomer to this town, despite the massive-sized baskets Falcon's welcome committee delivers.

"Oh, you're Steve's new business partner," Connie says. "Everybody in town is talking about the retail center you two are building on the corner of Eagle and Chinden. Say, any chance we can get a Brazilian steakhouse in there?" She turns to Jackie. “My sister, Tami Jae, says those restaurants are really popular down in Texas.”

“Here comes Pearl,” Aaron shouts. He points the camera in her direction.

I wave wildly, until a warm body seductively presses against mine.

Stunned, I turn to find my grinning husband.

“See, I got here on time.”

I give him a playful slap, and he brushes a light kiss on my cheek.

I try for a better look at Pearl, but a John Deere tractor pulling a tissue-decorated parade float blocks my view. On top, surrounded with girls in short skirts and waving pom-poms, sits Michael Warren—a man queen if I ever saw one, despite no crown could ever fit on that big head.

The crowd lining the street cheers as the coach waves and gives the thumbs up.

Aaron ducks past us and tries not to bump into bystanders as he videos the coach on the float slowly making it’s way down Main Street.

Steve gives me a squeeze. “Don’t worry. I’ll follow him.”

Connie clasps her hands, her face flushed. “I don’t know where this town would be without Coach Warren.”

She pulls her sunglasses from her face, then presses the stylish frames into a white case. “So, who’s meeting us at the Rotary Club’s appreciation dinner for the coach tonight?”

Paul and Jackie beg off, explaining they have another commitment.

When Connie looks at me, I quickly assure my friend that as much as I’d like to honor the coach, I have an appointment I can’t possibly escape.

Yeah, like washing my hair.

~

THE AFTERNOON GROWS MUCH COLDER. So, in addition to snacks and drinks, we pack the car with blankets before heading to Bronco Stadium for the big championship game.

"So Dad, do you think Coach Warren will have Craig run a bootleg pass in the first quarter?" Aaron says from the backseat.

"Naw, too predictable. I bet he has some surprises up his sleeve."

"Yeah, you're probably right," Aaron agrees, his wistful voice filling with confidence.

I pull the visor down to check my lip gloss in the mirror. "Remember, Coach Warren gets a lot of help from his coaching team. Winning is not a one man show."

Even Pearl seemed excited once news broke we were going to state. Lately, the sparkle has returned to her eyes and she's even acting genuinely happy.

Intuition tells me the glint in her eyes might be fueled by a new romantic interest, even though she vehemently denies it when I ask.

I've noticed she was almost late to school twice this week because of extra time in the bathroom primping. I press for details, but she gives me that look.

Despite wanting to know more, I back off. I know what it feels like to deal with a prying mother. *Believe me, I know.*

We arrive at the game and make our way into the stands with me lugging the blankets and Steve carrying the thermos of coffee and the binoculars. Aaron has the container of hot chocolate. Normally, bringing drinks into the stadium is prohibited. I guess they want you to patronize the concession stands, but they make exceptions for high school games. Good thing, because I could spend a small fortune trying to stay warm today.

As soon as we get settled, I scan the sideline for a glimpse of Pearl.

The dance team is wearing matching leggings and parkas,

compliments of AJ's Athletic Club. Finally, I spot her. "There she is." I point out our daughter to Steve.

"What?" He lays a blanket on the bleachers for us to sit on, then he too scans the field. "Oh, yeah. I see her. Is she going to be warm enough?"

I dig in my bag for the disposable hand warmers I'd slipped inside earlier. "I'll run these down to her."

Making my way down the bleachers, I pass familiar faces. I wave at Gary Mattson and his wife, Susie. "Hey there, Mayor," I call out.

"Are you ready for some football?" He hollers back.

I notice a reporter and his cameraman moving to where seven freshman boys hold their shirts up, revealing bellies painted with the letters C-O-U-G-A-R-S in our school colors.

Across the field, fans at the far side stand and raise their arms starting a wave that continues around the stadium, section by section. The drum corps beats louder and excitement pulsates against a backdrop of hot buttered popcorn and greasy fried burger smells drifting from the concessions.

I lean over the railing and call to my daughter. "Pearl!"

She turns her face in my direction and I wave her over.

She smiles and sprints to the railing, her blonde ponytail swinging. She reminds me of a puppy hopping back and forth in front of a smorgasbord of kibbles and chew bones—unable to choose which wonderful morsel to bite into first. The warmth I feel in my heart contrasts sharply with the frosty air.

"Yeah, Mom?" Pearl says, her breath creating a visible cloud.

"Here, take these. Your dad's afraid you're going to get cold," I explain, handing her the warmers.

My daughter smiles and thanks me, then lopes back to the others.

The Cougar football team bursts onto the field and our fans explode into cheers and applause. I watch Michael Warren and his coaching staff jog onto the field, stopping at the sidelines not far from where I stand.

Coach Warren barks into the mouthpiece of his headset, then focuses on a clipboard handed to him by the defensive coordinator, Rudy Foster.

As if sensing my disapproval, Michael Warren slowly raises his head and turns. When our eyes meet, an odd look briefly crosses his face. He frowns and quickly returns his attention to the players, leaving me staring at the back of his team jacket.

With a raised voice, Coach Warren shouts over the noise of the crowd. "Gentlemen, listen up. Tonight I ask you to look around and ask yourselves how much you're willing to sacrifice out there on the field? The answer to that question will determine the outcome of this game."

I shake my head, wishing I could motivate these young men to sacrifice for their academic careers instead.

A few minutes later, I make my way back up into the stands, steaming after I overhear Dan Taylor tell Todd Nord the booster club is purchasing three new flatscreen televisions for the coaches' audio-visual room, especially since the computer lab remains equipped with antiquated monitors and limited wi-fi. Of course, all the coaching staff are provided iPhones as well.

I slide in next to my family and immediately notice Aaron shoving a hotdog in his mouth.

"Hey, you just ate," I remind him, shaking my head.

He grins and chomps on his snack, a slight hint of mustard clinging to the corners of his mouth.

Steve holds up the thermos. "Ready for some coffee?" I shake my head. "No. I'm good for now."

He leans over and speaks over the loud din of the crowd. "So, I guess you heard."

"Heard what?"

"Coach Warren had to bench Cutler."

I blink. "What? Dennis Cutler? You're kidding. Why would he—"

Steve doesn't wait for me to finish. "Don't know how they've kept it out of the news, but apparently the kid got a DUI last night. Just got a text from Joe, which by the way, he and Connie want us to meet them out at their motorhome at half time for a tailgating get-together."

His face draws into a quick smile. "I told them I'd have to check with you before I accept."

I reward the remark with a kiss to his cheek.

Guess that explains the look from Coach Warren. He was probably wondering if I'd heard and was expecting me to gloat. But that's not my style.

To everyone's great disappointment, the Cougars lose the State Championship by one point in a double-overtime game.

A solemn mood descends over the town. Storeowners pull all the game banners down, and replace them with pine garlands and festive lights, and the residents of Falcon move into the holiday season, vowing to each other that no matter what it takes, next year the trophy will be ours.

8

The worst moment of my day is when the loud beeping coming from my alarm clock jolts me from deep sleep. This morning is no different.

"Steve." I give my husband a nudge. "Steve—it's five- thirty."

"Huh?"

"Time to get up." I throw back the covers, stretch my arms high above my head and then lean over and turn on the lamp.

A fleeting moment of guilt nags as I catch sight of the treadmill standing in the corner of the bedroom, a Christmas gift from Mother. Despite her good intentions, the machine serves as a place to hang extra clothes. "Steve, are you awake?"

"You go ahead and shower first, honey. I'm meeting Paul at the bank this morning, so I'm going to catch a few more winks." He turns over and pulls the covers over his head.

"Must be nice," I murmur as I turn the lamp off and pad across our bedroom to the adjoining bath.

Inside the shower, I bask in the pure joy of solitude and the warmth of the water as it pulsates against my back. The fancy showerhead was my Christmas gift from Steve.

I'd tucked my initial disappointment away upon opening it,

realizing yet again I was going to have to explain his gift to the women at school after cooing over their new jewelry. But right now, I wouldn't trade his practical gift for all the diamond bracelets at Macy's jewelry counter.

Finally, I turn the water off, ending my moments of bliss. After quickly drying off to avoid catching a chill, I tweak the bathroom window blinds open just enough to peek out.

Faint pink-tinged light outlines the serrated tips of the pines in our backyard, finally promising a break in the dreary snow-filled days of holiday break. Which just figures, now that it's time to return to school.

"Coffee?"

I turn to see Steve standing at the doorway. There's something about a man with mussed hair, his hand holding a Disneyland mug wafting with hot steam, that causes me to fall in love all over again.

"Thanks." I smile and plant a kiss on his cheek in gratitude. "Are the kids up?"

"Aaron is. And I hollered at Pearl. Twice." He playfully pops me on the backside before he heads back downstairs.

I finish getting ready and join him in the kitchen. Aaron leans against the stove, his wet hair brushed into place.

"Son, climb up to the counter and I'll make you some oatmeal." I head for the sink to rinse out my cup.

Steve walks over and kisses my cheek.

"You want me to cook you some eggs?" I open the cupboard door.

He checks his watch. "Not this morning. After the bankers, Paul and I are meeting up with a site engineer at the shopping center. We have to determine where that utility easement runs."

"Dad, can you drop me off at school?"

I pause, my hand still on a bowl. "What about breakfast?"

"Maybe we can stop at McDonalds." Aaron looks at his father. "Huh, Dad?"

Steve nods and ruffles his hair. “Sure, if you hurry.”

Minutes later, I’m alone in the kitchen, savoring a few minutes with a second cup of coffee before leaving for my early morning staff meeting. Grabbing the remote, I point it at the television on the counter and press the *on* button.

This morning we have a surprising story for you. Three men are under arrest after firing shots into a vacant lot . . . click.

We have a sad story to report this morning . . . click.

In other news, a homeless man was found dead in Garden City . . . click, click, click.

Today’s special value is a stunning Dooney and Bourke purse. Your choice of colors.

I lower the volume, then empty a packet of sweetener in my cup. I stir the dark liquid, wondering what kind of woman pays over three hundred dollars for a purse. Don’t they have utility bills and dentists to pay like the rest of us?

The thought still lingers when I finish my coffee and make my way upstairs. It’s not that I don’t like nice things. But with Pearl’s college expenses looming, designer anything is low on my list of priorities.

Before leaving the house, I peek inside Pearl’s room and find her still in bed, the covers tucked over her head.

“Pearl honey, get up. You’re going to be tardy.” I glance at my watch before closing her door and scurrying down the stairs.

All attendees know there is a totem pole of hierarchy when it comes to our high school staff meetings.

Let me explain.

First, these gatherings are held in the drama room, no pun intended.

Second, the principal fields questions and comments from her position on the raised stage. Department heads nearly always plant themselves in the first rows of chairs, teachers gather in groups in the next section, and the coaching staff saunters in last, capturing the back rows of seats nearest the exit.

Me? I sit to the right bordering the outside aisle, in a position where I can watch the others.

Each group comes to the meetings, carrying a load of personal agendas and opinions. Except for the coaches. Mostly, they bury their attention in their cell phones.

"Could I have everyone's attention?" Sharon Manicke pauses, waiting for the chatter to die down. A plastic-sleeved identification badge and a whistle hang from a long black ribbon-like cord draped around her neck.

"Excuse me." She waits again.

She clears her throat and begins. "Thank you for coming, especially at such an early hour. I know we all have a lot to accomplish today, so let's get started."

Sharon introduces her new Bell-to-Bell program, explaining no student should be outside a classroom without a written pass, and only then with good reason.

I scan the room. Each member of the staff is mandated to attend, so I'm a bit irked when I notice Coach Warren has failed to show.

Typical—that man believes he's the one exception to the every rule.

Sharon runs through her agenda items, then opens the floor for comments. "Now is the time if there's anything on your mind," she says.

Bill Miller stands. "I—uh, I'd like to discuss next year's budget. To the extent you have any sway with the school board, Sharon, I'd like you to convey the biology department is in need of additional funds." He pushes his thick black frames up on his nose. "How can I teach my students the difference between a vena cava and an aortic valve when we have only one frog for every three students?"

Sharon nods. "I understand your frustration, Bill. I'll see what I can do."

Before taking his seat, he adds, "The guys down at Davis Meat Packing provided cow eyeballs again this year. With a little luck, they might even have some hearts to donate."

"Yes, thank you, Bill. I know you do everything you can to stretch the dollars." Sharon lifts a file from the small table next to where she sits. She jots a note, before looking up. "Anyone else?"

As if on cue, Michael Warren saunters in carrying a stack of Krispy Kreme boxes. "Sorry I'm late. Traffic was a bear this morning." He slides the donuts into Bill's hands and motions for him to pass them on. "Help yourselves, everyone."

He finds his way to the empty chair in the front row, to the right of the principal. "Is that a new sweater, Sharon?"

Sharon Manicke blushes. "Why yes, a gift from my husband." She picks a piece of lint from the sleeve. "Thanks for noticing."

I cringe. Is no woman immune to this man's charms?

Scowling, I take a deep breath and speak up. "Uh, can we get back to things? I've got a lot of work on my desk."

Coach Warren holds up his hands. "Sorry, didn't mean to interrupt." He leans back my way and says. "The raspberry-filled chocolate one is for you, Barrie. Heard it was your favorite." He winks.

I rub my forehead, mentally pleading with Sharon to get on with the meeting.

The donut box reaches me and I pass the goodies on without taking one. Instead, I check my watch, hoping in the back of my mind that Pearl made it up and to school on time. Perhaps I should text her.

On second thought,I won't always be around. She needs to be responsible for herself.

The discussion drones on for another ten minutes, before one of the office workers enters the room. She glances in my direction as she walks up front and whispers in Sharon's ear. Something in her expression troubles me.

Sharon looks directly at me and slowly nods. "Let's take a quick break." She closes her folder and lays it on the table.

I glance at her, puzzled.

It isn't like Sharon to stop in the middle of a staff meeting, especially when we're going to have to wrap up soon. Classes start in a half hour.

Sharon clears her throat. "Barrie, Steve is here to see you. He's in the front office."

"Steve? He's here?" Everyone's attention drifts my direction.

A sudden uneasy feeling vibrates down my spine. The only other time I remember Steve coming to the school to see me was the time he wanted to tell me he'd been laid off. That was years ago.

I step into the hall to see Steve standing outside the front office. Next to him is the resource officer talking with a policeman. My heart sinks and every nerve ending in my body goes on high alert. Without thinking, I sprint toward them.

The school secretary points to an open door behind the counter. "Use Ms. Manicke's office."

"Steve?" My heart pounds wildly against my chest wall as he guides me past the front counter.

Ordinarily, I like it when Steve places his hand at the small of my back. It makes me feel safe somehow. Now it feels like a vise grip forcing me down a dark tunnel.

"Steve, you're scaring me. What is it? Are the kids—?"

He follows me into the office and shuts the door. When he lifts his head, Steve looks wrecked.

"Barrie." He moves next to me, pulling my body against him. "It's Pearl."

Steve's body shudders and I realize he's sobbing.

I pull out of his embrace. Slowly, I move several steps back, shaking my head. Fighting panic, I force the next words out. "What . . . happened?" My legs tremble. "Steve?"

He looks up, his eyes flooding with tears. "An accident. Pearl was hurt really bad. She—she didn't make it. She's dead, Barrie."

My eyes scour his crumbling face. "Dead? My—my, Pearl?"

The gravity of the words he'd spoken trickle into my understanding. The room darkens and the walls seem to melt. I feel my knees buckle and I slump hard to the floor.

I gasp, fighting for air through thick, bitter bile seeping into my throat.

My arms wrap tightly around my gut as if to hold dangerous emotions inside, thinking if I let any leak out, any at all—I might die too.

No! No! My mind screams. *Not Pearl. Not my baby girl!*

I sway back, then forward, the pain nearly choking me.

Seconds pass before I realize the loud guttural moan echoing in the room—is my own.

9

I don't know when I get up from the floor, or exactly when the officer joins us in Sharon's office. "Can we get you anything, Ms. Graeber? A bottle of water or something?"

I shake my pounding head. "I—I don't understand."

The officer pulls a chair up in front of me and sits down. He leans forward and speaks in a gentle tone. "Closest we can tell, the accident occurred about four-thirty this morning. The body —" The officer clears his throat. "I mean, your daughter was recovered from a field about a quarter mile north of the MacMillan and Star Road intersection.

"How can that be?" My eyes dart between Steve and the officer. "I saw her in bed this morning."

My mind leaps with hope. "You've made a mistake." I stand and raise my voice, as if volume will make my point. "Mistakes happen all the time. Pearl was home. In bed. I saw her myself." I shake my head. "And her car—her car was still in the driveway."

Steve stands and gently touches my shoulder. "Honey, it's no mistake."

The officer looks at me with compassion. "A sanitation

driver discovered the accident and called it in. She was driving a Jeep—registered to a Troy Hohman, I believe."

"What? No!" The information threatens to shatter the last remaining pieces of my heart. "You're not understanding. Don't you listen? It can't be Pearl—"

Within seconds my whirring mind slugs into slow motion. I sense more than feel Steve guiding me out of the office, down the hall and through the school's front doors.

I see faces, sad faces—and hear snippets of conversations breaching the fog that surrounds me.

Poor Mrs. Graeber.

Did you hear about Pearl Graeber? Didn't we just see her?

The words make their way into my consciousness, but I can't quite make sense of anything I'm hearing.

In the car, my thoughts clarify. "Steve, I want to see her. Take me to Pearl." Before he can respond, my mind races. "Where's Aaron? We have to get Aaron."

"Jackie is picking Aaron up and will take him home." Steve's voice grows shaky. "She promised to keep the news off until we get there and can tell him."

I look up, my eyes filling with tears. "Where's . . . Pearl?"

"When she gets to the funeral home, we'll be called and I'll take you there."

I feel panic seeping into my mind. "But, where is she now? Where is she?"

Steve reaches for my hand. "At the coroner's office, sweetheart."

I yank my hand from his. "Pull over!"

My outburst catches Steve off guard. He quickly glances in his rearview mirror, then slides the car to the side of the road.

We barely come to a stop before I unsnap my seat belt, open the door and scramble out. Blindly, I place my hand against the car to steady myself.

I lean over . . . and vomit.

ICICLES HANG from the Brannen's Mortuary sign as we pull into the parking lot, in stark contrast to the warmth inside Paul Hohman's Cadillac.

Steve and I sit in silence in the back seat for several long minutes after Paul cuts the engine. When neither of us move to get out, Paul also stays in the driver's seat, waiting.

I run my hand over the leather of the seat beside me, focusing on the soft feel and the heady new car scent.

This vain attempt to avoid what lies ahead fails. Finally I take a deep breath and squeeze Steve's hand. "Let's go."

"Huh?" My voice seems to bring Steve back from some distant place. Deep sadness washes over me as I realize the pain my husband is enduring. I quickly tuck guilty feelings away, unable to absorb anyone else's emotions right now, even his.

Paul moves into action. He climbs out and opens Steve's car door.

When I step from the car, a blast of cold air hits my face. I shiver, despite the fur coat Jackie draped across my shoulders before we left the house.

"Do you want me to go in with you?" Paul asks.

Steve nods and together we all move toward the entrance of Brannen's Mortuary, the dread I feel reflected on both their faces.

With each step, I feel something inside me dying, turning slowly to ash.

Inside, we're greeted by an older man with gray hair wearing a dark suit. He has a chiseled look, with sharp angles that suggest his face might crack if his mouth breaks into too wide a smile.

He extends his hand and introduces himself. It takes a few

minutes before I realize Mr. Brannen is the same man who arranged Daddy's funeral.

"We are so sorry for your loss. All of us here extend our sincerest condolences." The words sound as lifeless as the atmosphere inside this dreadful place.

Steve shakes the man's hand, but I ignore his formality and move past where they all stand. "Where is she?"

"We have her ready for you—down here." Mr. Brannen motions for us to follow him down a long dimly-lit hallway.

Overhead, the faint sound of an old hymn competes with the sound of my beating heart. We pass double doors to what must be a chapel of sorts. Just past a wall portrait of deer standing beside a creek, we stop in front of a door with burgundy-colored heavy curtains at the window.

Before he opens the door, Mr. Brannan issues a warning. "We have her covered and I must ask you not to remove the blanket." He looks apologetically at Steve. "I'm sorry. We didn't have much time—"

His voice drifts off as I watch his hand grip the knob. Behind that door is my sweet girl.

Paul speaks up. "I'll wait here." Steve nods and the door opens.

I hold my breath and step inside, not sure what I'll find.

The room is darkened, the only light coming from two floor lamps against the wall. An overstuffed chair in a floral print rests next to a small occasional table holding a box of tissues and a Bible. Beyond that stands an oblong table similar to a hospital gurney.

I pull my hand from Steve's and take a couple of tentative steps forward.

I see her beautiful blonde hair first. My breath catches and I move closer.

There she is—Pearl.

Still. Quiet. Perfect.

Suddenly, an inexplicable calm overtakes me. Everything the officer explained earlier melts away. The only thing remaining is me and my sweet girl.

My Pearl.

I sweep the hair back from her face, surprised at the coolness of her skin. She appears to be sleeping and I bend and gently press my lips against her cold forehead.

"Don't worry, baby," I whisper in her ear. "Mommy's here."

10

Barrie, honey . . . it's time."

Steve places his hands on my shoulders and gently draws me away from where I stand with my hand resting on the blanket covering my daughter's body.

I shake off his hands. "No, you leave. I—I need to stay."

"Sweetheart, we need to go home now."

"Huh?" His words seep into my head, but my feet remain planted. I let my face turn in his direction. "I don't want her to be alone."

"C'mon, babe. Let's go." The corners of his eyes are furrowed with deep lines I've never noticed before. His arm wraps firmly around my waist.

A deep feeling of exhaustion nearly bowls me over, and I allow myself to collapse in the comfort of his arms. I can't help but look back at Pearl as he guides me to the door.

"Wait!" I pull away and rush back to her side. Tucking the blanket in tight around my daughter, I whisper again how much I love her.

My feet take a couple of steps back. I draw several rapid

deep breaths in an attempt to gain control over the panic I feel inside, and my knees buckle.

Steve's arms appear out of nowhere and fold around me. I bury my head in his shoulder and together we exit the room, leaving Pearl on that table.

In the front lobby, several individuals are gathered talking in hushed voices.

Paul is speaking with two police officers. As we move into the room, Mr. Brannen stands on the far side of the front lobby engaged in dialogue with someone blocked from view.

"Direct all the bills to me. I will be taking care of the financial aspects."

I detect my mother's voice. "Mom?" I move in her direction.

Her head pokes from around the funeral director.

Our eyes lock, mine flooding with tears. "Mama?"

She walks toward me, her arms open.

I fold into her embrace, burying my face against her neck. Her smell, the faint scent of lavender and sweet powder, connects me to a time when I was little and she'd come to my room to comfort me when I had bad dreams.

A sob catches in my throat. No one warned me nightmares could get worse when you grow up.

She pats my back. "There, there."

The rare show of tenderness is more than I can stand. A river of pent-up emotion sweeps across me, and I give myself over to her comfort, letting tears flow. For a brief moment, I become a child again—a thirty-eight-year-old little girl who needs the solace found in her mother's arms.

She's the first to pull away when Paul announces he has the car warmed and ready for us.

Taking a tissue from her bag, Mother dabs at the large damp spot on her crisp, white blouse before turning to Steve. "I've arranged for Dr. Nazarov to meet us at the house."

"Mother, no. I . . . I don't need anything."

"Nonsense," she answers. "You're an emotional mess and he'll give you something so you can sleep tonight."

"But I don't want to sleep."

She looks at me like I'm a petulant child, before glancing back at Steve. "Take her home now." She pats me on the back. "I'll stay and deal with things here. News of the accident is bound to break by the evening broadcast, and I want to make sure these gentlemen understand our privacy is to be respected."

Before I can guard against it, my stomach tightens. This is one of a thousand times I'd been given a taste of my mother's softer side, only to have her yank the experience from my grasp, acting as if I'm another problem that needs managing.

On the ride home, scenes from the last hours replay in my head. Sharon telling me Steve needed to talk to me. A policeman standing at the end of the hallway, twirling his hat in his hand. And the room where I'd left my sweet daughter all alone.

Sifting through the limited information I'd learned about the accident, I try to make sense of all the pieces.

The police officer told us a sanitation driver was driving east on MacMillan Road in the early morning hours when he noticed deep tracks in the mud veering off the pavement. Despite the dim light, the sight of a flattened mailbox caused him to stop and investigate.

That's when he discovered Pearl's body in the field, several yards from where the mangled vehicle came to rest.

The mental vision of my little girl sprawled in that field all alone punches at my heart. I can't help but wonder, was she still —alive?

Despite the distant pounding in the back of my head, I squeeze my eyes closed and refocus my thoughts.

Why was she was driving Troy Hohman's Jeep? She had her own car, for goodness sakes. And they tell me she was driving nearly ninety miles an hour and didn't have her seatbelt fastened.

How can that be? Pearl knew better. I taught my daughter to wear her seat belt.

My hand wipes at angry tears rolling down my face. I'd have encased her in bubble wrap to keep her safe, if she'd have let me. What kind of a mother doesn't teach her child to take every precaution while driving a car?

Steve seems lost in his own thoughts. For a moment, I consider asking if he thinks the seatbelt might have released upon impact, but change my mind when I notice my husband's tear-filled eyes and quivering chin.

"You okay?" I ask.

"Remember that time right after I adopted her, when she was little and I had to swat her because she wouldn't stop stabbing things in the electrical outlet?"

I nod. "I remember."

He gazes out the window, a vague look painted on his face. "I remember too."

I finger his arm, and he grasps and hangs onto my hand so hard it hurts.

Still, nothing physical compares to the deep aching pain inside my soul.

WE DRIVE into the neighborhood to discover our street crowded with cars.

For a moment I'm confused, then it dawns on me people have assembled at our house because they've learned the news.

Joe Anderson's mud-caked Chevy truck is parked next to Connie's shiny red Beamer. Jackie's silver Jag is still in the driveway.

Unfortunately, I also recognize Dr. Nazarov's car amongst

those parked up and down our street, next to a media crew filming our house.

Reporters and cameramen rush forward when they see us get out of the car. Steve shields me with his arms and hurries us to the front door, while Paul stands like a sentinel near the mailbox, keeping the press from coming any closer.

I turn and see Callie standing on the sidewalk across the street, strands of red hair stuck to her dampened cheek.

My jaw tightens. I turn away and head inside.

A hush falls over the room as we enter.

Connie reaches me first. "Oh, honey." Her arms encircle me, and tears spill down her cheeks. Joe stands right behind her. He reaches and squeezes Steve's shoulder, but says nothing.

I hang my coat, aware friends and neighbors watch with worried glances. Steve shakes hands with his construction manager, a guy he's worked with for years.

Taking a deep breath, I move through the people gathered in my home. Amidst their whispered voices, floral arrangements of every size and color cover the coffee table and the fireplace hearth.

The sight makes my head pound. All I really want is be alone right now. That, and some aspirin.

"Where's my son?" I look around.

Connie wipes her face with the back of her hand. "He's in his room. Jackie's with him."

I politely thank everyone for their support, before I excuse myself and quickly move up the stairs, taking care to keep my eyes averted from the family portraits lining the wall.

Aaron's voice drifts from his bedroom door, which stands slightly ajar. "But where is Pearl?"

His question pokes at my heart. No eleven-year-old boy should have to wonder about these things.

Jackie takes on a tender tone. "What did your mom and dad tell you?"

"They said she's in Heaven. But—" Aaron's voice drops to barely a whisper. "—what if Sissy was bad? She snuck out without Mom and Dad's permission."

"That's not how it works, kiddo. We don't get to go to Heaven because we're good people. We all mess up sometimes. But the Lord loves us so much he paid the price for all the bad things we do. Because of that, we can join him in the special place he's saving for us—with him."

I hesitate outside the door, finding the words comforting somehow, despite the fact I haven't been in church for . . . well, in a long time.

A hand presses on my shoulder. I turn to find Steve. From the look on his face, he caught what Jackie said as well. Her words somehow soften the despondent look he carried earlier.

Together we move into Aaron's room. "Hey, buddy," Steve says.

Jackie stands. "How're you two holding up?"

I hear compassion in her voice, see it in her eyes. Any other time, I'd smile and assure her my family is doing just fine. Instead, I swallow a lump building in my throat and shrug.

She gently places her hand on my arm. With a sad smile, she tells me how deeply sorry she is.

Following an awkward silence, she adds, "Food and flowers have been arriving all afternoon. I'll head downstairs and pull one of the casseroles out of the refrigerator and get dinner ready." She leans and pats Aaron's back. "I'll bet you're hungry."

"Thanks, Jackie." Steve says, as he sits on the bed next to Aaron, his hand firmly grasping our son's. "We appreciate everything you and Paul . . ."

When he lets his sentence trail off, she gives him an encouraging smile before heading for the door.

Aaron's sweet brown eyes reveal he's been crying.

I join them on the bed. "Everything's going to be all right, baby."

Then more for my benefit than his, I pat my son's leg and add, "Somehow we'll make it through this."

"MOTHER, I told you before, I really don't want to take anything."

"Barrie, quit fighting me on this. Dr. Nazarov drove all the way here as a favor." She glances at our family physician. "Believe me, the shot will do you good. In the long run, you'll thank me."

Her argument is a familiar one. We debate the benefit of her advice every time life hurls any kind of hurt my way. Like the night I gave birth to Pearl and Evan showed up hours too late, smelling of pot and cheap perfume.

But, I'm not budging. Drugs didn't work when my baby girl entered this world, and no amount of sedative can possibly shave away any of this pain now that she's gone.

"Fine. Do things your way." Mother's jaw stiffens. "You always do."

"Honey, this time I think your mother is right," Steve interjects. "What can it hurt?"

In the kitchen, Jackie is busy loading the dishwasher. The wall clock reads ten o'clock, which means Aaron went up to bed over an hour ago.

I look my mother in the eyes, too tired to hang onto my resolve. In light of all that's happened, what does it really matter anyway?

With a heavy sigh, I concede. "All right."

Mother's chin lifts. She places her arm on Dr. Nazarov's. He nods and follows me up the stairs.

I can tell the moment the drug hits my system. My eyes grow heavy and exhaustion weighs down, pressing on me like a vise, until I can no longer stay awake.

Just before drifting off, I see an image of Pearl walking away down a beautiful path lined with brightly colored flowers, hand-in-hand with Jesus.

I struggle to stay awake long enough to form words.

Give her back.

11

Muted voices drift into the darkened room from downstairs, breaking into my sleep. I force my eyes open and glance at the clock on the bedside table. Five a.m.

My hand instinctively moves across the bed to the vacant spot next to me. Steve must've beat me awake. I smile and draw a deep breath, hoping for the smell of coffee.

Then I remember.

Immediately, I'm assaulted by an ache that pulls me back into the emotional abyss I'd escaped while asleep.

This is the first morning I wake without her. Of course, this time yesterday she might have already been gone. And I didn't even know.

Something deep inside me should have sensed the loss then. Instead, I drove to school with an insane sense of security. Why didn't my instincts register the moment her neck twisted, snuffing life from my precious girl's body?

Did she call out to me, in that instant just before?

Closing my eyes against the torment, I drag myself upright and swallow a sudden dryness in my throat.

It takes sheer will to lift from the bed and go through the rituals of brushing my teeth, washing my face and dressing, accomplishing these basic chores trying desperately not to think.

I skip the whole make-up thing, until I hear Pearl saying, "Mom, no one goes out of the house without at least a little mascara and lip gloss." Her voice in my head sounds as if she's here, standing beside me.

I choke back a sob.

I'll never hear her voice again. Not ever. That realization kicks my gut and tears flow again, making my raw eyes burn even more.

Ask any grieving mother and she'll tell you people lie when they say you can cry your eyes out.

I stop at Pearl's bedroom door, letting my hand rest on the knob several seconds before moving on, not quite ready to enter.

Downstairs I find Jackie at the kitchen sink and her son, Troy, by her side with a fork in his hand.

I clear my throat and Jackie looks up. "Hey, Barrie. Steve and Aaron already ate. Are you hungry?"

Troy peers at me from behind a shock of black hair hanging over one eye. "I made some waffles. And we have strawberries and real whipped cream," he offers hopefully.

I shake my head. "I'm sorry. I'm just not very hungry."

Jackie wipes her hands on a towel. "Of course, not a problem." She brushes crumbs from the front of a very expensive looking black sweater. Even at this early hour, she looks stunning.

"The waffles will freeze and so will the strawberries." Her face breaks into a weak smile. "If we can find room. People dropped off an unbelievable amount of food yesterday. I'm afraid many of us feel helpless, so we cook."

I try to return her smile, but the pounding in my head

forces me to the Tylenol bottle on the counter. I slip three tablets into my palm.

Troy speaks up, his voice timid. "Can I get you a cup of coffee?"

I pad across the floor toward the cupboard, the kitchen tile hard and cold against my bare feet. I grab a glass from the shelf and turn. "I need to understand why Pearl was driving your Jeep?"

Jackie carefully folds the towel and lays it by the side of the sink. She tucks her hair behind her ear. "We asked Troy the same question. He said—"

"I—I'm sorry, Mrs. Graeber." Troy's face pales, creating a stark contrast against his dark hair and clothes. "She just showed up late and asked to borrow my car. She wouldn't tell me how she got there or why she needed my Jeep. I should have —I mean, if I'd woke Mom up . . ." His voice drifts off and his eyes tear up.

Jackie rubs his back, her perfectly manicured hand making little circles. "Son, you couldn't have known—"

I interrupt. "Why would she need your car when she has her own?"

"It was late, like about midnight. I was tired—I don't know."

An irrational anger boils. "You didn't think, that's what."

Jackie's head jerks up. She opens her mouth to speak, but holds back. "Troy, honey. Let's allow Barrie some time."

A tense silence envelops the room as she hurries to wrap the waffles and places them in the freezer. Next, she snaps a lid on the bowl of strawberries and maneuvers them onto a shelf in the fridge, amongst the countless casserole dishes. Before leaving, she walks over and gives me a little hug, reminding me she's only a phone call away if I need her.

As I hear her car pull from our driveway, I feel awful. After everything she's done, I should have curbed the edge in my voice. But frankly, my emotions are raw and being politically correct isn't exactly my top priority right now.

Outside the kitchen window, the bare limbs of Mrs. Otis' cherry tree appear stark against the backdrop of the frosty January morning.

I move to the sliding doors that lead to our patio. Steve sits on the trampoline. Aaron is sprawled on his back, his head in Steve's lap. Neither one is talking.

I rub the chill from my arms, thinking I should join them. Instead, I make my way back upstairs. To Pearl's room.

Her closed door mocks me, dares me to grab the knob and turn. Several seconds pass before I muster the courage to enter.

What appears as a form under the covers draws me to her bed. My hand grabs the duvet and I yank, exposing two pillows laid end-to-end.

So, this is what I believed was my daughter.

My knees buckle under the wave of emotion that washes over me.

Sinking to the bed, my eyes scan her room. Her slippers are tucked neatly against her dresser. Her pretty lavender robe drapes across the back of the armchair to the right of the window.

I pull one of the pillows against my face, taking in the smell of her. The sweet scent of her shampoo, the heady smell of rose petals mixed with a hint of creamy vanilla. I close my eyes and let her form in my imagination. She smiles at me in that way that so reminds me of Daddy. A mouth that curls up slowly, before breaking into a full grin set inside parenthetical dimples.

"Honey?"

The sound of my husband's voice cruelly jerks me back into reality and I open my eyes to see Steve standing behind me, his chin shaded with unshaved stubble. He points to his wrist-watch. "We agreed to meet your mother at the funeral home in a couple of hours.

"Steve, I don't understand."

"Barrie, we talked about meeting your mom to plan the memorial—"

"No, not that. I'm talking about this." My arms wave across the bed and the charading pillows. "None of this makes any sense, Steve." My eyes search his, hoping for answers.

He runs his hand through his hair and stares out the window, as if the answer might be found in the street where he taught our daughter to ride her bike.

Finally, he turns and admits he's as confused as I am. "Guess it doesn't matter a whole bunch now."

I stand. "Of course it matters. A nearly four-point student who has everything going for her, deceives her parents into thinking she's in bed, sneaks out—" I pause, placing my hands on my hips for emphasis. "And where was she all night?"

Steve hangs his head and quietly says, "I—I don't know. All I do know is she's gone and nothing we find out is going to bring her back. Ever."

A strange mixture of anger and sorrow flashes in his eyes. "Please, Barrie. Let's just get through these next few days. There'll be time for sorting all this other stuff out later."

He walks out of the room, leaving me staring at the empty frame on her dresser, the one that once held Craig's photo.

Answers to all these questions may not bring Pearl back. But, if it takes every ounce of my being, I am not going to leave my daughter down in the cold, dark earth without understanding why this happened to my little girl.

12

We ride to the church in silence as Mother's town car snakes through nearly empty streets.

I consider asking Mother's driver to make a quick stop so I can quickly grab another bottle of Tylenol, but the stores have all closed early for the service. Instead, I lean back into the deep leather seat and work my temples with the tips of my fingers.

"What is it, dear?" Mother asks, even as she pulls a jewel-encrusted pillbox from her purse and thrusts the tiny container in my direction. "There will be water at the church."

The parking lot in front of Grace Community Church is full, as well as the surrounding streets. Several orange cones block an empty area adjacent to the front door. Two men spot Mother's car and move the cones, waving us into the reserved space.

"Boy, there's a lot of people here, huh Dad?"

Steve squeezes my trembling hand. "Yeah. A lot of folks loved our Pearl."

Inside, the sanctuary is filled with teenagers, teachers and neighbors. Some I barely recognize. Many I've known my whole life. My own fifth grade teacher, who retired years ago and moved to Florida, extends her hand as I walk by. "Honey, I'm so very sorry."

The look of sadness in her eyes threatens the wall I've built around my emotions. My breath catches. "Thank you, Mrs. Mecham. You didn't have to come all this way."

"Nonsense." She covers my hand with her fleshy palm and the scent of her signature rose petal fragrance wafts across my nostrils. Or maybe it's the mass of flowers stationed at the front of the room, I don't know.

Steve's hand moves to the small of my back, and he guides me and Aaron to our designated seats up front. Mother follows close behind, her heels making a light thumping sound against the carpeted aisle. I draw a deep breath and silently pray I'll somehow get through the next couple of hours without falling apart.

As soon as we're seated, I let my eyes sweep over the easel holding the blown up photo of Pearl, the one taken last year at our neighbor's wedding. I picked out the blue sweater she wears. That shade sets off the color of her eyes beautifully. And I'd had to help her curl the back of her hair into those large drooping curls all the girls wear.

I quickly divert my gaze to the large baskets of lily-of-the-valley, her favorites. Mother had the bouquets flown in special. The tiny white blooms must have cost a fortune this time of the year.

To the right, hangs her empty dance team costume, her pom-poms rest in a carefully maneuvered pile at the base of the stand.

Mother wanted a more elaborate affair and didn't hide her disappointment when we chose not to have a full-blown funeral at a *real* church. "This one doesn't even have stained glass windows," she said, shaking her head. But Steve remained adamant he wanted to use the Hohman's church. Said he'd liked their pastor when he came over that first night after we'd learned Pearl died.

I'd appeased her by offering to let her priest officiate at the private family burial. And I'd further appeased Steve by consenting to Troy Hohman speaking, which should send Mother to the moon once she gets a look at him.

The pastor steps to the podium, welcomes everyone and opens his Bible. After a short reading from the book of Romans, he invites us to bow our heads.

At the close of the prayer, Aaron reaches for my hand and I give a little squeeze. Steve stares at a copy of the program, his thumb slowly moving across Pearl's photo.

When the room darkens for Pearl's memorial video, I brace myself knowing the images set to the song *Remember Me*, can potentially rip any emotional resolve I've hidden in my heart.

Her baby picture is the first, the bare-bottomed variety I'd threatened to show to her prom date. Next, an adorable toddler with curly blonde hair takes uncertain steps, her arms outstretched waiting for me to catch her. Ah . . . then the one we took outside the courthouse on the day Steve's adoption was finalized.

Steve draws a quick breath and I feel his shoulders tighten. One by one, images appear then fade—each capturing a moment in my precious daughter's life. And then, just like her physical being, the screen fades to black.

The lights in the room brighten again and I notice Mother sits with tear-pooled eyes directed straight ahead, her fingers knotting her handkerchief into a tight wad.

Next, four of Pearl's classmates she's known since second grade sing a beautiful a cappella rendition of *Amazing Grace*.

When they finish the final strains, the pastor returns to the podium. "Before our service concludes, one of Pearl's friends would like to say a few words and close us in prayer."

Troy makes his way up front. He steps to the microphone, and clears his throat. "Uh, I'm a little out of my element here. If anyone had told me I'd be wearing a suit and speaking to a bunch of people, I'd have laughed and said no way. But that was before I lost my friend, Pearl Graeber."

I shift uncomfortably in my seat. "Pearl was very special to me."

The words catch my heart and I turn my full attention to Paul and Jackie's son.

"Many of you have known Pearl a lot longer than I have. Some of you would say she's smart. And she is. Some would claim she's pretty. No one could argue that. But in the short time I've had the privilege of being Pearl's friend, I have come to understand how beautiful she is on the inside."

Troy shifts at the podium and sweeps his jet black hair from his face.

"I don't always understand God's ways," Troy continues. "But I know Pearl recently trusted Him with her eternity." The dark-haired nose-pierced boy's eyes glisten with tears. "I just didn't know how quick her eternity would start."

With that, Troy bows his heads and prays.

"Lord, our hearts hurt over the loss of Pearl. And we don't understand. But we trust You. Thank you I'll get to hang with her again someday—in heaven. Amen."

The pianist takes her cue and gentle music filters through the sanctuary, competing with muffled crying. Steve offers his hand and I stand and follow him down the aisle.

Pearl would approve. I can almost hear her say, "I liked the service, Mom. Tasteful and not overdone."

We exit the sanctuary, walking past a blur of faces.

I spot Mr. Jackson, the pharmacist at the new drugstore out on Sunnyside Road. And the Otis family from next door. Ralph

Otis's eyes are red, his veined hand sweeps across his balding head as we pass.

Near the back, two rows from the double doors leading to the front foyer, is Craig Ellison. Pearl's former boy friend sits alone, his head tucked.

13

What is *he* doing here?"

I nearly choke on the whispered words, glad my dark glasses hide the angry tears that follow.

"Barrie—" Steve reasons, pulling me through the doors and out of earshot of the crowd.

"Don't Barrie me." I raise my voice and pull away.

Mother's voice intercepts my tirade. "I'll take care of this." She firmly grasps my arm and leads me to a small office off the front foyer. I hear the door close behind us. "That's enough, Barrie."

Her words are a shot of ice water flung against my flaming temper, instantly dousing my outburst. I rub my temples and try to collect myself. "Mom, I don't want him here."

"That may well be, but I will not allow you to behave in an undignified manner in public."

I pull the glasses from my face, no longer holding back the tears. "No, Mother. My daughter is laid out in that box up at the cemetery and soon I'll be watching them lower her into the ground and cover her with dirt. But let's not act undignified."

I see a momentary flicker of hurt in her eyes, and I realize

I'm misdirecting my anger. She's not the one I'm really upset with.

I'm angry at that Ellison boy who broke my daughter's heart. I'm angry that my daughter turned to Troy Hohman, a kid she barely knew, instead of me. I'm angry that my mind is filled with questions—and no answers.

I take a deep breath, and reach for the tissue Mother offers. Pressing my glasses back in place, I collect myself and let her guide me back to the foyer. We join Steve and Aaron, who both eye me nervously.

After what seems like hours of endless hugs and condolences, the crowd finally dwindles. I glance at my watch and motion to Steve, pointing to my wrist.

He scans the foyer and waves to Aaron, motioning for him to join us.

"Barrie?"

I turn to find Michael Warren and his wife. Pearl's friend, Rebecca, stands next to them clutching a large-sized photo album, her eyes brimming with tears. Her light brown hair has been flat-ironed, like Pearl often wore hers.

Lisa Warren extends her hand. As soon as I reach out, she covers my palm with her own. "Barrie, we simply don't know what to say. We are so very sorry."

Coach Warren shifts uncomfortably. "Yes, we are all—" his voice cracks and he pulls at his neck, like the collar of his starched white shirt is suddenly cutting off his air.

He stares at me and I find myself wondering what he sees. A woman wracked with sorrow can't be a pretty picture.

Steve appears by my side. "Hey Coach." He shakes hands, then his arm goes around my waist. "Aaron is with your Mother. He'll meet us at the car."

Rebecca thrusts the book she's been holding out to me. "Uh, some of girls got together and made this last night. It's a scrapbook."

"Why thank you, sweetheart." I take the book, pulling it next to my chest.

"We all recorded our memories of Pearl. I—uh, I'm really going to miss her." Fresh tears form in her eyes.

I nod and swallow hard, trying to keep my own emotions at bay.

"We should get going." I hear Steve's voice, and mumble in agreement.

Excusing ourselves, we make our way to Mother's town car. Inside, Mother and Aaron sit in silence, waiting to make the trip to the private family burial service.

None of us say anything as the driver maneuvers down the lengthy driveway onto Main Street. Seconds later, he turns on Cemetery Road and heads west.

A faint violin melody fills the vehicle, a sad tune that matches the mood of the occupants. I stare out the window at the gray sky, aware rain droplets have begun to bounce off the glass. Fitting, I think, that the clouds cry for me when my eyes are spent and no tears come.

As we make the last bend into Memorial Cemetery, I see the white walled tent positioned on the far hillside, nearly indiscernible against the backdrop of snow. The structure will provide warmth and privacy for what comes next.

Mother tried to talk me into something more traditional, but I remained adamant I wanted these last moments for our family alone, away from staring eyes. I requested the casket remain unsealed until we said our goodbyes. Finally, Mother gave in and the funeral director was directed to accommodate my wishes.

I feel the car come to a stop. The engine cuts.

"You okay, Mom?" I hear Aaron's young voice and throw him a weak smile.

He pats my hand. "I think Sissy would have liked the flowers, don't you?"

Aaron hasn't called Pearl that in a long time, but that's the second time our son has recently reverted to using that term. I nod and intertwine my fingers with his. "I sure do. And she'd like all this fuss, wouldn't she?"

He looks past me to the driver opening the door for us. "Yeah."

Steve helps Mother from the car. Aaron and I follow and together we walk up the green turf path lined with black plastic posts and chains.

Halfway to the tent, I notice a small green sedan meandering up the roadway. The vehicle pulls up and parks near the town car. The door opens and out pours a woman wearing a bright turquoise wrap and a skirt that sweeps the top of the snow as she moves. She waves wildly.

My breath catches. "Tess?"

"Mom?" Steve cocks his head to one side, then breaks away to meet her as she rushes up the path. "I didn't think you'd come."

"Of course I'd come." She embraces my husband. "Anthony couldn't. He had to stay with the sailboat."

Tess Graeber never changes. She looks exactly as she did two years ago, and eerily like Meryl Streep in the movie *Mama Mia*, her deep Cabo tan completely out of place here in this frosty Idaho late afternoon.

I move to give her a hug.

In response, my mother-in-law pulls me into a deep embrace and I find my face buried in her long blonde hair, which smells of patchouli and coconut.

She pulls back, and reaches to brush the hair from my forehead. "Baby, I'm devastated by all this." Her eyes glisten. She quickly waves away her tears and adds, "What was our girl thinking?"

She moves to Aaron, bends and gives him a tiger-sized squeeze. "How's my favorite boy in the whole wide world?" She lowers her voice. "Grandma Tess brought you a surprise from Mexico."

His face instantly brightens, then just as quickly a shadow blankets his features again as if he believes he shouldn't feel happy today.

"Hello, Tess." Mother removes a handkerchief from her bag and dabs at her nose. "It's good to see you again. What's it been —two years?"

A wide smile breaks across Steve's mother's face. "Greetings, Elaine. You look nice. Black is your color."

I suppress a smile and follow Steve and Mother to the tent. Tess and Aaron are in the lead, her hands on his shoulders.

Inside, Pearl's white casket perches in the center, the base of the stand lined with dainty lily of the valley blossoms. The lid is open. I hold back while Steve leads his mother and Aaron forward.

For a moment, I wonder if I should join them, be there for Aaron as he sees his dead sister for the first time. To my relief, I see Steve's hand go to our son's shoulder, which allows me to stall the inevitable.

There are people who claim to have had an out-of-body experience. Before this, I've scoffed, believing the notion silly. But standing here watching each of my family members move through their own grief-filled goodbyes, I can somehow relate.

My raw feelings separate from my body and it's as if I'm in two distinct places at one time. Standing near the door and simultaneously hovering over the open casket.

The experience shakes me to the core and I struggle to collect myself. Perhaps this is what schizophrenics feel like.

I now understand how a person could escape emotional pain by leaving.

Aaron reaches out and touches his sister's hand. Tess sniffles, then falls to wailing. Steve hurries them both toward the door. Tess wipes her arm across her face, apologizes and assures us she's got a hold of her emotions now.

After the priest says a quick prayer, Tess offers to drive Aaron home. Mother stands on the other side of the tent, tears streaming down her face. I walk over and hug her, offering what comfort the token might provide.

She immediately straightens, takes a deep breath and says, "Well, I'll let you two have some time alone. I'll be in the car waiting." She stops at the open door, checking the darkening sky, then pulls on her gloves and strides out, her quivering chin held high.

Steve steps up to the casket next. He reaches for me, but I shake my head. I'm not ready. He turns, his voice quivering. "How do I do this, Barrie?"

I purse my lips and bite at the inside of my cheek. I can't lose it.

"How do you say goodbye to—" His question is interrupted by a deep wracking sob. I move to him and bury my face against his back, holding him from behind as if to brace a man about to melt with his emotion.

Finally, his shoulders quick shaking and he sniffles. "Honey, why don't you head to the car?' I lightly caress his back. "I need a few minutes with her. Alone."

"You sure you'll be okay?"

I nod.

The priest, who has been standing quietly next to the open tent door, suggests he stay with me. I assure him I want to be alone.

With a conflicted look, he tells me he'll be right outside if I need him.

Steve presses his head against my forehead. "I love you, Barrie."

"I love you too. Very much."

A strange calm settles when I'm finally alone with Pearl. On purpose, I've kept my eyes averted from the open casket, until now.

The simple, pure beauty of the girl lying in the bed of white satin stuns me. I straighten her blouse, her hair. My fingers lightly trace the features of her face, in an attempt to commit every inch to memory. This last look has to last a lifetime.

Finally, I reach around my neck and unhook the strand of pearls my Daddy gave me on my sixteenth birthday. I scrunch them in my hand, then reach and gently lift Pearl's fingers, draping the keepsake through her forefinger and thumb.

"I was going to place these around your neck on your wedding day—" I press down the emotion that rises in my throat, not wanting to waste a precious second of this time.

Finally, I hear Steve at the door to the tent asking me if I'm ready.

I nod.

Leaning over, I kiss my daughter's cheek for the last time. "Goodbye, my sweet. My heart goes with you."

14

In the days that follow Pearl's memorial, each of us copes with her death in different ways.

Tess stays with us and busies herself trying to keep Aaron's mind focused on board games and root beer floats, anything but the sadness that permeates our home. Perhaps she believes ice cream chases away bad karma. And maybe it does. Sure beats sitting around in your pajamas staring at wilting flowers and stacks of unopened cards.

I met Tess Graeber the morning I married her son. Like today, she drove into town, arriving at the last minute, only that time in a Volkswagon bus. A blue one, painted with butterflies and flowers, the rear-end cluttered with bumper stickers.

Back then, she lived in Seattle, I think. And I don't remember the name of the guy she lived with, only that he was one in a string of men that followed. She made her living as a birthing doula, a good deal of her income coming from a rather lucrative side business of encasing placentas in resin. For what reason, I can only imagine.

Despite her odd nature, I'm glad she's here. Tess is a natural born nurturer, and Steve and Aaron are benefiting from her doting.

Steve spends his days buried in work, hiding from how awful all this feels. To pretend things are normal, when our lives are anything but, is clearly unhealthy, and I suppose I should challenge him to face his emotions.

Frankly, I don't have the energy.

Instead, every morning he grabs his mug of coffee and tucks rolls of plans under his arm.

I give him a weak smile and say, "see you tonight" and he grunts and heads out the door.

Aaron is the one I'm particularly worried about. Despite the treats from his Grandma Tess, his world has been turned upside down with this loss.

Last night I went in to kiss my son goodnight and found him asleep with one of Pearl's pom poms on his pillow.

I wonder, does Pearl have any idea how badly we're all hurting? And where is heaven exactly?

I'm jerked out of these thoughts by laughter drifting from the dining room.

Tossing the afghan aside, I slip my bare feet into slippers and lift from the spot on the sofa where I'd been perched for the last several hours.

At the table, Tess and Aaron are embroiled in a highly competitive game of Scrabble.

Aaron draws two tiles. "Ah, not more vowels." He sighs and slides the letters onto his little wooden rack. He tucks his leg up in the chair and leans on the table with his forearms.

Tess, on the other hand, maneuvers her tiles onto a triple-score, spelling out the word *zit*. "Ha! Thirty-three points." She looks up and notices me in the doorway, rubbing at the back of my neck.

"I could give you a massage," she offers, and moves to get up. "My oil is in my bag."

I motion her back down. "Not tonight. But thanks."

My mother-in-law knots her long blonde hair at the nape of her neck before she speaks again. When she does, her voice is filled with compassion. "I know you guys are hurting right now, Barrie honey." She pats Aaron's hand. "I want you to know our girl is not far from us. She's perched on the moon, looking down smiling. And she wouldn't want to see all of you this wrecked."

My mind tells me her words are meant to comfort. But my heart screams in protest. Really? She thinks my dead daughter is sitting on the moon?

I force a smile for Aaron's benefit. "Who wants pizza? Aaron, why don't you call in an order? I'm sure Grandma Tess wouldn't mind running you down to Luigi's to pick up dinner."

She nods and scoots her chair back from the table, looking relieved to be able to do something to help me.

Later, as we stand around the kitchen counter, waiting for Steve to cut the pie into slices, I find myself frowning.

Why have I never noticed before how much a pepperoni pizza looks like the moon?

THE NEXT MORNING, I watch the clock on the kitchen wall slowly tick thirty-two minutes past the time Steve promised he'd be home.

Feeling anxiety rise in my gut, I try diverting my attention outside the window where snow flurries threaten to add to the already frozen landscape. When that doesn't work, I drum my fingers on the kitchen counter and try to focus on Tess's incessant chatter.

"Honey, why don't you and Steve bring Aaron to Mexico for a family vacation? Get away from all this for a little while.

Anthony and I would love to have you." She lifts the teapot from the stove and moves to the sink.

My mother-in-law's suggestion sits on my chest like the chunk of ice out in the birdbath. How does one do that, I think. No, really. How do you escape the fact your daughter is dead and you're expected to go on with your life, as if your world hasn't cratered?

I try to picture Steve and me sitting under an umbrella on a white beach, fruity drink in hand, watching Aaron in the surf. The image is marred by the person missing from the scene—the one who will never be in our family portraits at Christmas, the young woman who won't be standing next to us at Aaron's graduation and wedding. Or, ever have her own.

I shake my head. "I don't think so, Tess."

My mother-in-law studies me. "Yeah, I suppose getting Steve away from his business venture right now would be like bulldozing Houston into the Gulf of Mexico." She turns off the faucet and places the pot on the stove. Her hand reaches and turns the flame on the burner.

A couple of crumbs left on the counter from Aaron's breakfast catch my attention. I sweep the surface clean. "Where *is* Steve? He needs to get home. Our meeting at the prosecutor's office is in less than an hour."

Nothing I'd said this morning had convinced my husband to stay home. I'd argued it'd only been a week since Pearl's accident, that surely Paul could handle things for one day. But no amount of argument kept Steve from his chance to escape back into some aspect of normal.

As if our lives could ever be normal again.

Tess opens the cupboard door and grabs a mug. "Join me for some tea, honey?"

I decline, glancing at the clock again.

"Honey, he'll be here," she assures me. Then, as if to change the subject, she adds, “I like Steve’s new business partner, and his wife.”

Jackie Hohman dropped by night before last, her hands filled with a crock pot of chili. Paul followed, his hands carrying a pan of cornbread, and a jar of Jackie’s special honey butter tucked under one arm.

“I infuse the mixture with a touch of vanilla bean,” Jackie confided, after which she and Tess launched into a lengthy discussion over where you find the best beans, Madagascar or in Mexico, while I wondered, was there anyone Jackie didn’t find a way to connect with?

At the sound of an engine in the driveway, I jump from my perch at the kitchen counter. Grabbing my purse, I scurry for the front door. “We won’t be gone long,” I call back over my shoulder.

The Ada County Prosecutor’s Office is located on Denton Street in west Boise, about forty minutes from our home in Falcon. We arrive and walk through the front door of the sprawling brick building two minutes before our scheduled appointment.

Steve and I cross a shiny linoleum floor to a reception window where a heavy woman ruffles through a stack of papers from behind the tiny counter, her shirt buttons fighting to cover her ample bosom. Her name tag reads *Deputy Sheriff Medlin.*

“Excuse me,” Steve says, a bit too breezily. “Can you direct us to the prosecutor’s office?”

The woman doesn’t respond right away, instead she remains completely focused on her task. Finally, she lifts her head and points to the elevators across the lobby. “Take the last one on the left to the second floor.” She tucks her head, returning to her papers.

We ride the elevator in silence. When the bell dings and the gray panel slides open, Steve takes my hand and together we head for the open door at the end of the second floor hallway.

In sharp contrast to the woman downstairs, we're greeted by a young woman with kind eyes. As soon as we introduce ourselves, she tells us Mr. Voorhees is expecting us and leads the way to an office with a gold-tone name plate that reads *Garrett Voorhees, Ada County Prosecuting Attorney.*

Mr. Voorhees looks to be in his early forties. Laugh lines peek out from the corners of his glasses, softening the angular jaw line and precision cut of his slightly graying hair. His white shirt has been pressed crisp, but oddly I find myself fighting the urge to straighten the knot on his tie, which he wears loose with his collar unbuttoned.

He extends his hand. "Thank you both for coming." He offers us a beverage.

Steve sits in one of two metal armchairs. "Uh, no thanks."

I shake my head. "Not for me."

I take a seat in the chair next to my husband, resting my purse in my lap. Fighting to keep my nerves in check, I let my eyes wander to a large family portrait on the wall. The shot was taken much earlier, when Mr. Voorhees' hair was much darker. He and his wife and three young sons are dressed in matching blue sweaters, their faces displaying wide smiles. On the credenza below, frames in various sizes display what must be more current photos of his sons, one in a graduation cap and gown, one in football gear and another standing in front of a shiny black car.

No daughters.

"Nice family," I comment, trying to make small talk.

Mr. Voorhees sits on the corner of his desk. "Thanks." Beneath the forced smile, he wears a strangely solemn look.

I recognize his face from television. Last summer, he gave several interviews during a high profile trial relating to a horrendous murder of a child out in Kuna. The stepfather was accused of the crime.

I remember my mother's comment at the time. "If I sold

that man for what he thinks he's worth, I'd make a fortune," she said, clearly not impressed with Mr. Voorhees' crass political positioning in front of the camera.

Mr. Voorhees pulls a file from the center of his desk. Without breaking eye contact, he takes a deep breath. "Well, I'm sure you're wondering why I asked you to come in."

I swallow against the nervous feeling buzzing in my gut. Ever since we received the telephone call from his assistant, my mind's been racing down a road of possibilities as I've wondered what might warrant this meeting.

Steve voices my concern. "Yes, we're anxious to know what this is about."

Mr. Voorhees clears his throat. "As you may or may not know, any time someone dies of what could be determined unnatural causes, the coroner is required to perform certain tests in order to establish the exact time and cause of death. In this case, the deceased—"

"Pearl."

Mr. Voorhees and Steve turn and look at me.

"Her name is Pearl," I explain, my voice barely above a whisper.

The prosecutor's brows knit. "Yes, of course. Pearl." He lifts his chin and continues. "When routine blood analysis revealed your daughter, a minor, had a blood alcohol finding, the coroner was required to notify us."

My heart pounds and I feel Steve's hand grab my own. "She was drinking?" he says.

Mr. Voorhees drills his gaze in Steve's direction, as if perhaps a man-to-man discussion might be more appropriate at this juncture. He stands and moves to the chair behind his broad wooden desk, the top cluttered with similar files and empty Styrofoam cups, some lying on their side. He clears a spot for the file in his hand, opens the front cover and studies the contents for several seconds.

Steve and I exchange a quick glance.

Mr. Voorhees unbuttons his cuffs, and rolls up his sleeves. First one arm, then the other, never taking his eyes from the papers.

Finally, he looks up. "I have to be frank. Her alcohol levels were very low, well within the legal limit. True, she's a minor, but there is no evidence of a crime. What we have is a minor who snuck out of her house and got in a fatal motor vehicle accident. The matter requires no further investigation, from a criminal standpoint."

Steve lifts his chin and he fingers his jaw line. "But, aren't you going to look into who provided the alcohol?"

Mr. Voorhees looks to Steve, then to me. "Do either of you have facts that would substantiate a person over the age of eighteen purchased alcohol for your minor daughter?"

Steve and I glance at each other. We shake our heads.

At this point, Mr. Voorhees directs his attention back to his file. "Look, without any evidence to suggest otherwise, these things tend to be a wild goose chase. Unless we have something concrete that leads us to believe otherwise, this could just have easily been a case where a minor snuck into her parents' liquor cabinet."

I scowl. "But, we don't drink."

Mr. Voorhees reaches for his phone. He presses a button. "Gladys, could you bring the Graeber girl's belongings in?"

Mr. Voorhees removes his glasses. He pinches the bridge of his nose, takes a deep breath and closes the file.

"Let me get to the real reason I asked you to come in." He draws a deep breath before going on. "A slip of paper from Planned Parenthood was retrieved from the floorboard of the vehicle, which led the coroner to pull some vitreous—," he pauses. "—uh, do some extra testing."

Steve interrupts."What are you implying?"

A flash of sympathy crosses Mr. Voorhees' face. He pauses briefly, glancing first at me and then back at Steve.

"I'm afraid your daughter—was pregnant."

15

Steve leads me into the elevator, down past the fat clerk and into the parking lot. I focus on breathing, and try to feel nothing.

The instant Steve helps me into the passenger seat of his truck and I hear the door close, I can no longer hold in my emotions. Sobs buried deep in my soul make their way to the surface.

I cry my eyes out, my face buried in my hands. Steve strokes my hair and says we'll make it through this too. I cry until I can't. When no more tears come and I've worn myself out, I lean against my husband, letting the warmth of his chest counter the icy chill in my heart. "Why didn't she tell me?" I whisper in a hoarse voice. "I'm not like my own mother. I wouldn't have called her baby a mistake."

We sit in the truck with the engine running and the heater blasting for nearly an hour, rehearsing what we've been told. She'd made an appointment to terminate the pregnancy, thankfully one Pearl never kept. I've seen the emotional repercussions when desperate young girls make hasty decisions without proper counsel. But I never thought my own daughter—

"Oh, Steve," I mutter in a choked voice, my shoulders shaking. "Do you think that was why she snuck out?"

"What do you mean?"

I lean back and swipe my arm across my runny nose. "It had to have something to do with why she was driving like a wild cat that night, don't you think?"

Steve rubs his chin, slowly, his eyes pooled with pain. "We shouldn't jump to any conclusions."

Ignoring his sensibilities, my mind races through a mental calendar. That baby couldn't be Craig's. They broke up too long ago.

An image of Pearl's former boyfriend at the back of the church hints of another possibility. "Steve, do you think Pearl tried to reconcile with Craig? Maybe gave in physically to win him back? Girls her age stumble into those kinds of emotional traps, you know."

Steve leans back against his seat, looking more tired than I've ever seen. "Oh, c'mon. I don't think she'd do anything to take him back, after what he pulled."

I slowly shake my head in agreement. "You're right. Why would she hide the fact she was back with Craig?"

My husband releases a heavy sigh. He straightens and clicks his seatbelt closed. "Well, we aren't likely to ever know the answers to all our questions. All we do know is our baby made some mighty bad choices. And the cost was extremely high."

My eyes burn with tears as Steve pulls out of the parking lot and into traffic.

He's right, we may never reconstruct all this fully. But, our daughter was seeing someone. And if she wasn't with Craig, then who?

~

At home, Steve and I walk in the door with normal plastered on our faces.

Both of us know nothing good can come from revealing what we've learned. So, we do what families everywhere do. We hide the shameful truth and tell ourselves we are protecting our daughter's reputation, that Aaron has enough to deal with, and that no one needs to know our family's business but us.

We pass the tuna casserole at the dinner table and try not to think about how our daughter must have suffered when she found out she was pregnant. We smile and congratulate Aaron on his spelling test scores, and secretly wonder if the baby was a boy or a girl. And when our eyes accidently meet across the table, we avert our gaze and bury our thoughts in what we could've said that might have let her know she would be loved, regardless.

We pretend. Something I'm fairly new at, given what an advocate I am for open and honest communication. And while I try to convince myself that this time, things are different. I wrestle with a heavy thought that weighs on me like cement.

The white casket buried up on the hill contains not only the body of my precious daughter, but my first grandchild.

I feel Tess watching me. "Honey, are you okay?" She glances at Steve, her eyebrows knit with concern. "You both look awful."

She's right. Steve's face is clearly troubled, his eyes tormented. I guess we both need more practice at hiding our pain.

I assure my mother-in-law we're fine, just tired.

She doesn't look entirely convinced. Regardless, she claps her hands together with enthusiasm, "Jackie dropped off a pineapple upside down cake. Who wants some?"

My eyes fall to my plate, where I've barely touched a bite. "I'm sorry, Tess. Thank you for cooking, but I guess I'm really not that hungry tonight. I think I'll head to bed a little early."

I stand and give Aaron a peck on the top of his sweaty head.

Tess extends her arms for a quick hug and promises she'll clean up, no worries.

At the same time I start up the stairs, Steve retires to the living room and grabs the remote, leaving Aaron and Tess to enjoy Jackie's treat by themselves.

Granted, I'm exhausted and should go straight to bed. Instead, I stop and slip the yellow bag Mr. Voorhees gave me today from where I'd tucked it in the hall closet. Funny, even though there is no one upstairs but me, my eyes still dart up and down the hall, as if to make sure my actions have not been detected.

Pearl's room has remained closed off since the memorial service. As if it's a sanctuary deserving a certain reverence, everyone in the family quiets our voices when moving past.

My hand trembles slightly as I grip the knob. Inside, I flick the light switch and her presence hits my senses with unexpected impact. The way a hint of last summer's suntan oil drifts in the air. The brush filled with her blonde hair lying on the dresser.

My eyes drift to a wadded tissue on the floor near her trash and I can't help but wonder how many of my daughter's dried tears surround the fibers.

After quietly slipping the door closed, I plant myself on the floor, legs crossed and work to untie the bag lettered with the word GRAEBER.

The contents are carefully folded. I pull gently and lay the articles of Pearl's clothing on the carpet in front of me.

Each piece is labeled and dated. Her jeans. The pretty lavender button down sweater my mother gave her for Christmas. Both caked in dried mud. Surprisingly, there are no visible blood stains.

Wrapped with a red tag is a gold bracelet I'd never seen. My fingers slide over the shiny gold metal.

The bracelet is made of eighteen carat gold. Not a piece my own pocketbook could easily afford, let alone a boy in high school. Then again, you should see the cars a few of them drive.

Engraved inside are the words *Forever Yours.*

I pull the tag off and slide the pretty trinket onto my own wrist. Somehow the small gesture makes me feel closer to her, even though in some ways this piece of jewelry represents so many secrets.

Shaking, I take a deep breath, determined not to fold with emotion. Despite my intentions, tears swell and I have to swipe my hand across my eyes before I can continue.

Her socks are tucked inside a pair of sneakers, the Nikes she often wore, even when I suggested snow boots would be more appropriate. Wrapped in clear plastic, are her undergarments. How many strangers handled these private items?

The last thing inside the bag is Pearl's Coach purse. This too has dried mud clinging to one of the sides.

I dump the contents, sifting through two tubes of lip gloss, her wallet, a scattering of coins and a tiny bottle of lotion. My hand lands on her cell phone. Lifting it from the pile, I finger the face of the tiny pink device, holding it like a treasure from a hidden pirate's chest.

How many times had Pearl argued for one of the new iPhones? Convinced she had to have access to her email account at all times, she even offered to pay for half.

Why didn't we give in and let her have it? Such a small thing, and it would have made her happy. Now I'll have to live with the fact I'd withheld that small pleasure from her, and so many others.

I shake my head, knowing I'd do things differently, if given the chance. With the power to turn the clock back, I'd throw sensibility to the wind and spoil her rotten.

I turn it on and flip her phone open, hoping the battery hasn't worn down.

A wallpaper photo of Steve jumping his snowmobile in the McCall snow appears, bringing a smile to my lips. Pressing the settings button, I click through the menu selections until I finally land on her recorded greeting. I pull the phone to my ear and wait until Pearl's sweet voice fills my head.

Deep down, in a place I rarely acknowledge, my soul aches with a force that throws me into a vortex of anguish, spinning my thoughts so fast I barely catch the words she speaks. *Hi, this is Pearl. I'm away from my phone right now, so leave a message.*

When I hear the beep, I sit mesmerized.

I press the button again, listening to my sweet girl's voice, letting the sound filter into my consciousness, indulging a fantasy she's standing in front of me and not back in that white satin-lined box, forever silent.

My mind loses track of the times I repeat that process. Finally, a thought occurs to me and I press the button that takes me to her call history. There, a phone number I fail to recognize appears multiple times.

My heart pounds. I hold my breath and click to the home screen. Seconds later, I return and stare at the numbers.

Should I?

Before I can mentally answer my question, my finger presses the call back button and I pull the phone to my ear. The ring tone sounds and I nearly hang up. I mean, what am I going to say when someone picks up? *Hi, I'm the dead girl's mom—?*

"Hello?"

My heart moves into my throat. I swallow, my mind racing through the rolodex in my mind, searching for a hint of familiarity of the female voice.

"Honey? What are you doing?" Steve stands in the doorway, a look of concern on his face. "I thought you were going to bed."

I quickly click the phone off and shove Pearl's cell phone back in the bag. "Nothing really. Just—"

He gently takes the bag from my hands. "Barrie, don't torture yourself. Pearl chose not to tell us. We'll never know why. The only thing we can do is move on from here." He opens Pearl's closet door and tucks the bag on the top shelf, next to the box holding her Beanie Baby collection.

"But, Steve—"

He moves to me and takes me in his arms. "Honey, don't you know I would fix everything if I could? But, it's too late. We can't do anything to change what happened," Steve's voice is filled with regret. He rests his head against my hair. "Right now our focus needs to be on Aaron."

I allow Steve to guide me from Pearl's room. But I can do little to turn the thoughts off in my head.

Like a mama bear, my job was to protect my little cub. Instead, I somehow allowed my daughter to place her paw in the same trap that amputated my own self-respect all those years ago.

Steve's been a great bandage, but nothing completely heals the shame that slices into your life like being pregnant and alone, and the fear of not knowing where to turn. And nothing is going to lessen the sting of knowing I failed my daughter when it mattered most.

Which is why I sneak back into her room in the middle of the night. I sit on her bed, staring into the darkness, mentally rifling through possible answers to a myriad of questions.

We'd have heard her car if she attempted to drive that night, so she likely walked the thirty-minute distance to the Hohmans. Troy claims she showed up shortly after midnight.

But, where was she between then and the time she ended up in that field?

Apparently, Pearl confided in Troy that she was pregnant. He was with her when she cancelled the appointment. So, did she sneak out that night to tell the baby's father she'd changed her mind? Did the boy get mad? Did they fight?

My mind paints a picture of Pearl, upset and crying. Climbing into Troy's Jeep and driving, not even taking the time to fasten her seatbelt. Going faster, and faster . . . until she loses control.

The image forces a fresh ache in my heart.

We'll never know for certain the details of those final hours, or the answer to the entire mystery. But my imaginary scenario fits the few facts we do know. But, even if I'm square on with all this, the puzzle still has a huge piece missing.

My eyes drift to the closet door.

Who did she go see that night?

The nocturnal clouds outside the window shift. A sliver of moonlight sifts through the bedroom window, casting shadows across Pearl's empty bed.

My hand slowly caresses her empty pillow.

I've not disturbed anything in here, wanting to preserve her bedroom the way it had always looked. But, in my need to feel closer to my baby, I pull back the comforter, and her sheets. I climb inside placing my head where hers had rested so many nights.

My mind wanders back to a night years ago, when a four-year-old girl snuggled tight against me in bed after a loud clap of thunder caused her to be afraid.

My throat pulls tight.

I promised Mommy would protect her from the storms.

16

I follow Aaron as he lugs an oversized and well-worn piece of luggage to the curb in front of our house. "I wish you didn't have to go, Grandma Tess."

Steve reaches for the bag. "Here, Scoot. Let me help with that."

"Nah, I got it, Dad." Aaron gives one final heave and plants the suitcase next to his grandmother.

Tess' eyes twinkle. "As fast as those muscles are growing, by the next time I see you, my little guy will be able to carry *me* to the car."

In an unexpected show of affection for a boy his age, Aaron grabs her, wrapping his arms tightly around her waist. The sudden movement causes the fringe on her leather belt to swing wildly. "I'm really gonna miss you," he says, his face buried against her chest.

The sight stirs a heaviness, as I consider how often I'd not been there for him myself since Pearl died.

Tess struggles to catch her balance. "I'm going to miss you too, honey." She reaches and lifts his chin so that they can make eye contact. "Who's going to play Xbox with me in Cabo?"

Aaron releases his grip and grins. "But you'll be marlin fishing anyway."

She ruffles his hair. "Maybe we can talk your dad into bringing you for a visit. Nothing like sailing to heal the soul."

Aaron turns to Steve. "Can we, Dad? Please?"

Tess places her hand on her son's face. "It wouldn't hurt, you know." She kisses Steve's cheek. "Might do you some good."

"We'll try. I promise." He gives his mom a hug. "As soon as I get things under control at work."

"Maybe that nice Paul Hohman could cover for a week?" Tess chides. "Oh! I nearly forgot." She throws her hands up in the air and turns to me. "Barrie honey, don't forget to give Jackie the jars of salsa I left in the pantry. I wrote down the recipe on a card and set it on the second shelf right next to the salsa."

I move into her embrace. "I won't forget."

A smile tugs at my lips. Who'd have expected Jimmie Choo's and Birkenstocks could sit on the same shelf?

Minutes later, we wave our goodbyes and watch Tess drive away, then we make our way back in the house.

A twinge of guilt runs through my mind when I consider the way Steve and I avoided her questions after we returned from the prosecutor's office yesterday.

My mind rationalizes it's not that we lied exactly. We just elected to keep some information buried with our daughter.

Steve leaves for work, even though it's Saturday. I tell Aaron I'm really tired and move for the stairs. Lately, I wake as exhausted as when I slip in bed the night before.

"But Mom, I'm bored."

"Just play with Omelette or something. Can you do that?" As soon as the words leave my mouth, I regret my tone. "I'm sorry, kiddo. I feel out of sorts this morning."

"That's okay, Mom. I understand." Aaron pets the top of Omelette's head. The dog rewards him with a tail wag that waves as wildly as a flag at a Nascar race.

Instead of heading for bed, I reach the top of the stairs and slip into Pearl's room, walking straight for her closet and the cell phone. Despite Steve's attitude, I've got to know.

My fingers tremble as I scroll to the number I'd called last night. Taking a deep breath, I press the send button—and wait. Within seconds, a warning sounds.

Your call cannot be completed as dialed. Please check the number and try again.

I whisper an expletive and pull the phone from my ear.

My eyes stare at the screen, a sinking feeling churning in my stomach. Obviously, the boy doesn't want to reveal his identity. And the female voice from last night—a girlfriend perhaps? Which provides a hint as to why he's reluctant to step forward. And, the reason he's eliminated the possibility of Pearl's mother ever calling again.

After slipping the yellow bag back on the closet shelf, my feet trudge toward my bedroom for that much needed nap.

A sense of hopelessness washes over me as my head hits the pillow. Without that link, we may never have the answers to all our questions.

Hours later, I wake realizing I've slept longer than I'd intended. Still groggy, I skip my shower and pull on jeans and one of Steve's t-shirts. I gather my hair into a ponytail and quickly slide my toothbrush across my teeth before heading downstairs.

"Aaron?" I call out.

Hearing no response, I move to the window and move the curtains to find an unfamiliar car parked on the street in front of our house. Aaron is talking with a man. A stranger.

I rush to the door.

"Aaron, honey?" I scramble down the steps, glaring at the thirty-something man dressed in a leather bomber jacket and loafers. "Excuse me—who are you?"

Aaron pipes up. "He's from television. The news."

"The news?" I manage to say, my voice frosty as the cold morning air. "Aaron, in the house." I give my son a slight shove, pushing him in the direction of our front door. "Now."

I turn back to the guy, who is leaning against his car, arms folded. I notice he's holding a small spiral notebook. My eyes narrow with suspicion. "What do you want?"

Despite my obvious anger, he calmly extends his hand. "I'm Chad Nelson. KING News Network."

When I fail to shake, he slowly drops his arm. "What do you want?" I repeat.

He runs his fingers through his collar-length brown hair. "Following up on a lead I got this morning." He reaches in his jacket and pulls out a pen. "I understand you recently had a meeting with the prosecutor's office regarding your daughter's accident."

The information hits me hard as the cement sidewalk I'm standing on. Despite my wildly pounding heart, I force a poker face and respond the way I'd seen on television so often. "No comment. Now if you could please leave—"

The reporter's thumb clicks his pen closed. " I apologize. I didn't mean to upset you. But—"

Like that mama bear protecting the opening to her hidden cubs' lair, I lean forward and snarl. "Hasn't this family been through enough? This kind of reporting is abusive. Sneaking around talking to my son without my permission. Shame on you!"

Never flinching, he jots something on the paper before looking up. "I think you'd be interested in—"

"We're finished here." I turn away, praying the fact Pearl was pregnant remains buried with her.

Before I even take a step, a car pulls up. Mother climbs out of her town car and tells her driver to wait before moving in our direction. "Barrie? What's going on?" Her eyes quickly assess the circumstances I find myself in. "Dear, go on in the house. I'll take care of this—situation."

Suddenly exhausted beyond comprehension, I follow her directive. As I near the door, I notice Aaron's face plastered against the living room window.

All this is entirely too much. Less than two weeks ago, everything was normal. Now we're in serious jeopardy of becoming the next Dr. Phil family. If this reporter has his way, our private business will be displayed for all to see. Pearl's secret will be revealed.

The old Barrie Graeber would never long to crawl in bed to sleep the dark, dreamless sleep of the sedated. Nor would she have let a jerk reporter rattle her. I used to be on top of the game. Filled with hope for the future. Confident and happy. And I used to know things. The times I wasn't sure, I'd take hold of my unwritten rule and fake it.

Now? Well, now I'm forgetful and have trouble concentrating. I cry all the time and I'm—afraid.

My gut tightens when I think of Mother talking with the reporter. Why can't everyone just mind their own business?

Aaron pulls away from the window when I enter. "Did I do something wrong, Mom?"

I grasp Aaron's shoulders with both hands, hard enough to make my son's eyes fly wide open. "You know better than to talk with strangers."

Tears pool in my son's eyes, sending remorse coursing through my mind. I relax my grip, but before I can apologize, the door opens and Mother walks in.

She hesitates. After quickly running a disapproving look up and down at what I'm wearing, she tells my son to run upstairs. "Aaron, your mom and I need to talk. Alone."

He nods, sniffles and says, "C'mon Omelette. Let's go play Xbox." Before heading upstairs, he casts a look my way—one that clearly says he's mad at me.

I sigh, knowing I was wrong to yell at him. Yet, I need to help Aaron understand how risky it is to talk to someone he doesn't know. Especially some guy who just drives up in front of our home and asks questions.

"So, it's true then." Mother's question sounds more like a statement.

"What?" My masked response has nothing beneath it, and Mother knows it.

"Barrie, don't be coy with me. All of that—" She nods in the direction of the door. "—all that business with the reporter could have been avoided. Must be avoided."

She sets her purse on the entry table and follows me into the living room. "Use your head, Barrie."

The way she says my name reminds me how often I've missed the mark in her eyes. Of composition papers graded B and ironed shirts without enough starch. Lipstick shades that never matched my outfits and beds not made properly. Yes, long is the list of ways I've disappointed my mother.

"Do you know who the father was?"

My head jerks up. "How did you—?"

"Don't be naïve. Of course I know. Do you forget Voorhees plans to run for governor next term, and he wants my support?"

"That reporter knows nothing substantive—yet." Mother moves for the phone. She removes the beaded clip earring from her lobe, before reaching for the receiver. "Still, I need to call Gary Swensen."

My mind fumbles to comprehend what Mother intends. "The former White House press secretary?"

She squeezes the earring in her palm and lifts her chin. "I know his father."

"But, why are you calling him?"

"He owns the largest publicity firm in New York. We'll need advice on how to handle all this—" Her voice drifts, as if even she struggles to admit out loud that Pearl was pregnant when she died. "The media could sensationalize this situation, if given the chance. Underage drinking is barely newsworthy alone, but this added drama could play well in an otherwise lack-luster news week."

The front door opens, interrupting our conversation. "Hey, you two."

When I hear my husband's voice, I glance at my watch. "What are you doing home this time of day?"

"Took off and left the lease for the in-lines," he explains. Mother steps aside to allow him access to the papers on top of the counter.

He grabs a large stapled document off the stack and glances between Mother and me. "What's going on?"

I stroke my forehead. "Mother is contacting a publicist."

"A publicist?" He flashes a look at my mother. "What for?"

I stare at a dark spot on the carpet I'd never noticed. "She knows about Pearl."

"How the—?"

Mother squares her shoulders. "I'm going to ask the Swensen firm to prepare a written statement. In case."

Steve's jaw twitches. "In case of what?" He looks at me for an explanation.

I tell him about the reporter, watching as emotions similar to my own parade across his face. When I finish, he walks to the kitchen, opens the cupboard. He fills a glass with water while Mother explains the potential dangers the press poses.

He lifts the drink to his mouth and drains the glass, his face pulled into a dark scowl.

"I want you to trust me on this," Mother tells him. "Obviously, someone in Voorhees' office has loose lips."

Steve slams the glass to the counter, shattering it. "No."

Startled, I jump back. "Steve!"

Blood emerges where the glass cut his palm. "Elaine, under no circumstances will I allow you to proceed with any of this.

As far as I'm concerned, everything surrounding this thing with Pearl is to be left alone. Do you understand?"

Her mouth draws into a thin line, the only signal her idea has met a hostile reception. "Fine."

Moving for her purse, her back to Steve, Mother turns to look at me. "You might think of your daughter's reputation. News of this sort is like a fine perfume. Once the bottle is opened, and the wind catches the scent—there will be no collecting the fragrance back again."

For emphasis, she pulls her signature cologne from her purse and spritzes her neck. Placing the cap back, she returns the bottle to her bag.

"Take care, dear." A light kiss to my cheek, then she turns to my husband. "Steve."

She walks out and draws the door closed, leaving behind the faint smell of Givenchy—the perfume my daddy used to buy her for Christmas every year.

17

If I needed my own personal cheering squad, the ladies sitting around the country club's linen-covered table would definitely fit the bill.

My tastes run closer to grilled hamburgers, loaded with cheese and bacon, but today my friends are treating me to tea sandwiches and scones served on dainty floral plates.

"Honey, I'm so glad you finally decided to get out of that house." Connie Anderson reaches for the honey bowl. "Joe and I were beginning to think y'all had fallen off the face of the earth. Since that awful—" Her heavy sigh mixes with the thin sound of ice tinkling in stemware at the table behind me and strains of a string quartet playing faintly in the background. "Well, since all this happened."

"Here, let me," I say, keeping my game face in place while I pass the container her way, taking care to avoid the tiny vase of purple hyacinths in the center of our table.

Connie surveys our surroundings and comments how she much she likes the new color they've painted the dining room, telling us that particular shade of green reminds her of a photo she'd seen in her Decorating Today magazine. "They called it *celadon,*" she reports, quickly scooting the conversation to a lighter subject.

Somewhere in the back of my mind, the notion dawns how little I'd seen Connie since Pearl died. How uncomfortable she seems even now, as if my horrible luck might be contagious or something.

I look around the table at the gathered women. Maybe she feels there is safety in numbers, at least where confronting my grief is concerned.

Connie turns to Lynne Matheson, a friend from our Bunko group. "Joe and I just got back from Dallas last week." She scoops honey from the delicate bowl, using a tiny silver spoon. A wide smile spreads across her face, as she stirs the amber liquid into her teacup. "My sister, Tami Jae, got married."

"Again?" I pull the thin cucumber slice from my sandwich and place it at the rim of my tiny plate. "What's that make now —four times?"

Connie chuckles. "You know what they say, everything's worth doing up large in Texas. She turned in that skinny engineer for a big strappin' former football jock. Rich as black oil, too." She leans over to me, cupping her mouth, but speaking plenty loud for everyone at the table to hear. "He's chummy with Jerry Jones."

Robin McBride, a sugary woman we know from the Women's Auxiliary, dabs at her mouth with a napkin. "Who's Jerry Jones?"

Connie's hand slaps to her chest. "Are you kidding? He's the owner of the Dallas Cowboys."

Lynne raises her perfectly shaped eyebrows. "Wow. Bet Joe appreciates knowing his new brother-in-law has those kinds of football connections."

Connie nods. "That'd be the truth. Y'all know I'm his second love," she says, mimicking a Texas drawl. She laughs and draws the dainty cup to her lips, taking a sip. "Ooh, this

Earl Grey is yummy," she says, taking care not to make eye contact.

I paste a smile on my face, doing my best to join the "*let's cheer up Barrie*" party. Inside, I feel detached from the conversation, wishing I could spend the afternoon taking flowers to Pearl's gravesite instead. Late February is unpredictable when it comes to weather here in Idaho, and I hate to waste this sunny day. One of the first, following weeks of gray skies and freezing temperatures.

Outside the floor-to-ceiling paned windows, a gentleman steps up to a tee box in the distance. He takes several practice swings before lining up to take his shot.

Lynne asks when I'm returning to work. "Soon," I tell her. "With the vacation I had built up, I didn't have to hurry back. I'm scheduled to start on Monday."

"I'm glad you aren't letting all this pull you down." Robin dabs the corners of her mouth with a napkin. "We've all known people who use a loss as an excuse to wallow. Our deacons had to pull the stopper on the grief recovery group at church. None of the members were getting any better. It was as if they just wanted to stay victims of their circumstances."

Connie's eyes went wide. "Well, but sometimes these things take time," she says, looking at me apologetically.

I give the women a weak smile. "Eternity couldn't be enough time for me to fully recover."

Robin winces. "Oh, I didn't mean you guys are acting like that," she adds quickly.

A white-gloved waiter steps to the table with a tray of tiny petit fours, little bite-sized cakes decorated with stunning precision. "Ladies?"

I help myself to several, not caring how the gesture might look to the others. On some occasions, food is the best medicine. That, or alcohol. And since I don't drink, these desserts will have to do.

Without waiting for the others to finish being served, I sink my teeth into a tiny cake with white frosting adorned with thin slices of strawberry.

Pearl would have loved these fancy desserts.

Once, when she was twelve years old, I treated her to a trip to Portland, Oregon. I had a counseling conference and Steve and I both decided it would be fun to show Pearl the big city while Steve and Aaron went fishing on the Middle Fork.

I got paid for presenting a workshop and splurged on a dinner at the Heathman, a luxury downtown hotel, which boasts "*where service is still an art.*"

When the server placed the triple chocolate truffle topped with cream ganache and berries on the table, I thought my daughter's eyes would pop out of her head. I ended up ordering a second serving boxed to take with us, just so I could see that joy on her face a second time.

"You should sign up for the bible study class at my church."

It takes me a second to realize Robin's suggestion is directed to me."I—ah. I think I'm going to pass. I have a lot on my plate right now, what with catching up at school and everything."

Robin rests her hand on my arm. "Oh, honey. It'd do you good, don't you think?"

Her touch bristles. I understand why she might believe a good dose of God might move me out of this grief faster, but frankly the woman doesn't get it.

I don't want to let go of this pain. No matter how raw, this hurt somehow connects me to her—to Pearl. Every time my heart weeps, the pain signals something precious was ripped away.

I'm torn and no amount of stitching, even if the Almighty were doing the sewing, will ever weave the fabric of my being back in place.

"Look, I've got to go." I pull my wallet from my purse and ruffle through my credit cards.

"This one's on us." Connie looks at the others for confirmation. They all nod their heads, sympathy oozing from their eyes.

I stand, feeling a bit awkward. A day with the girls used to be fun, but now, my mood seems to burst everyone's party bubble.

As I weave through tables and make my way outside, I catch a glimpse of a guy with shoulder length brown hair sitting alone in the corner. His eyes follow me as I make my way to the door. As I near his table, my muscles tense.

It's the reporter. The one from the curb.

"I'M TELLING YOU, Steve, that reporter is following me." I grab a grocery cart, tossing my purse in the place where I used to seat my children when they were toddlers.

"Aren't you overreacting a bit?" Steve reaches for the printed advertisements stacked in a rack to the right of the automatic door. He scans the front page as he follows me into the store.

"Sure. The guy always has lunch at a dining room filled with women," I counter, rolling my eyes. I push my cart toward the produce section, planning how best to approach the next subject. I stop in front of the romaine. "Maybe we should reconsider Mother's offer."

Steve shakes his head. "Barrie, I don't want any part of that nonsense."

"But, what if she's right?" I argue, my voice lowered. "What if we come home one day to find our lives are splayed across the televisions all across the valley—telling every intimate detail of how my baby stumbled into a bad situation.

I grab some lettuce and toss it in the basket, followed by a bag of tiny carrots. "I mean, think about what something like that could mean. Think about Aaron."

I know I'm playing a little dirty with that last comment, but Steve has to admit the risk and what all this could do to our son.

"It's not like I want to admit Mother is right, and let her take over. But, why else would that reporter be following me? There is simply too much at stake."

"Hey, you two."

I startle and turn to find Robin McBride, her cart loaded with hamburger, buns and chips. Her young son follows her with a second cart filled with soda pop. She notices Steve and I staring at her purchases. She explains she's hosting a little get-together to celebrate her husband's job promotion at Hewlett-Packard.

"He finally made VP. We considered inviting you both, but wondered if it might be too soon." She gives me a sympathetic look. "I mean, you seemed to have a really hard time at lunch yesterday."

I nod. "Oh no, that's okay. You're right, I—"

"How's Brian?" Steve interrupts, saving me.

"Good. He's so excited about everything at work. Oh, I almost forgot to tell you." She leans forward and lowers her voice. "Did you hear about Lisa Warren, the coach's wife? She just got out of rehab." She shakes her head. "It's just a shame. Guess you don't know what people battle with behind closed doors." She waves off her comment. "But I guess you guys really don't want to hear all about that right now."

When Robin finally pushes her cart on down the aisle, Steve scowls. He leans close to my ear. "Okay, I get it now. The last thing I want is for this town to chatter about our daughter around their dinner tables. Maybe I will talk to your mom. See what she has in mind."

I nod. "I think that's a good idea."

In this situation, Mother is right. When it comes to gossip, the best way to keep honey from oozing out the jar is to keep the lid tightly screwed on.

As soon as Steve and Aaron leave for the hockey game, I take advantage of the time alone and get Pearl's laptop. Wedging it on my knees, I lean back into the sofa and lift the screen.

When the boot-up process is complete, I take a deep breath and swallow the notion I'm intruding on my daughter's privacy. In reality she's no longer here, but somehow I get the sensation she's watching.

Despite my discomfort, I fumble through her files looking for something I can't put a name to. Mostly, I find school essays and reports. Study notes.

I pull the mouse to the email icon and click. A box appears where I must type in a password I don't have. Chewing at my lip, I move on and click through her music collection, past a few videos, and finally to her Facebook.

Quickly scrolling through the posts on her wall, I scan for clues. Anything that might shed light on . . . I shake my head, knowing that stumbling on who fathered Pearl's baby is a long shot, at best.

I click to her friends. Classmates, the people she babysat for two summers ago, even Grandma Tess. Near the bottom, a name appears that makes me pause.

Michael Warren.

I frown and open to his wall, where most of the posts are from students.

"Hi, Coach. Thanks for the ride last night. And you're right—grilled chicken pizza is the best!

You rock, Coach! BTW, we're all checking out the new Twilight movie on Friday. Wanna come?

I frown.

Opinions vary on this matter, but many educators believe this chummy kind of interaction with students isn't wise. I know I've read articles warning against blurring these lines. I guess I could slip one of those magazines in his mail cubby, with the page tabbed. Knowing my luck, he'd discover who placed it there, and the last thing I need right now is another battle with the coach. I have enough to deal with right now. And so does he, with his wife and all.

By the time Steve arrives home with Aaron, I'd found nothing that shed any light on my daughter's secrets.

My son's arms are loaded with game souvenirs. Omelette stands near, eying Aaron's half-eaten candy apple. The sight makes me grin. "So, buddy. Looks like you had a good time?"

"Yeah," he says, tossing the mementos onto a chair. "You should've seen the way the Hawks' forward slammed into the plexiglass, right in front of us. Huh, Dad?"

Steve tosses his keys on the counter. "Is that Pearl's laptop?"

Feeling caught, I nod and shut her computer down.

Steve sends Aaron on up to bed, then he joins me on the sofa. "Barrie, even if you find answers, then what? Will the knowledge of who Pearl was sleeping with bring any difference?" He draws me against his chest, nestling his face in my hair.

"Please," he whispers. "Let it be."

18

Nearly eight weeks have passed since the morning we learned of Pearl's death. The day my world crashed. And even though I long to stay home with no pressure to dress or wear make-up, the day I'd scheduled to return to work arrives, about as welcome as a door-to-door salesman.

I'll especially miss my afternoon naps, when I slide under the covers and blot out thoughts of what might have been—*if only*.

I maneuver my car into the Sawtooth High parking lot. After cutting the engine, I check the rearview mirror once more to make sure my makeup covers the dark circles that have become permanent fixtures, shadowing pain I can't keep from reflecting in my eyes.

The last thing I need this morning is another pity party. Don't get me wrong. I appreciate that people care. But, if someone asks me how I am even one more time, I think I'll scream. And I don't want our family tragedy added to any more prayer chains, which is really just another name for holy distribution centers.

Shoving these thoughts from my mind, I run lip gloss over

my mouth, paste on my most convincing smile and take a deep breath.

Well, here goes.

Stepping into the chilly morning air, I make my way to the teachers' entrance. Normally, I'd be juggling books and files, but this morning I simply carry my purse—and the memories of that morning.

I arrive early on purpose, wanting time to myself before facing the mass of students and teachers scurrying to get to the next class before the tardy bell. A wise decision, it seems.

I step into the hallway and immediately envision Steve with the policeman and the resource officer standing outside the administrative offices, waiting to crush the blissful ignorance of a mother who didn't realize her world was about to change forever.

I force my thoughts back to the present, batting my eyes several times to stave off tears. If I keep letting my head drift, I'll never make it through this day.

My desk is remarkably clean, likely straightened by the substitute counselor who spent two days a week covering for me over these last weeks. I need to send her a thank-you card.

I sink into my chair, the one really nice piece of furniture assigned to me, and the result of a push by the state's education department to be more ergonomically minded. Or, perhaps the genesis was really the rise in worker comp claims filed by teachers with bad backs.

"Hey, there you are." Sharon Manicke peeks her head inside my door. "Welcome back. How a-a-a-re you?"

"Just fine," I say, using the cheeriest voice I can muster. "Glad to be back."

"Well, we missed you around here. But don't feel you have to tough it out if things get too hard." She looks at me like I'm a puppy with a sore paw. "We can manage if you need to ease into things a bit."

I avert my eyes. "Thanks, I appreciate it. But, I'm good." I pull some papers from the neat stack and grab my reading glasses, praying she doesn't notice my hands are trembling. "Really."

Sharon nods. "Well, okay then." She raises her arm and looks at her watch. "By the way, we have a department head meeting at noon. In the teachers' lounge."

The morning slips by faster than I'd expected. With no student meetings, I'm able to review all the notes the substitute left and get back on top of things. In fact, this afternoon I think I'll schedule appointments for later this week with the few remaining seniors who have yet to cement their post-grad plans.

Out of nowhere, a thought slams into my heart. I need to call and cancel Pearl's application to UC Davis. And her teeth cleaning appointment. Surely it's been six months since she was in. But then again, Dr. Madsen's staff must know what happened.

I picture that lady at the front desk, the one with the really wide behind that barely fits into drawstring pants, pulling her file and shaking her head in sadness. Where do they put files for people who have died? Do they just throw them away?

I'm obsessing again. I chastise these careless thoughts and pull myself together. Organizing my pen and pencil drawer seems to help.

Minutes past twelve o'clock, I shuffle the loose pages on my desk back into the neat pile, grab my purse and head into the hallway, angling my way through hungry sophomores making a beeline for the lunch room. Outside the door to the teacher's lounge, I overhear my name.

"I hear she still cries at the drop of a hat."

"That's crazy." Bill Miller, the biology teacher, clears his throat. "She lost her daughter, for Pete sakes. Of course, she's going to cry sometimes."

"I know but—"

The chatter quiets the instant I walk into the room. Everyone sitting around the tables and on the sofa stops what they are doing and stares.

Frances Webber is the first to break the awkward interlude. She stands and moves to me, arms outstretched. "Oh, Barrie. Welcome back. Things haven't been the same around here without you." She gives me a hug.

When Frances releases her grip, Sandy Martinusen follows with several pats on my back. "We've had you on our prayer chain at church, honey."

I sigh and give her a weak smile.

Let the pity party begin.

"Hi, Emily. Thanks for coming in." I greet the Jorgenson girl with a warm smile, and motion for her to take a seat.

"Welcome back, Mrs. Graeber. Everybody really missed you." She drops her loaded backpack on the floor and sits.

"Thanks," I say, grabbing her file from the top of the stack on my desk. "It's good to be back." Okay, that statement is not exactly true, but there's no purpose served in burdening this young girl with my troubles.

"I see here, you've made some changes in your college plans that frankly surprise me." I look up at her.

Is she wearing eyeliner?

Emily leans forward. "Oh, yes! I'm so excited."

"But, you're declining your Harvard Scholarship . . . so you can attend Syracuse?" I shake my head. "I don't understand."

"Syracuse has the best communications slash broadcasting program in the country. I'm going to be a sports announcer," she says, grinning.

"A what?"

"A sports announcer. Do you know that in the top twenty-five announcers of all time, not one of them has been a woman?" Emily's head bobs with excitement, sending her long ponytail swinging.

"But, that's a long way from biomathematics, and—" I pause. "Emily, what do your parents say about all this?"

"At first they were confused, and a bit upset," she admits. "But after Coach Warren talked to them—"

"Coach Warren?"

"Yeah, he called and explained how lucrative a field this can be for a woman willing to do the hard work to break in and make a name. And he says with my smarts and natural, sporty look, I have a real shot."

I lean back in my chair and rub at my temples. So, now Michael Warren thinks he's fit to advise students on career choices. "But Emily, you've never even played sports."

The girl stands and grabs her backpack. "Thanks for everything you've done for me, Mrs. Graeber. Someday when I'm famous, I'll give you a shout out in front of the camera." She giggles and heads for the door. At the last minute she turns back. "I'm really sorry about Pearl, and everything."

I nod, and watch as she moves into the crowded hallway. I sigh and close her file, feeling defeated.

Last fall I would have known what to say to counter this girl's change of plans, would have charged into the fray with the coach and battled the notion a smart girl like Emily should drop her dream of becoming a research doctor. Regardless how much money a network might throw her way.

Slowly, I move to the cabinet and open the second drawer. I slip Emily's file in with the other students whose last names begin with the letter J, knowing this is just one more way I've lost my footing since my baby girl died.

Even so, I try to take the matter up with Sharon before I head home.

Unfortunately, she doesn't share my concern that Coach Warren overstepped his bounds with Emily. And nothing I say convinces her his interaction with the students on Facebook might be inappropriate either.

"Barrie, you've been through an awful lot. I hate to see you spending all this emotional energy fretting over the coach. Let's just chalk some of this up to the fact you guys don't see eye-to-eye."

She pats me on the back and walks me out to the parking lot. "Go on home, Barrie. You don't need to take the entire world on your shoulders. At least not so soon after suffering the loss of your daughter."

I wander to my car, feeling disqualified to make a difference. If Sharon Manicke no longer trusts my judgment, I might as well hang it up. Perhaps it's not too late to pursue a different career. I know—maybe I'll become a sports announcer.

Mother always wanted a famous daughter on television.

19

Each of us must find her own path, and my mother-in-law's has always been a different one. When Tess calls me on my way home from school, I learn she's been exchanging emails and text messages with Jackie Hohman. And get this—she's become a born-again Christian.

Tess. A bible-thumper.

She tells me she's been longing for unconditional love her entire life. Even though I try to change the subject, she goes on and on, explaining how Jackie helped her see she's been looking for that love in all the wrong places.

Yeah? No kidding.

When Tess finally ends the call and tells me goodbye, I toss my phone in my purse and roll my eyes. So, Tess's latest boyfriend is Jesus. Go figure.

As soon as I walk in the door, Steve greets me with a peck on the cheek. "Hi Babe, how was the first day back?"

I shrug and follow him into the kitchen. "Oh, I don't know. About like I expected, I suppose."

I tell him about the teachers' lounge and how the comments rubbed me wrong. I explain how no one can possibly understand what things are like for a mother who loses her daughter. How I wish I could just stay home and escape all the nonsense.

Then I report what happened with Emily. How in my brief absence, the coach somehow convinced not only my brightest student, but also her parents, to walk from the Harvard scholarship I'd worked so hard to secure—and why. "Steve, this girl planned to be a doctor."

Steve wipes his hands on a kitchen towel. "Honey, you can't build everybody's house for them. Sometimes you just have to be content knowing you've handed them the best hammer and nails available. If they build a structure that blows down—," he shrugs. "Well, there's very little you can do."

Perhaps Steve is right. But somehow it feels like the coach has talked Emily out of a house, and into a tent.

"By the way, Steve. Have you talked with your mother lately?"

A buttery lemon scent hits my nostrils about the same time I notice the dining room table is set to look like something out of a Martha Stewart television show. "Hey, what's all this?"

White plates perfectly accent a floral tablecloth in a pretty design containing blooms in shades of pink, coral, and light yellow. At the center of the table, someone parked a basket filled with spring flowers. Daffodils and tulips. And some delicate white flowers I don't know the name for.

"Jackie thought you'd be tired on your first day back and wanted to do something nice for you."

"Oh no." I shake my head. "Uh-uh. This has got to stop. I am not another of Jackie's projects. And I can feed my own family, thank you."

Steve lifts his eyebrows. "What are you saying? She's just trying to be nice." He runs his fingers through his hair. "She was being thoughtful. At least I thought so."

"I'm sure you did," I say, unable to keep a hint of accusation from my voice. I flip around and head for the refrigerator, my back to him. I duck my head inside and scan the bare shelves of our Amana side-by-side.

There has to be something here to eat besides what that woman brought over.

Before the thought can fully gel, my eyes drift to the pan of tantalizing smelling food bubbling on the stove. On the counter are three individual bowls of what looks like pear walnut salad.

"You're being a bit dramatic, don't you think?" Steve moves to the stove. "She calls this chicken scallopini." As if to emphasize how ridiculous I'm being, he makes a production of scooping the thin slices of chicken breast dripping with sauce and lemon slices onto the serving platter she'd left on the counter. He marches and places the steaming entree on the table, then moves to the bottom of the stairs. "Aaron. Dinner."

I respond by serving up a steamy retort of my own. "Did you know Jackie has been corresponding with your mother? That she's convinced Tess she needs to see the light and be saved? Or, some such nonsense." I follow him back to the dining room. "Seems your new partner's wife is a Tammy Faye Baker or something."

"I kind of admire Paul and Jackie's faith."

"Well frankly, turning religious isn't going to fix what's wrong in my life. Maybe that makes you and your mother feel better, but I don't need people telling me God can make any of this better. He's the one who let my world crumble in the first place."

Steve plants his hands on the back of a dining chair. "Why are you acting so mean, Barrie?"

The comment slaps me in the face. His words couldn't hurt more if he'd hauled off and popped me one with his hand. I glare back at him. "Excuse me?"

"You heard me. Jackie and Paul have done nothing but to be

kind. Even before Pearl died, you had a chip on your shoulder. And Aaron. You barely notice he's around any more."

"That's not true!"

"Sure it is." He yanks the chair back from the table. Before he sits, he takes a deep breath. "Look, I'm sorry for my tone. But Barrie, you're not the only grieving one in this family." He lets his gaze drop to the floor and lowers his voice. "I just wish you'd at least try to move past some of this."

"Oh yes, let's move on and pretend everything's rosy. The Steve Graeber method for coping."

Aaron appears and Steve motions him to take a seat. Our son quickly glances between the two of us. He sits across from his dad without saying a word.

"This conversation is not over." I grab a roll from the bread basket and march upstairs.

With tears stinging at the back of my eyes, Steve's accusations replay in my head as I stomp my way to our bedroom and slam the door. Something I don't ever remember doing before.

More than once, I consider going down to help clean up. I even get as far as the top of the stairs. But something stops me when I hear dishes banging.

I can count on one hand the number of times my husband has used that tone with me over the course of our marriage. He's what my dad used to call, a slow boil. I wear my emotions on my sleeve, but Steve—well, sometimes I don't know anything is bothering him until he blows.

My mind obsesses over our heated exchange, turning the words over and over, examining each like a piece of fruit on the verge of going bad. If I can isolate the spoiled portions, perhaps there's hope for the part remaining. But as Steve's words ring in my ears, a part of me gets mad all over again.

How dare he accuse me of being a globehead—only thinking of myself? He may not have said those exact words, but clearly the meaning was there.

Frankly, he has no idea what all this has really been like for me. In my own defense, I'm truly doing good just to get out of bed each day. But I guess that's not good enough.

Hours pass before Steve joins me upstairs. As he enters our room, I lean against the bed pillow and flip the magazine page with all the dignity I can muster. Over top of the pages, I watch him get undressed, waiting for him to break the silence.

Truth is, he might be right to some tiny extent. Not about the Jackie Hohman stuff, but I admit as of late, the line of folks ready to bestow a Wife of the Year award would be pitifully short.

And Aaron.

My gut tugs as I consider how absent I've been when my son has needed me. Seems I'm officially now the one who fails everyone. It's in my job description.

Steve opens the sheet and climbs in bed next to me. My stubborn streak takes over and I flip another page, not venturing to say a word.

"Barrie, we need to talk."

A sigh of relief courses through my body. "About what?" I casually flip another page.

He reaches and pulls me next to him. I drop my magazine, and my defenses.

Resting my head against his shoulder, I try to explain. "Steve, I didn't ask for this journey."

"None of us in this family did." He kisses the top of my head.

"I'm not like you, Steve. I can't just roll with the punches."

He pulls back. "Is that what you think? I lost her too, Barrie."

"Oh, please. You ran right back to work as fast as you could. And you sleep like a baby every night—I listen to you snore."

He looks at me with disgust. "Is that what this is? A contest over who misses her more?"

"No, but—"

"But, nothing. I'm getting through this one day at a time, just like you. But Paul and Jackie have helped me to understand—"

I eye him with suspicion.

"Oh, don't give me that look. There's a lot in the Bible that comforts me."

We fall silent, avoiding each other's gaze until I say, with a bit more sarcasm than I intend, "Well, sure. If that helps."

Confusion and sorrow cloud Steve's expression. Before I can follow up and soothe the cut I know my words have made, a loud knock interrupts. The door bursts open and Aaron scrambles over, breathless.

"Mom. Dad. Come quick—"

Steve throws the covers back and grabs for his pants. "What is it, son?"

Aaron's eyes grow wide. He points in the direction of the street.

"Someone just ran over our mailbox."

20

With only one leg in his pants, Steve stands and scrambles to get dressed. Like a madwoman, I grab and throw on my own clothes. In our slippers, we both follow Aaron into the hall and down the stairs.

"Hurry," I say, as we head for the door.

Outside, a woman has already climbed from her vehicle, which rests partially on our sidewalk. She rubs the top of her head, and looks at the downed mailbox as if she's just run over a dog.

I rush across the lawn, the grass crispy with frost. "Lisa?" I say, surprised to see the coach's wife standing in our front yard. "Are—are you hurt?"

Steve rushes to her side. His eyes quickly scan her up and down. "Do you feel pain anywhere?"

Lights flick on in the upstairs windows next door. Mrs. Otis presses her face to the window.

Tears pool in Lisa Warren's eyes. "I'm soooo sorry," she says, her words thick with slur. "I just needed to say I'm—I'm sorry.

"Don't worry about it. It's just a mailbox." I tell her,

watching as Steve checks her over. "Maybe we should call an ambulance?"

Her head bobs up. "No. No, don't call—" She reaches for me. "Your little girl . . . I'm soooo sorry."

Has she been drinking?

I look at Steve, his expression tells me he's wondering the same. "I don't think she's hurt. Let's get her inside."

"Is she gonna be okay, Mom?" Aaron looks at me, worry etched across his face.

A gray pick-up pulls up to the neighbor's curb and screeches to a halt. Out climbs Coach Warren. He rushes over, sirens wailing in the distance. "Lisa?"

He tries to take her arm, but she pulls away. "No!"

His face grows dark, and he grabs her shoulder. Hard. "Look honey," he says, looking up at us. "You've taken a hit to the head. You're not making sense right now." He slides his arm around her waist and guides her toward his truck as flashing lights approaching from the end of our street send eery blue shadows across the lawn.

Steve places his hand on my shoulder. "Why don't you take Scoot and go inside?" He looks over at our son.

Aaron's eyes widen. "Is she in trouble?"

I nod at my husband and place my hand at my son's back. "C'mon sweetheart. Dad's got this handled."

Upstairs, I tuck Aaron into bed. As I reach and turn off the lamp, my son's voice breaks into the darkness. "I think I'll pray for Mrs. Warren."

His words stab at my heart. Especially as I remember my heated words with Steve earlier. For just a brief moment, the hole in my heart grows a little wider, and I'm jealous of the faith my little boy seems to embrace.

I bend and kiss his cheek. "That would be really nice, son."

When Steve finally joins me upstairs, he looks exhausted.

He gets undressed for the second time. I open the covers, and he clicks off the lamp and slides in beside me.

"What do you think all that was about?" I ask.

Steve lets out a heavy sigh. "I don't know, but the coach has got his hands full. I think he plans on taking his wife directly back to rehab tonight, after he bails her out, that is."

I moan. "Oh, no. They arrested her?"

"Afraid so."

"What did Coach Warren do?" Despite my dislike of the man, I wouldn't wish this set of circumstances on anyone.

"He seemed really worried."

"Honey," I say, snuggling closer. "About earlier. I'm sorry." Steve's arm moves across me and he pulls me tight. "I know."

I lean against his warmth and whisper. "I love you."

I drift to sleep with the image of Lisa's Warren's glassy eyes playing in my mind.

Who would ever have expected this beautiful young woman struggles? But then, as I've recently become painfully aware with our situation with Pearl—some things are not always as they seem.

21

Life goes on. Garbage cans still overflow, bills have to be paid and there's yard work waiting to be done. I'd like to press some cosmic pause button. Instead, I force myself from bed and fix my family French toast and sausage for breakfast, I take Omelette to the groomer, and I drive to Home Depot to buy petunias and little tomato plants. All things that must be accomplished, no matter the fog I still live under.

Grasping the trowel with my gloved hand, I plunge the blade into newly tilled earth in our backyard. My other hand plucks a tiny plant from its plastic container, lowering the tender stem with tiny green leaves into the hole I've made. With my teeth, I free my gloved hand so I can use both hands to scoop dirt around the roots.

Pearl and I used to do this together.

Nearly finished, I lift my face to the sun, feeling the warmth of the late spring day against my closed eyes. A warmth I wish would melt the cold ache I still carry.

"Hey, Mom."

Aaron slides the back door closed. "Need some help?"

I pat the ground beside me. "Sure."

He plops down and starts digging with his hand. I hand him the trowel. "Here honey, use this."

After finishing the bedding area, we move to the little garden spot at the rear of our small yard. Aaron carries over a flat of tomato plants that'd been on sale this week. Together, we dig and plant.

There's something about gardening that comforts me. I like knowing if I plant a tomato start, I won't wander to the garden in August to discover green peppers.

I wish mothering promised the same.

"Don't plant them too close together, sweetheart." Aaron nods and fills the hole he's just created.

I expected to feel better as time passes. But in these last weeks, I can barely get out of bed. I cry a lot and even lost weight, something I hate to admit is fairly unusual. Saying these days are hard is an understatement.

Some days, I call in sick and all I do is sit in Pearl's room in tears.

Steve, on the other hand, finds solace in his work. If my husband can't fix a problem, he figures the best approach is to simply ignore the situation. At least on the surface. But I know many nights, he lays awake beside me.

Grief can be a lonely walk.

I finally gave in and agreed with Steve. We need to focus on getting life back to some kind of normal—for Aaron's sake. Mourning a loss is a process, and everyone at the Compassionate Friends meeting we attended last week tells us working through the stages will take time. There's no sense in allowing our lives to completely unravel. Still, a stiff upper lip makes it really hard to smile.

These last months have changed me. I barely have enough tenacity to pull myself from the sofa on weekends after hours of watching QVC in my slippers.

But, like Steve says—it's over. There's nothing to be gained by keeping a chokehold on these bad feelings.

Maybe my husband's right. It's time to move on. We need to leave what's happened behind us and get back to some level of normal. Again, for Aaron's benefit.

My head understands. I wish somebody would tell my heart.

"There, how does that look?" Aaron stands over his work, pride evident on his dirt-smeared face.

I paste a smile. "Looks great. Just think of the tomatoes we'll have this summer. Maybe we can make homemade salsa."

"Yeah. And can you fry some tortilla chips?"

"Maybe, but remember, I nearly caught the kitchen on fire last time, when the grease spattered."

Aaron nods. "Oh, yeah. That's right." He brushes the dirt from his knees. "You hollered for Dad and Pearl grabbed the extinguisher and sprayed that white junk all over. You got all mad 'cuz the kitchen was a mess."

I briefly shut my eyes and nod, letting the memory form. When I open them again, sadness flitters across my son's face.

"I miss her, Mom."

"Me too, baby." I give him a quick squeeze, and together we head for the garage.

"Once, she bossed me so much, I got mad and told her I wished she was dead." His words weigh heavy with guilt. "But, Mom. I didn't mean it."

I stop walking, and place my hands on both his shoulders. "Aaron, people say things they don't mean all the time. She knew you loved her."

Tears form in my son's eyes. "But—what if she didn't?"

His question grabs my heart, squeezing it tight. Hadn't I asked that same question in my own mind? Worried she never knew how much I really loved her?

I search for a way to reassure him. "See that bird up there?"

Aaron looks to the tree where I'm pointing. "Uh-huh." "Every morning, that momma bird flies off—"

"Yeah."

"—and she goes all over looking for worms. And when she spots one, she swoops down and pulls it from the dirt with her beak." I look at Aaron. "Sometimes it's not easy. Every once in a while, it takes everything she's got to yank that earthworm free. Then, she chomps it all up and carries the tiny pieces back to her much loved babies."

Aaron sighs and rolls his eyes.

"No, now wait. There's a point." I lean against the door into the garage, my arms folded. "You see, that's love in action. That bird didn't sit in the nest, cheeping "I love you."

"Yeah, so."

"So, you may not have said the words *I love you.* But I know you cleaned the toilets that time for your sister, so she could say her chores were done and meet her friends at the mall."

"You knew that?"

"Yup." I clasp Aaron's chin, and lift his face until our eyes meet. "You showed Pearl love in action. More than once." I kiss his sweaty forehead. "She knew, Aaron."

The concern in his face softens. "Yeah, you're probably right."

"Hey, what's going on out here?"

Both Aaron and I look to the patio in the direction of Steve's voice. He stands with his hand shading the sun from his eyes.

Aaron bolts in the direction of his father. "Look, Dad. Mom and I planted all this." His hand makes a wide sweep across the yard.

I join them, and Steve kisses my cheek. "Looks like you two have been busy."

Steve slides the glass doors open, and I follow him inside. "What time are we supposed to show up at the Hohmans?"

"Six o'clock." He grabs the stack of mail from the kitchen

counter, and rifles through the envelopes. "Sure you're up for it?"

I tell him I am, hoping that by accepting the dinner invitation, he'll recognize I intend to hold up my end of the bargain.

Aaron pulls a glass from the cupboard. He opens the refrigerator door and retrieves the pitcher of lemonade. "Do I have to go? Ricky wants me to spend the night." He looks at Steve as he pours.

I grab the dishrag and mop the floor behind him, where he's splashed the sticky drink all over the tiles. "Honey, I don't think that's a good idea."

Steve shoves the mail behind the phone, then wanders over to where I'm wiping at the floor on my hands and knees. He squats, and with a lowered voice, he says, "Barrie, the kid hasn't done anything fun with his friends since—well, since all this started. Let's not be too over-protective."

I stand. "I'm not being over-protective. I just think—"

"It's okay, I don't have to go, Mom." Aaron places his glass on the counter. "Really."

Steve gives me a look.

Before the collective mood in this house turns as sour as that lemonade, I change my mind. "No, honey—your father's right. I bet you'd really enjoy some time with Ricky." I look at Steve in resignation. "I'll call his mom and confirm the arrangements and Dad will drive you over."

Aaron's face brightens. "Yes!" He makes a pumping motion with his fist.

I give my son a weak smile, kick off my loafers and head for the shower.

See? I'm good at this normal stuff.

22

The Hohman's dinner party is in full swing, when Jackie pops into the dining room carrying a chocolate raspberry torte, drizzled with chocolate genache and heaped with real berries.

A collective sigh of admiration sifts through the room as Paul helps her place the massive cake on the sideboard, between the small floral arrangements placed at each end, which perfectly match her table arrangement—votives, twigs and small round stones strewn around a vase of flowers. As if spring marched down Jackie's dining table.

Darrell McDonald, a guy the Hohmans know from church, is the first to take a bite. "Oh, Jackie. This is outstanding." He closes his eyes. "Paul, you're a lucky man."

His wife, Carolyn, frowns. "Hey, now. I may not bake, but I ride a Harley."

Her husband winks at her. "Yep, I got me a biker babe."

Laughter breaks out around the room. Jackie licks a bit of stray frosting from her finger. "Darrell surprised his wife with a Harley and lessons for Christmas," she explains. "And a full set of leathers."

Carolyn leans in my direction. "Liked to have scared me to death, learning to ride that thing."

Darrell wipes his mouth with his napkin. "But man, there's something about seeing your wife in tight black—"

She slaps at him. "Darrell!"

Everyone laughs. I glance across the table and catch Steve staring at me. He smiles when our eyes meet.

It turns out this normal thing is working for him. I know my husband's still hurting, but lucky for him, Steve has the ability to adapt to any situation.

Maybe that comes from being raised by someone like Tess, a free spirit who drew no boundaries and imposed no limits, leaving Steve to often find his own way.

The upside? Steve's ability to shift his expectations. To live in relative peace, even when hard things try to knock him down. But, there's a downside as well. He never stays in a difficult situation long enough to really feel and let his emotions heal.

Steve thinks it's time to pack up Pearl's things. But, I'm not ready.

I work hard to react appropriately to the conversation around the table.

When Darrell mentions he read an article in the Idaho Statesman announcing the grand opening of Steve and Paul's shopping center, I feign interest and join in the con- gratulations. As the discussion turns to the difficulties businesses face in this tough economy, I knit my brows in concern. And, I'm quick to express delight when Darrell and Carolyn announce they will soon be grandparents—even though the news cuts like a knife.

Jackie glances over at me. "Barrie, are you okay?"

Everyone stops talking. I muster a weak smile. "Sure, yes. Of course."

Carolyn pushes her empty plate back. "But you haven't

touched your cake, and you barely ate any of Jackie's famous crab cakes. Maybe you are coming down with a stomach bug, or something?" She turns to Paul. "Remember, the pastor's wife was down for two days last week with something going around."

Paul's face goes soft, his eyes filled with empathy. "Okay, you guys caught us. The cat's out of the bag. Huh, Barrie?"

Confused, I open my mouth to reply, but he cuts me off. "Barrie and I snuck and ate more than a few samples in the kitchen while the rest of you were out here nibbling on goat cheese."

"That was goat cheese?" Steve asks, his face looking a bit soured.

Laughter breaks out, a welcome diversion. I glance at Paul, sending a silent thank you across the table. He smiles in return.

After dinner, we join the Hohmans at the front door and tell the McDonalds goodbye. Steve reminds Darrell he'll see him at Bible study. I lift my chin slightly.

My husband sees the question in my eyes. "We all meet for breakfast at the church on Tuesday mornings. I told you that."

I nod, thinking perhaps he did. I don't remember. Still, the knowledge leaves me feeling a bit unsettled. It's not that I don't think studying the Bible is a good idea. But, a person can carry that kind of thing too far. And it's just one more way Steve is moving on, without me.

"Steve, what did you do with my jacket?"

"Honey, would you mind if Paul and I review some last minute changes in the lease language? We meet with the attorney first thing in the morning."

I shrug, knowing any objection would appear rude. Instead, I offer to help Jackie with the clean up. She waves me off, saying her housekeeper will help put things away in the morning, then adds, "I'll send some of that cake home for Aaron."

"Is there any left? I thought Darrell was going to eat it

gone." I smile and follow her into a room with overstuffed cream-colored sofas lined with accent pillows in shades of aqua. A pretty room, one made for holing up with a good book, or perhaps a close friend.

Jackie pours us each a glass of sparkling pomegranate cider from a delicate decanter on the coffee table. I saw the empty bottle on her kitchen counter, and recognized the brand as one I'd seen in the upscale market over on Jefferson—the store where it's impossible to find processed cheese spread for my celery.

Finished, she kicks off her rhinestone-studded flats, a pair Pearl would've loved, and sits, pulling her feet up. She pats the cushion next to her.

"Dinner was great, Jackie. I've been struggling with my appetite lately, but everything tasted delicious." My attempt at small talk fails to squash my desire to get home and climb in bed, with the promise of the blissful nothingness of sleep. I lower myself at the opposite end of the sofa. With the tip of my finger, I stir the juice.

Jackie sips her drink in silence for a few moments, then looks up at me. "Are your days getting any easier, Barrie?"

Her question catches me a bit off guard. I muster all the fake gaiety I can find and paste it across my face. "Oh, sure. I mean, I still struggle at times. But, like Steve says, you have to take some steps to move on."

She nods, and chews her lip, deep in thought.

"The books on grieving explain all this will take time." I sip my drink and look past her, out the window to the black night sky. "I've got that. Time, I mean."

Jackie fingers her necklace, a big chunky gold thing like I see on the women in the daytime soaps I've taken to watching, a fact that would rub my mother raw.

Without warning, tears form. I say nothing, despite my deep longing to talk about Pearl. No one wants to discuss a dead daughter. Even Mother changes the subject when I mention her.

I glance around the beautiful room, the cream-colored drapes hanging at the windows, pulled back with ties the exact shade of the pillow I lean against. The matching lamps. The art on the walls.

Despite the fact my heart longs to tell someone how I miss the sound of Pearl's music blaring from her room while I cook dinner and even her hair clips left on the kitchen counter, how could this woman, with her impeccable life, possibly comprehend how I feel?

The worst thing you might say about Jackie Hohman is that her son has too many tattoos. In a million years, she could never know what I'm going through now.

Could she begin to grasp how disoriented I've become? Does she know what it's like to walk on shifting sand? That no matter where you step, trying to find a firm ground, there simply is none?

Only months ago, I took for granted my daughter's voice drifting through the house. Now, the walls echo silence.

"Listen, I'm not going to pretend to understand how you feel." Her voice is composed as she tucks her long blonde hair behind her ear. "But I bet at times, the happiness of others must twist that rag a little tighter."

I shake my head. "Oh, no—I, uh . . . I need to be around people who are enjoying ordinary things. You know? It's just that—"

"Your heart won't cooperate?" Jackie swirls the pomegranate cider in her glass.

"Yeah. Something like that." I sigh, a small sound, and stare out the window. I wait for what I know is coming—the Jesus talk, or something.

Instead, Jackie reaches for my hand. "I'm here if you ever need anything. I mean that. And you *will* get through this."

Eyes lowered, I jiggle the ice in my glass.

For a brief moment I consider confiding in the woman at the end of the sofa. Just as quickly, I dismiss the idea. No one needs to know Pearl was pregnant, not even this sympathetic woman with her stunning house, fancy shoes and perfect crab cakes.

I finger Pearl's bracelet on my wrist.

Not even this sincere woman would understand that despite my promise to Steve to set aside the unanswered questions and move on, I'd poured over the photos in the scrapbook Pearl's friend, Rebecca, presented to me at the funeral, trying desperately to find some clue.

How, like some obsessed woman, I'd examined each one for some hint of who Pearl might have been with, who she probably snuck out to see the evening she was killed. Maybe even to tell him she was pregnant.

Looking up at my hostess, I smile and thank her. Yes, I know we'll all get through this horrible time, I tell her.

What I don't say is that I even called Rebecca—twice. That I'd decided to back off, after overhearing her tell another girl in the hall about my calls, characterizing them as "creepy."

I drain my glass and set it on the coaster. "Maybe I could talk to Troy? See if he remembers any more details about—"

"Hey, Barrie. You ready to go?" Steve enters the room, followed by Paul. "We have that early meeting."

I jump to my feet. "Sure, honey." I straighten the pretty blue sofa pillow before following Steve into the entry foyer.

At the door, Jackie gives me a warm embrace and whispers in my ear. "Remember, I'm here if you need anything."

On the way home, Steve goes on about how much he enjoyed getting to know the McDonalds. "Pretty funny stuff about those Harleys, huh?"

"Uh-hum." Distracted, I look out the car window at the black sky dotted with stars. At times, the lights from the city can dim their brilliance, but here in the foothills, the view looks like someone sprinkled thousands of tiny diamonds above the horizon.

The sight makes me feel insignificant. Like somehow in the vastness of it all, I could easily get lost.

In some ways, I guess I have.

STEVE CHECKS THE LOCK, and together we head upstairs. I can't stop myself from opening the kids' doors on the way to our room. Why, I don't know. My head knows both rooms are empty.

Steve is propped on his pillow, reading over the lease one more time while I get ready for bed. At my vanity, I rub cream across my décolletage, making wide sweeps up toward my neck like the label on the jar recommends.

Never one to spend much on vanity items, I succumbed to the QVC host when she promised the elixir would shave years off my appearance, leaving me feeling younger.

Who couldn't use a little of that?

Massaging the remaining creme into my hands, I lean closer to the mirror and examine my reflection. Several new wrinkles and under-eye circles the color of cigarette ash stare back, mocking me. The image eerily resembles my mother's features—something I'm not prepared to see.

I close my eyes, envisioning the way I used to look—how I used to feel. Somehow, I've lost the girl in me, let spontaneity slip through my fingers. That realization takes hold of me like a cold hand around my heart.

I've morphed into a woman mired in grief, and every minute of despair I've felt these last months shows on my face. I used to be pretty. I used to be—a little daring. There was a time I'd have ridden a Harley.

I don't even know who I am anymore.

When I buried Pearl, I guess a part of me stayed in that casket with her. Somehow I've got to find a way to resurrect the woman I once was. I'm tired of feeling this broken.

Without fully comprehending the need, I stand and turn out the light.

Finding Steve dozing, the lamp still on, I pull the paper from his hand and toss it on the floor.

His eyes open in surprise.

My mouth presses against his with an insistence that surprises even me. I take in the smell of him, a man's smell. His chest hair brushes against my bare skin and a slight shudder trickles down my stomach.

I reach beneath the covers, letting my hand wander. Steve's breath catches. He lifts, but I slam his body back against the bed, pressing myself against him with an urgency I've not felt for some time.

Minutes later, we lay staring at the ceiling, drenched in sweat.

"What was that?" Steve's face breaks into a puzzled grin.

I wait for my breathing to slow. A tear forms and trickles down the side of my face as I take a deep breath and search for the words to explain.

"I just didn't feel like being myself tonight."

23

We survive Pearl's birthday week by painting the house, inside and out. Like Daddy used to say, a good coat of latex enamel covers up almost anything.

Almost.

After days of non-stop taping, rolling and cleaning brushes, we finally finish. I'm labeling containers of left over paint in the garage and Steve's storing the cans on the top shelf, above where we hang the ladders and yard tools, when Steve's cell rings.

"Barrie, there's a problem with the building permit on the corner parcel. Radlin Drug will walk if we don't get started on time. I need to go."

I shrug. "No problem. I'll store the painting equipment." With my forearm, I brush the hair back from my sweaty face.

"Sure you can handle getting up in the attic?"

I wave him off. "Of course. Now go take your shower."

It takes three trips to carry the drip pans, brushes and tarps up the narrow folding steps to the small storage area above our garage filled with boxes.

Only minutes into the process, I remember why it's been so long since I've ventured up here, and why I always let Steve be the one to maneuver the cobwebs and dust.

With the last of our painting supplies tucked on a shelf at the back of the small space, I hurry for the exit before I go into a sneezing fit. My foot lands on something that makes a crunching sound under my weight. I look and groan, realizing I've broken a set of Christmas lights. The ones Pearl begged me to purchase when—

Out of nowhere, fresh tears appear and my heart sags under the weight of yet another memory. I bend and clutch the strand of lights in my hands, not caring that glass shards slice into my palms. The sting doesn't compare to my lacerated emotions. I slump to the grimy floor, letting the tears I'd held back for weeks flow freely down my face.

We decorated our tree with those lights. Back when I still thought Pearl would wear a gown, fix her hair and we'd laugh together and take photos of her pinning a boutonniere to the lapel of some lucky boy's rented tuxedo? Before the dream of her marching down the aisle to strains of Pomp and Circumstance in her cap and gown hadn't been ripped from my reality?

"Mom?"

I hear Aaron's voice below in the garage and quickly wipe my face. His head pops up through the opening. "Mom, are you okay?" He climbs on up and joins me on the floor.

I pull my son into a tight embrace. "Yes, I'm okay. I just—well, sometimes my heart hurts really bad and I need a good cry. Know what I mean?"

He hugs me tight. After several seconds, he winds a strand of my hair with his forefinger, a habit from younger years when he'd nestle in my lap for comfort. "Want me to get Dad?"

"No," I say, assuring him everything is fine now. I stand and brush off my pants, determined to sweep away the unpleasant outburst.

We both climb out of the attic and I glance at my watch. "You're home from soccer practice a little early, aren't you?" Then I remember he'd told me at breakfast I needed to pick him up an hour earlier today. "Oh, son. I'm so sorry. I forgot—"

"Jason's mom gave me a ride."

"Everything all right in here?" Steve stands at the door into the house, concern written on his face.

Before I can respond, Aaron answers. "She just needed a good cry, Dad."

When Steve focuses his gaze in my direction, I see the disappointment in his eyes, feel his impatience. He directs Aaron inside, and tells him to straighten his room, promises when he gets home they'll go fishing at the pond east of town.

As soon as we're alone, Steve turns his attention to me. "Barrie, I know this is a hard week, but you need to keep it together. For Aaron's sake."

Deep inside, I feel the truth of what my husband is telling me. I know I've not been there for Aaron like he needs. Still, Steve's statement whips at my already raw emotions.

I tighten my jaw and force out words. "Do you not think I want to be happy?" Anger burns at the back of my throat. "I've lost my daughter. She's not coming back. I'll never see her get married. Never hold her children. I won't—"

"Don't you think I feel the same?"

I clamp my lips shut, waiting for what I know will come next.

"I hurt too, Barrie. So does our son. You don't have the corner on the pain market." He raises his voice. "But this isn't healthy. We can't keep dwelling on all this. Aaron needs permission to be happy."

Steve's reaction, the tone in his voice, catches me off guard. "Well, I guess an apology is in order. I didn't realize my inability to box up my emotions and hide behind some building permits and site plans wasn't working for you."

I feel myself losing control. The voice inside my head warns me to step back from this ledge. Even though I know a fall is coming, months of pent-up anger propels me forward, and I jump.

"You got a magic pill I can take, Steve? Some tablet I can swallow so my eyes don't search for her in the halls at school? A prescription to keep my stomach from lurching when another envelope from some college arrives addressed to her? If there's a medication that will keep me from waking up in night sweats because I'm haunted by the image of her stone cold body at the mortuary, then give it to me."

My fists clench and I lean forward, my voice growing so loud the neighbors likely hear every word. "Better yet, let's just march down to church with Paul and Jackie and God will fix me."

"This is what I'm talking about, Barrie. It's impossible to have a conversation with you. Both Aaron and I need—"

"Why don't you go ahead and say it, Steve? I mean, who is Barrie Graeber if she's not the woman failing everyone?"

Steve's eyes soften. "Is that what you think?" He shakes his head. "I'm worried, Barrie. You—it feels like I'm losing you."

For the first time in this conversation, Steve lands square on the truth. Because ever since we buried Pearl, I've been lost.

The problem is, I don't know how to be found.

STEVE HASN'T BEEN GONE twenty minutes, when Mother calls. "Hello, Barrie dear. I'd like to take you for dinner tonight."

"So, Steve called you?"

"He's worried about you."

Inwardly, I groan. He must be worried if he's joined forces with my mother. "Mom, I don't think so. I'm really tired—"

"Nonsense. Reservations are made. I'll pick you up at five." Click.

Well, there you have it. Dinner with Mother, thanks to Steve and his concern. The idea makes me even more exhausted.

I hang up and move into the kitchen, my shoes making a gritty sound against the floor tiles. For a few minutes, I ponder grabbing the mop and bucket.

In the end, I go upstairs and crawl into bed.

24

Along the Boise River, the day's light fades to evening, the fresh smell of spring leaves vying for space in chilled air filled with the intoxicating scent of lilacs.

From the restaurant deck where Mother and I sit at an outdoor table, we see a duck waddling along the foliage and tall grass growing along the bank, followed by three tiny ducklings. She searches for a safe place to enter the water with her offspring, but the fast flow of the spring runoff changes her mind and she leads her young family back onto the footpath where no danger lurks. I send up a silent prayer, hoping the little momma is granted the ability to keep her babies out of harm's way.

"I'll have the almond crusted trout salad, and a glass of club soda with a lime twist. Plenty of ice." Mother tells the waiter.

He takes her menu, then directs his attention at me. "Ma'am?"

"Oh, uh." My eyes quickly scan the selections.

The Cottonwood Grille is one of my favorite restaurants. I look forward to the signature lobster risotto every time Steve and I come here for a special occasion. But this evening, I'm not up for Mother's disapproval, so I pass on the calorie-laden entrée, selecting a safe choice. "I'll have the same salad. With iced tea."

As soon as our waiter is out of earshot, Mother removes her reading glasses. "Steve tells me he's worried about you."

I watch a girl about Pearl's age walk in the restaurant behind her parents, her blonde ponytail swinging. "Yeah, I know."

Mother opens the linen napkin and removes a roll. "Should he be?" She offers me the basket.

I shake my head. "If you're asking if I'm still grieving the loss of my daughter, the answer is yes."

Mother's perfectly manicured nails break open the crusty bread. She slowly butters the steaming roll without speaking. Finished, she lays it on her bread dish. "It's understandable you are still hurting. But a person can get mired down with their emotions." She says this carefully, as if speaking with a child that could erupt into a tantrum at any moment. "You mustn't let Pearl's tragedy redefine who you are, Barrie."

I turn my full attention on her, my eyes glistening with held-back tears. "No one could possibly go through something like this and not be different, Mother."

We're interrupted when the waiter appears at our table with our drinks. He promises our entrees will be out shortly.

When we're alone again, Mother stirs her soda. "They never put in enough ice," she says.

"Mother, when did you realize Daddy was an alcoholic?"

She stops stirring. Raising her gaze to meet mine, she places her spoon on the table next to her plate. "Barrie, I'm surprised at you. Your father wasn't an alcoholic."

"What do you mean he wasn't an alcoholic? He passed out sitting in his chair every night after drinking umpteen cocktails."

Mother tosses me a stern look and lowers her voice. "Your father was not an alcoholic."

Her response is one I fully expected. Still, I press on. "Do you suppose he was too scared to admit he had trouble with his drinking? I mean, maybe he'd have sought help if he knew he had our support."

Mother threw her napkin to the table. Her words become as brittle as the bread crust. "Look Barrie. I know you have been struggling with . . . well, with everything. But I won't stand for Jack Taylor's name to be denigrated, not even by his daughter."

"Mom, surely after all this time we can—"

"That's enough, Barrie." She gives me a warning look as the waiter steps to our table, his arms laden with plates and a pepper mill tucked in his arm. He places our salads. Both Mother and I decline pepper.

"Anything else I can get for you ladies?"

We shake our heads and wait in silence until he smiles and retreats back to the kitchen.

"Next Saturday morning, my car will pick you up. I've arranged for a day at the spa for you and that nice Jackie Hohman. A pedicure and a massage will do you good." She lifts her roll. Frowning, she examines my hair. "And perhaps the salon can give you some of those pretty highlights?"

COMPASSIONATE FRIENDS MEETS every Tuesday night in the basement of St. Luke's Hospital.

Steve attended one meeting with me in the early weeks after Pearl died, then claimed it wasn't his thing. But he encouraged my attendance. "I know how you need to talk out your feelings," he said, while clicking through the sports channels.

The printed brochure handed to me at the door says tonight we'll focus on the unexpected waves of grief.

I fill a Styrofoam cup with coffee tinged with a slight burnt aroma, then make my way into the room and take a seat in the third row, next to a young Hispanic woman, her dark brown eyes layered with pain. She gives me a timid smile as I sit. I nod in return, at this stranger who understands the depth of the emptiness I feel.

The meeting opens with a few brief announcements. After the speaker, we'll move to sharing time, an opportunity for people to share their struggles with other parents who have lost children to death.

The speaker walks to the podium, a man who is simply introduced as Chuck. He clears his throat. "How many of you have been surprised by your grief? By that, I mean your emotions have a will of their own no one else seems to grasp."

Hands go up across the room.

Chuck nods. "People in life experience death in various forms. They lose friends, they lose relatives. Some think losing a child is the same. And it's not. It's very, very different." He takes a deep breath. "Others assume it's like any other death. In time you'll get over it and move on. But our grief is not like that."

I let the speaker's words wash over me like warm rain, cleansing away the notion I've lost my mind. All because I can't let go of this pain.

After sharing time, I light a candle to my daughter's memory—in honor of her birthday. I see several mothers, and a few dads, cry in solidarity. They know. They understand what I feel.

And it helps.

25

"Choose your color." Jackie pulls a peachy looking shade from the rack of nail polish.

Overwhelmed by all the choices, I lean forward for a better look before reaching for a bottle of nail lacquer. Way more fancy than the regular bottle of polish in my bathroom drawers.

Not wanting to hold things up, I select a shade called Holy Pink Pagoda and follow Jackie to the back of the salon.

Soon, I'm sitting in a black chair with rollers kneading up and down my back, my feet tucked into a warm tub of bubbling water. I can't help but sigh. A gal could get used to all this pampering.

"This your first pedicure?" Jackie asks from the seat next to me.

I lift my head. "How did you know?"

She grins. "Pearl told me she'd given you a gift certificate and you'd never used it."

My mind flits to the desk drawer where I'd tucked the little silver envelope, thanking my daughter profusely and promising I'd use it soon.

How had I forgotten?

"I'm sorry, Barrie. I didn't mean to mention her and make you sad."

"Oh, no. That's okay. Really." I feel the pedicurist lift my foot from the water. "No one ever talks about her anymore." My eyelids drift closed. The soothing atmosphere teases me into dropping my guard a bit. "She really liked you, Jackie." I take a deep breath, before adding, "In some ways, I actually felt a little jealous."

"You had no reason. Pearl admired you very much."

Leaning back into the massaging rollers, I let out a sigh. "Don't go bestowing any undeserved Mother-of-the-Year awards on my head. I failed her in plenty of ways." I'm surprised when a lump forms in my throat.

"You did the best you knew to do." Jackie says firmly. She pauses, as if contemplating what she wants to say next. "Years back, I got distracted and left for the grocery store. It wasn't until I climbed out and opened the back door to retrieve my son that I realized I'd left him strapped in his car seat in the middle of our living room." Jackie falls silent, deep in thought. Even the pedicurist stops clipping.

"What happened?" I ask, masking my shock.

"Well, I rushed home, of course. And there he was, sound asleep. In his car seat—right where I'd left him." Jackie takes a long sip of her water bottle before twisting the cap back on. "The perfect parent thing is a myth."

I let my head fall back against the chair, pondering this surprising revelation. "Wow, remind me to avoid deep conversations about motherhood with *you* again."

Jackie busts out laughing, spewing water from her perfectly glossed lips. "Oh, I'm so sorry." She quickly leans and grabs a tissue from her purse, offering it to the lady bent at her feet. She turns to me, her lips curled in an apologetic smile, and mouths "*oops*".

I laugh as well. Before we know it, both of us are cracking up. The pedicurist, who doesn't seem to understand much English, smiles and nods her head.

"Troy was a good friend to Pearl," I say. "I don't know if I told you this, but I talked to him several times about those last days. Even asked him if he was the one who gave Pearl this bracelet." I hold up my wrist encircled by the gold band.

Jackie smiles. "Yeah, he told me. I think he might have liked to have had that kind of relationship with her. She was a lovely girl. But, he assures us Pearl was dating someone—and it wasn't him."

"And he doesn't know who?" I prompt, sounding hopeful.

Jackie shakes her head. "No. He doesn't know."

Later, as we walk our pretty toes to our cars, a pickup with the back end loaded with cheering students passes, honking. Jackie sighs and rolls her eyes. "Looks like somebody is enjoying their Saturday night."

I nod. "Appears that way."

She gives me a quick hug. Leaning close to my ear, she says, "Pearl admired you, Barrie. She loved your courage." She pulls back, and her face lights up with a ready smile. "She was at our house one evening with Troy, and bragged nothing could interfere when you set your mind on a mission."

"Yeah? I thought my soapboxes annoyed her to no end."

Jackie winks and blows me a kiss. She slides rhinestone-studded sunglasses onto her face and gets in her silver Jaguar.

Before closing the door, she promises to call me soon. Her words mull inside my head as I watch her drive away.

She loved your courage.

I take a moment to appreciate newly planted red geraniums and blue lobelia in the pots at either side of the spa doorway, while letting that thought sink in. I wanted to be a courageous mother, but often I'm afraid many of my actions were motivated by fear.

Fear she wouldn't excel in school.

Fear she would follow my footsteps and make choices she couldn't take back.

Fear she wouldn't be . . . as perfect as I wanted.

The often tense relationship with my own mother moves into my thoughts, and I whisper a curse.

Jackie's right. Maybe we all just do the best we know to do.

I'M on my way home when Steve calls and tells me he and Aaron are going to play another round of golf, not to worry about them for dinner. He says he'll take Aaron for pizza. I listen for his standard I *love you* before hanging up, but this time the phone goes straight to click.

Last week, Steve suggested a trip to Mexico might do Aaron some good. He said the final four leases weren't due to close until late summer, which would allow him to sneak some time off when Aaron gets out of school in a few weeks.

At the time, I'd brushed the idea aside. Days cooped up on a boat with his mother did not sound like my idea of fun.

But, maybe time away would do us good after all. An opportunity to reconnect could help with some of the tension that is building between the two of us. Floating on azure water off the shore of Cabo could be tolerable, providing I take enough novels and sunscreen.

The idea of surprising Steve with my decision adds to my already buoyed spirits.

I fought Mother on this whole spa day idea, but things turned out better than expected. Especially laughing with Jackie. Frankly, I don't remember laughing since . . . well, since Pearl died.

Immediately, I feel guilty about how good I feel.

The words of the leader at the Compassionate Friends

meeting sound at the back of my mind. It's *okay* to enjoy life again. The fact you feel happiness does not mean you don't still mourn the loss of your child.

My head gets that, but in the deepest part of me, I still struggle with the truth of that sentiment. My daughter died nearly five months ago, and one thing I have learned is this—life will never be the same.

Steve still pushes for me to let go of this pain. I agree, I've not been available to Aaron, physically or otherwise. What my husband doesn't comprehend is every time I see Aaron, I also see the beautiful blonde haired girl who no longer stands beside him. And it's almost more than I can bear. I understand that it's different for him. But I'm her mother, the one who carried her for nine months within my own body.

The Compassionate Friends group helps. Lately, I've felt hopeful. Even though life is forever altered, if all those people can survive severe loss, maybe in time I'll learn to cope better as well.

I turn my key in the ignition and jazz filters from the speakers. My hand reaches and turns up the volume. Before pulling out, I text Steve a message telling him I won't be home until later.

Not wanting to return to an empty house, I drive around for hours listening to soulful melodies of Billie Holliday and Dizzy Gillespie—the old greats Daddy used to listen to on his LP turntable in the den.

I drive by the new Walmart on the other side of town. A young woman struggles to load bags of groceries while keeping an eye on two little boys who seem bent on escaping her watchful eye.

At the stoplight, an expensive-looking red sports car edges up beside my Acura. Inside, a guy in a crisp suit with a neatly trimmed goatee smiles in my direction—one of those "hey babe" greetings. I can almost hear Pearl's teasing voice, "He's checking you out, Mom."

I avert my eyes, focusing instead on the radio's search button. Two quick clicks and a favorite Eddie Van Halen song blasts through the speakers. Feeling youthful, I crank up the knob, letting my mind drift back to a time when my only concern was the color of my lip gloss.

Down the road about a quarter mile, I pull into Paul and Steve's new shopping center, surprised at how many establishments are now open.

The pylon and monument signs glow bright in the dark sky, appearing much like the prototype drawings Steve showed me early on, when he'd barely been able to mask his excitement over the whole project.

When Steve first broke the news of his new deal with Paul, I'd been anything but supportive.

"We did it, Barrie. Paul and I won the bid."

I looked across the restaurant table to where Paul and Jackie sat, beaming. "That's wonderful."

He squeezed my hand. "Paul called Don at the bank and it's a go. We're on a fast track, so we arranged to sign papers early next week increasing our construction line."

"Increase?" I retracted my hand. "How much of an increase?"

Steve avoided my gaze and instead reached over to pull some bread from the steaming loaf the waiter had just set on the table.

Paul spoke up. "Two million."

"Two million?" I choked out.

Steve quickly nodded. "I know it seems like a lot of money, Barrie, but a project of this size requires a substantial amount over what we're used to carrying."

"The bank's going to lend us two million dollars?"

"It's a matter of perspective, Barrie. Paul's numbers project we could almost double our investment."

"But there's got to be some risk," I argued.

"Well sure, there's always risk," Paul explained. "But I assure you this project is as solid as they come. Once we signed the grocery anchor, it was like money in the bank."

From the looks of things, they were right. Steve says the last of the leases will close by the end of summer. Then he and Paul will be able to perm the loan. Nearly all the risk will be gone and our bank accounts will show the fruit of their labor.

Steve was so worried about the expense of sending Pearl to school. That doesn't matter now. The money can be used for something else—our trip to Cabo, I suppose.

Out of the corner of my eye, I notice a familiar blue Honda Civic pull from behind the shopping center. An uncomfortable feeling wedges between my shoulders. The car is Callie's.

Inside, a guy sits in the driver's seat. In the dim light from the street lamp, I can barely make out his hand reaching over and stroking her hair, her cheek. I look closer, vaguely aware the profile doesn't match Craig Ellison's.

Oh, Callie. Who have you gone off and hooked up with now?

I ease my car out of the parking lot and onto the street, pulling behind Callie's vehicle at the stoplight.

Callie brushes something from the guy's shoulder, then tosses her head back and laughs. He turns and the illumination from the corner street lamp lands just right.

My heart lurches as recognition washes over me.

Despite the cap he's wearing, there is no doubt. The man sitting in Callie's Blue Honda is Michael Warren—the coach.

26

My jaw tightens and my heart pounds. Despite what I know what I see, my mind argues. *This can't be. Surely, he knows better than to—*

The light turns green. Callie's car makes a left turn onto Fairview, heading west.

For several seconds, I sit stunned. The beat of the music on my radio fades as if the notes are being filtered through layers of cotton before reaching my senses. Tiny beats of sweat form along my hairline. I lean against my seat, fighting overwhelming emotion that nearly chokes the breath from my lungs.

As if in a time warp, my mind races through a litany of events. The Facebook interaction. The way Michael Warren always seems to be around young girls. I remember the comment Emily said he made about her looks. I notice her eyeliner.

The car behind me honks.

In an instant, I know what I must do.

I jam my foot down on the gas pedal, sending my car lurching forward. Gripping the steering wheel like it was the coach's throat, I give a yank, sending my car screeching into the far left-hand lane.

The driver of the pickup I barely miss lays on his horn and gives me the finger out his downed window.

I gun my car, my eyes locked on the tail lights ahead. When Callie's car moves into the inside lane, I follow, not bothering to signal.

Suddenly, a small red sedan pulls out in front of me. I slam my brakes to keep from hitting the car. An expletive flies from my mouth, a word I've not uttered since before I met Steve.

Move. Get out of my way.

With a quick motion, I whip around the intruder. For a few seconds, panic sets in when I fail to see my target. Then, my sights land on tail lights heading north on Cloverdale Road.

That must be them.

I lean to my right, trying to see around the car in front of me. My eyes follow the lights, desperate not to lose sight of Callie's car.

Suddenly, a severe jolt throws me forward, followed by a flash of light. A hard punch knocks me back against the seat at the same time the deafening sound of crunching metal and exploding glass drowns the radio. For a brief moment, fear clutches my heart. My lungs fight for oxygen against the deployed airbag.

I scream, but no sound leaves my lips.

"FOLLOW the light with your eyes please, Mrs. Graeber."

A bright light flashes against my pupils, sending pain pounding in my brain. Trying my best to comply, I let my vision focus on the tiny pin light the doctor shines across my face. Finally, he clicks the light off and tucks the instrument back inside the pocket of his white coat.

"You're a very lucky woman, Mrs. Graeber. You've suffered a concussion, and there's going to be a pretty good headache over the next twenty-four hours. But nothing a little pain medication won't take care of."

A commotion out at the nurse's station pulls my attention to the open door. Steve's voice drifts from the hallway. Through the glass panels, the nurse points and I watch as my husband scurries in our direction.

"Barrie? Are you all right?" He rushes to my side, clutching my hand with such force it hurts. His lips are pulled into a tight line and his neck pulses in that way I know happens when he's stressed.

I nod. "I'm fine."

The doctor pats Steve's back. "Your wife lost consciousness, but only briefly. We've run a cat scan and all appears fine. She'll be sore and will probably suffer a headache for the next while. But we're going to release her and let you take her home tonight."

Steve's eyes flood with tears. Embarrassed, he wipes at his cheeks. "Thanks, doctor."

Steve runs his free hand through his thick dark hair. As soon as we're alone, he turns to me. "What happened?"

I tell him the full story, stopping several times to emphasize that the coach was with Callie and what I saw.

"Barrie, what the dog pete were you thinking? You could've killed yourself. Or someone else."

I pull my hand free from his and press the button on the side rail, letting the gurney raise my head a bit. The movement makes my head pound harder. I blink the pain aside, and meet my husband's stern gaze. "Thanks, I appreciate your support."

"Blast it, Barrie. Cut the nonsense." Tears well in his eyes a second time. "Do you know what another tragedy would have done to me? To Aaron?"

"How do you know all this was my fault?"

"The police told me you were seen weaving in and out of traffic, that you were driving well above the speed limit."

My chin lifts. "I had a good reason."

"No reason is worth the risk you took tonight," he thunders. "The thought of losing you after . . . well, after all we've been through—I just couldn't survive it."

Guilt wells inside my gut. I hadn't thought about what it was like for Steve to get a call telling him I'd been in an accident. I reach for his arm, caressing it gently. "I'm sorry, honey."

I sit up, leaning on one elbow. "But Steve, I've got to stop him."

Steve's eyebrows knit. "Stop who?"

"Michael Warren. Steve, I told you already. I saw the coach with Callie tonight. The two of them were nestled in that car behind the shopping center doing who knows what. They pulled out and didn't even know I saw them." I take a quick breath. "Steve, I've got to do something."

A thunderous dark moves over my husband's face. His jaw sets. He opens his mouth to respond, but before he can speak another word, Mother marches into the room.

She removes her hat and cape and drapes them over the stiff vinyl chair with metal legs perched against the wall. "Steve is absolutely right on this, Barrie. What you did tonight is pure foolishness."

Mother appears shaken, despite her take-charge demeanor. She touches Steve's arm briefly, before moving to me. Leaning down, she brushes my cheek with a kiss, then sweeps several damp strands of hair back from my face. "You're going to have black eyes."

I sigh, and lean back. The move sends a spasm of pain coursing through my shoulders. The doctor warned how sore I'd be, and the tell-tale signs I've been in an accident are showing up fast.

Steve and Mother stand on either side of where I'm laying.

Like two chaperones guarding the last strain of good sense in this room, they chatter on about how in the future I must use better judgment. That I need to stay out of Warren's way. It's not my job to protect every young girl. I've been through enough. *Aaron's* been through enough.

How can I make them understand?

Someone has to stop Michael Warren, before he goes too far.

I need to inform Sharon and the school authorities. Michael Warren must be reprimanded for his complete lack of judgment. Maybe even terminated.

27

Aaron leans over and kisses my forehead. "I could stay home from school if you need me, Mom."

I squint against the bright light from the lamp on my bed table. When I see the concern pouring from my son's eyes, my hand reaches for his. I give a little squeeze and coerce a smile onto my face. Using an elbow, I struggle to raise myself. "No honey. You don't want to miss field day.

Steve leans over and adjusts my pillow, helping me nestle into a more comfortable position. "She'll be okay, Scoot. Jackie is on her way over." From the look on his face, I've slipped another couple of notches on his *good mother* scorecard.

"Steve, surely Jackie has better things to do than to spend her day over here." Giving in to the pain pressing at the back of my head, I let my head sink into the pillow.

My eyes follow my husband as he reaches for his jacket from where he tossed it on top our dressing table last evening. My fragrance bottles clink together as he pulls the coat. I want to tell him to be careful, but think better of it. He's clearly in a mood.

"I can't stay. I'm meeting with an electrician at noon and

Paul and I have a meeting with the bank after that. I don't want you alone with that concussion."

Steve frowns at my silence. "I could call your mother—" Our eyes meet and he quickly looks away.

Aaron stands near, his eyes nervously sizing up the tension between Steve and me.

Steve digs his hand deep into his jeans pocket and removes my cracked iPhone. "I'll stop by and pick you up a new phone on my way home." He tosses the broken one on the dresser. "Hopefully our service contract defines accident in broad terms."

Before leaving, Steve moves the bottle of pain pills and my glass of water so I can easily reach them. Aaron walks over and gives me a quick hug. When I wince, he pulls back. "Oh sorry, Mom."

"That's okay, baby. I'm just a little sore is all."

Steve glances at his watch. "C'mon, Scoot. Time to go." He motions and together they head into the hallway.

They hadn't taken but a few steps when Aaron glances back in my direction. "How long will Mom have black eyes?"

I see Steve's arm go around our son. "In a couple of days, no one will be able to tell she once looked like a raccoon."

Aaron's giggles fade as they move down the stairs at the end of the hall.

Glad to be alone, I close my eyes, mentally calculating how long before I can take more pain medication. Every muscle in my body aches. Reaching for the bottle, I try to focus on the tiny print on the label. The instructions clearly state I must wait another half hour before taking another dose. Fumbling a bit, my fingers unscrew the top of the bottle. My head is pounding so hard, the Bakers must feel the beat all the way from their kitchen table next door.

I toss a pill in my mouth and grab for the glass of water.

Somehow, the small act of defiance makes me feel powerful. Some rules are meant to be broken.

Like when a coach acts inappropriately.

A woozy feeling forces me back against the pillow. Perhaps if I close my eyes for a few minutes, the pill will kick in and the pain will subside. I'll just rest for a little while, then I'll figure out what to do.

There must be a way to stop Michael Warren. All I need is a plan.

A SCRAPING SOUND punctures my sleep, pulling me from deep dark nothingness. My eyelids feel weighted as I struggle to pull them open and focus.

"Oh, Barrie, I'm sorry. I was trying my best to be quiet." Jackie stands next to the windows, one hand pressed against her chest. "I came up to check on you and saw the open draperies. I was afraid the light would wake you, so I wanted to shut them."

"What time is it?"

"Nearly noon." She pulls my sweater off the bottom of the bed and folds it neatly. "I used the key Steve dropped off and came on in when no one answered the doorbell. Steve warned you might be asleep."

"That's okay. I need to get up."

Jackie returns to the window and pulls the curtains wide open, letting the morning sun spotlight the accumulation of dust on my bedroom furniture. "I wanted to rush over last night when I heard what happened, but Paul convinced me you weren't badly injured and that all you needed was a chance to get some sleep. Barrie, I'm so sorry this happened." She sits on the end of my bed. "Especially after all you've been through."

I lift myself from the pillow, trying to ignore how I must

look with my matted hair and black eyes. "It was my fault really."

"Still—" She pats my leg. "Are you hungry? I baked a coffee cake this morning and brought it over."

"No, I'm good." I swallow a cottony taste that's formed in my mouth and pull back the bed covers. "I need a shower."

"Goodness, no. Barrie, the doctor said you're to take it easy. You suffered a concussion." She maneuvers the bedcovers back in place. "Just rest today."

I shake my head and push her hands away. "I need you to drive me somewhere." I swing my legs to the floor and stand. The room spins and I reach for the bed table to steady my quivering stance.

"Whoa, girl. You don't look ready to go anywhere." Jackie's arm bullets forward, providing much needed stability. "What is so important that it can't wait a day?"

I straighten, mustering all the strength I have. The effort delivers, providing a physical resolve that up until now, failed to match the conviction deep within my spirit. "I've got to talk to Callie's mother."

Jackie slowly nods. "Oh—I see. Steve told me what you thought you saw."

"What I *did* see," I argue, pulling away from her grip. "I can't let another mother suffer not knowing what is happening to her own daughter without her knowledge."

"Listen, Barrie. I understand—"

"Are you going to take me? Or, am I going to drive myself?"

Jackie takes a deep breath and shakes her head. "Oh, all right. But you don't need to be standing in that shower where you might fall. Here, let me brush your hair and then you can wash your face and we'll go."

She bites at her bottom lip. "And we need to have you back in bed before Steve gets home." As if to herself she adds, "He'll have my skin for this."

She stomps her sporty knee length boots across my carpet, and disappears into my bathroom. "Where do you keep your hair brushes?"

I smile. "Top drawer, left of the sink."

Less than an hour later, Jackie pulls her Jag into the parking lot in front of Boxer's Bar and Grill on Chinden Road. "Somebody might want to fix that sign."

My eyes follow where she's looking. One of the neon letters has burnt out, leaving the banner reading *Boxer's Bar and G ill.* I sigh and reach for the door handle, ignoring the fact Jackie watches as if I might drop to the cracked pavement at any moment.

Jackie pushes her sunglasses up on her head and moves next to me. She looks with disgust at a beer bottle littering the weed-infested sidewalk. "Are you certain you want to do this?"

I give the heavy front door a heave and step inside, with Jackie close at my heels.

The immediate darkness feels thick, and several seconds pass before my eyes adjust. Just as dense is the smell of stale cigarette smoke mingled with a lingering aroma of human sweat.

The place is empty, except for two guys sitting up to the bar. Despite the fact it's summer, a dusty holiday wreath fights for wall space with a neon Budweiser sign.

Jackie places her hand on my shoulder and leans close to my ear. "Nice place."

"I take it you've never been dancing at Boxer's?" I whisper back.

"Oh sure. Me and Paul pull on our boots and boogie down here every Saturday night, before we get up and attend church on Sunday."

Her smart-aleck tone makes me smile.

A balding man in his late forties or so, crosses the empty

dance floor, wiping his hand on a bar towel. "What can I get for you ladies?"

Both men sitting at the bar drill us with their stares. One wears a green John Deere cap and the other has a comb-over so extreme, it looks like a wind storm hit the left side of his head going forty miles an hour.

I clear my throat, acutely aware I sport two very black eyes. Make-up only covers so much. "Uh, yeah. Is a—I'm looking for MaryAnn Pratt. I understand she works here?"

The bartender grabs a ten dollar bill off the counter and slides it into his apron pocket. "Well, if it's MaryAnn you gals are lookin' for—" He reaches for a glass and places it under a spout. "—she ain't here."

Drawing on the lever, he fills the glass about halfway before tipping the glass, reducing the amount of foam collecting on the amber liquid.

"She doesn't work here? Or—"

"Went home with Jim Tigert last evening after her shift ended. Today's her day off."

Jackie leans over and whispers, "Let's go."

I give her a pointed scowl before asking the bartender if he knows where Jim Tigert lives.

"Are you out of your mind?" Jackie rubs her forehead. "Your husband is going to blow his gasket, Barrie."

We learn Jim lives in a trailer court south of the airport. Twenty minutes later, we head that way, stopping at the first Starbucks we pass. Jackie says if she's going to be a part of this foolishness, she's going to need a double shot Skinny Cinnamon Dolce Latte—grande size.

The entrance to the small enclave of mobile homes reads Holly's Gardens. Despite the name, the place is seriously void of any foliage. There is, however, an abundance of concrete and broken pavement.

Jackie presses a button on her steering wheel, silencing the computerized voice on her GPS system.

"Look for the blue one on the right," I remind her.

"Would that be turquoise blue, or peacock blue?"

I wave off her sarcasm. True, there are several blue trailers, but only one with an air conditioner mounted in the front window. I point. "There, that one."

Jackie drains her drink and wedges the empty cup in the holder on the console. "This should prove interesting."

A quick rap on the dented metal door starts a cacophony of barking. Inside, a woman's voice shouts, "Knock it off, girls."

The door opens, and we're greeted by a heavy woman wearing a housecoat in a brightly colored floral print—the kind that closes with snaps down the front. "Yes?"

I clear my throat. "Hello. Uh—we were told we might find MaryAnn Pratt here?"

"She got red hair?"

I nod.

"She just left with my Jimmy. They's going to pick up my Prilosec down at Walgreens. Got me the heartburn something fierce." She opens the door and waves us in. "They'll be back any minute. C'mon in and sit."

Jackie and I exchange glances. I step inside and she reluctantly follows.

Two Chihuahuas dance at our ankles, yipping so loudly I can barely collect my thoughts.

"Hush. That's enough, girls," the woman shouts. The dogs immediately quiet and sit at her feet. She rewards their obedience with two tiny dog biscuits she digs from her housecoat pocket.

Within minutes, the sound of a truck pulling up outside the window draws her attention to the window. "Well, look it there. There's Jimmy and his girl now."

I try not to be too obvious as I peek out the window, sizing up the guy climbing from the shiny black truck. With his camo print shirt, jeans and boots, Jim Tigert looks like a guy you'd see on the cover of any hunting magazine.

He spits the match stick in his mouth to the ground, and offers his hand to his female passenger. She slides from the seat, grinning when he plants both his hands on her hips and lifts her from the truck. He gives her a quick pinch on the rear. She giggles and rewards him with a kiss on the mouth.

I quickly avert my eyes when the scene gets a bit more amorous than I'm comfortable watching.

I'd met MaryAnn Pratt only one other time when I'd dropped off my daughter's friend after a birthday party. Even back then, I'd been struck by the extraordinary resemblance between Callie and her mother. In some ways, MaryAnn Pratt could pass for an older sister. Especially today in that sleeveless top that stretches tightly across her perky assets. Despite the warm afternoon, surely she could find something a bit more modest to wear.

When the couple outside the window finally quit kissing and make their way inside, Jackie's face breaks into a broad grin. Undoubtedly, she's noticed MaryAnn's upper arm tattoo—a rendition of a bright pink hibiscus bloom with the words *HOT MAMA* engraved directly below.

Jim's mother tosses more biscuits to the dirty carpet. "These ladies are here to see you, Marilyn."

"MaryAnn," her son corrects.

The woman waves him off. "Oh right—sorry."

MaryAnn gives me the once over, before recognition finally dawns on her face. "You're Pearl's mama."

I nod. "Yes. Uh—can I have a minute? Could we talk?" I motion to the door. "Alone?"

MaryAnn glances back at Jim.

He shrugs.

"Sure, what's up?" She bends and strokes the dogs' heads, sending them into another barking fit.

"Hush!" Jim hollers. "Ma, put Chi-Chi and Rita in the back bedroom, would ya?"

The woman scoops up the pups. "Sure, Jimmy." She gives us an apologetic look. "Then I'll get our guests some refreshments."

Outside, I look Callie's mother in the eyes and come right to the point. "MaryAnn, last night I saw Callie with Coach Warren."

"With the coach?"

"Yes. Rather late in the evening, really. I saw them in Callie's car. They pulled out from behind some store fronts and—" I take a deep breath. "—and I have good reason to suspect they are inappropriately involved."

MaryAnn looks at me like I've grown two heads. "What exactly do you mean *inappropriately involved*?"

I look to the sky for strength, before pulling my attention back. Letting my gaze drill into MaryAnn, I answer. "I saw them alone in a car, late at night. He reached and tucked her hair behind her ear in a very intimate gesture."

Callie's mother pulls a pack of Camel Lights from her jeans pocket. She pats her other pockets until she locates her lighter. Her eyes never leave mine while she lights her cigarette. She takes a deep pull, letting her eyes nearly close while she holds the smoke in. Finally, her smoky pleasure escapes her lips, slowly. "Look, Barrie, isn't it?"

I nod.

"Well, Barrie—it's like this." She takes another drag, then tosses the cigarette to the ground and grinds her foot over it.

"Callie isn't that kind of girl."

28

Technically Sharon Manicke is my boss, but in many ways Sharon is also a friend. Knowing I have such good rapport with my school principal makes what I have to do a lot easier. "Sharon, do you have a minute?"

She looks up from her desk. Her expression immediately fills with alarm when she notices my blackened eyes. "Barrie. What happened?" She closes the file on her desk, giving me her full attention.

I ease her office door closed. "My face looks worse than I feel." I tell her all about the accident and my trip to the hospital. "But that's not why I came to talk with you. I need to talk to you about Michael Warren."

The memory of the coach caressing Callie's cheek plays in my head as I settle into Sharon's office chair. I look directly in her eyes, and make my plea. "I need your help."

Sharon frowns. "You need my help? With the coach?"

I know what she's thinking. She believes I have another ax to grind, but once she fully understands the situation, Sharon will be my ally. Once I explain what I've seen, she'll be as incensed as I am and take the necessary steps to remove Michael Warren from his position.

As school administrator, and especially in today's environment with so many inappropriate teacher-student relationships hitting the news, she'll want to take appropriate action against any staff member who crosses the line with students.

I take a deep breath, before launching into what I'd seen. Over the next minutes, I give her a detailed account of everything. "So, as you can see, he's clearly crossed the boundaries of propriety with a student—especially a female student." I stand. "I'd like to see him terminated. You've got to stop him, Sharon."

She promises she'll do everything she possibly can. First, she must prepare a written report. I assure her I will attest to what I've seen.

"I have to warn you, Barrie. I won't be the one calling the shots here. All this will have to be run through legal. Coach Warren is held in high regard by the school board, and this town. Any action taken against Michael Warren won't be popular."

"But we don't have a choice. Not when it comes to these kinds of things."

After giving my shoulders a hug, she urges me to take the day off and go on home. I start to argue, then realize she's probably right. The last thing I need is to run into Coach Warren before they're able to put him on leave and ask for his resignation.

Sharon promises to call me as soon as she knows anything. Seeing the elation on my face, she warns these things can take time. She might not have anything definitive to report for a couple of weeks.

That's why I'm surprised when she calls just as we're sitting down to eat supper.

"Barrie, I'm afraid I have troubling news."

The tone in her voice frightens me. I brace myself. "What is it?"

"The school board called an emergency meeting. I'm not at liberty to disclose the details of the investigation or discussions, but suffice it to say, both Coach Warren and Callie deny they were ever alone in a car together. After deliberation, the board feels this is a *he said she said* situation. Given the history, the allegations you've made—"

"Allegations? Sharon, I know what I saw."

"Barrie, I'm sorry. My hands are tied. There's nothing I can do."

My body tenses. "Just tell me this. How did Joe Anderson vote?"

"You know I'm not allowed to reveal that to you."

"Fine. Don't tell me. It's not as if I don't know the chairman of the school commissioners isn't one of the most dedicated Cougar boosters around. That the new football uniforms were financed by a 'secret' donation from his jewelry store."

I hear the escalation of my voice, see Steve wave Aaron upstairs and head toward me. But something inside won't let me stop. "Sharon, if you go along with their decision and don't fight the good 'ole boys, you are as pathetic as the rest of them."

I don't need to see Sharon's face to know the effect of my words. Each syllable has hit its mark, I'm sure of it.

Steve's hand grips mine and he takes the phone from my hold. I hear him apologize to Sharon. He listens briefly, then tells her again he's sorry. Before hanging up he promises he'll help me understand. No, he agrees she's not the villain in all this.

I lean against the counter, shaking.

He ends the call. "Barrie, what in the world were you thinking?"

Before he can say another word, I launch into my argument. "Steve, they aren't going to stop him. It's all about football. The whole entire school board is willing to forfeit this young girl for the sake of a championship title."

"Barrie, stop it!"

My husband rarely shouts. The fact he's raised his voice gives me pause. I take a deep breath, blinking back hot tears. I bite my lower lip and try to collect my composure. I must choose my next words carefully—make him understand the gravity of what's at stake.

Bile rises in my throat and a wave a deep grief washes over me fresh, leaving me feeling as wounded as in the hours after her death. "Steve, do you wonder what was going through her mind, if she was crying when she dialed the number and made that appointment?"

He flinches, as if my words burn. Shaking his head, he slumps against the wall. "Barrie, what is it going to take for you to understand? I can't take this anymore. I don't want to dwell on Pearl, what happened to her." He drops his hands and stares at me with eyes that plead for me to listen.

"The good memories are all I have room for. This other stuff —" He waves my phone in the air. "—we have to let it go. For all our sakes." Steve tosses my phone on the counter. I startle at the sound the impact makes and watch as my cell slides across the granite top, finally landing against the phone book.

Out of the corner of my eyesight, I see Aaron descend the stairs, pausing between each step as if to size up whether or not he can break into our discussion without suffering repercussion. Timidly, he asks, "Can I grab a plate and take it upstairs, Dad? I'm hungry."

"Of course, come on down." Steve meets him at the stair landing and gives our son a tight hug, assuring him everything is going to be all right.

I watch the two of them make their way back to the dinner table, knowing Steve is entirely wrong.

Nothing is going to be all right.

29

It feels like months have passed, but it's only been a little over three weeks since our blowup when Steve and I pack the car with lawn chairs and a picnic basket brimming with food and head for the annual Falcon River Festival.

In the time following the final day of school, I'd purposed to lay low. Let things settle down a bit. During those endless days of mowing lawns, taking Aaron to his swim lessons and staying out of Steve's way, I'd unsuccessfully tried to formulate a plan.

Over and over, I played out an imaginary scene where I'd had the good sense to take a photo of what I'd seen that night with my cell phone. In my daydreams, I emailed the proof to every single school board member and their legal counsel.

I found it easy to think about their reaction, how my pretend scenario left no wiggle room for exposing the coach, forcing those football-crazed morons into taking the proper steps to severely reprimand him for the sacred boundary he'd crossed.

Unfortunately, reality always set in. I hadn't taken that photo.

There is only my word. And no one believes me.

All my adult life, my focus has been on guiding young adults away from danger and pushing them toward a life filled with possibility. Yet, somehow I failed my calling. Even with all my training, I neglected to discern my own daughter's terrible choices before it was too late. Her future will never be. And now I'm professionally bankrupt as well—deprived of even the ability to secure safety for the girls in my high school.

Steve says I'm not responsible for the school board's decision, that accountability for their actions rests solely on the shoulders of those with the power to change the situation. He even spouted some scripture about justice being in the hand of the Lord. Seems after attending those weekly bible classes with Paul, he has all the answers.

Steve shoves the cooler of sodas into our trunk. "Did you remember the sun screen?"

I nod.

"The bug spray?" I nod.

Aaron's worried face brightens. "I'm going to buy you both some cotton candy with my allowance money."

Steve slams the trunk door shut. I look at him in silence, then move for the front passenger door of the car. "What did you say, Aaron?"

Our son scrambles into the back and buckles his seat belt. "Remember how much Pearl liked it? She said it reminded her of eating clouds made of sugar."

Pearl's bracelet dangles from my wrist as my hand pulls the visor mirror down to check my face. "Yes, I remember."

In the reflection, I see Aaron settle back into his seat. His face breaks into a slight grin. "And she liked corn dogs and hot buttered corn on the cob."

Steve moves into the driver's seat, starts the ignition and slowly backs down the driveway. "Is your mother still planning on meeting up with us?"

"No, she doesn't feel up to fighting the crowds."

The parking areas lining the river are packed on this sunny June afternoon. It takes nearly twenty minutes driving up and down the narrow lanes between the rows of cars and pickup trucks before Steve locates a spot and pulls in.

For the past thirteen years, and ever since the festival's inception, we've attended the annual event with our close friends, Joe and Connie Anderson. This year we let go of that tradition for obvious reasons. Joe is chairman of our school board, and Steve knows I'd never let the issue of Michael Warren rest.

Instead, we head in the direction where Paul and Jackie have parked their motorhome. We'll sit under the awning to watch the hot air balloon launch, and later join all the other "Parrottheads" for this year's headline entertainment—Jimmy Buffet.

A perfect day for an outdoor event, the air is warm and slightly breezy, with the early summer sun high and bright. The sky is completely cloudless, perfect for the balloon launch.

As we approach, Jackie exits the motorhome carrying a tray of iced tea and glasses. Despite the warm temperatures, she looks cool and relaxed in a crisply pressed pair of linen capris topped with a nautical looking red and white striped top. Her hair is pulled back into a ponytail. Paul follows her. He too looks relaxed, in a pair of khakis and a light yellow polo.

"Hey, you're just in time," Jackie sets the tray on the tiny patio table. "The first balloon is scheduled to launch in minutes."

She pours me some tea, just as a loud whoosh sounds and a large red balloon holding a pilot and a passenger slowly ascends over the tops of the trees along the river.

"I wandered through the craft booths earlier and found the most gorgeous quilts." She hands me the tall tumbler, its glass sides already dripping condensation. "They'll make perfect Christmas presents." After placing the pitcher back on the tray, she tilts her head back, her hand shading her eyes. "Oh my, how pretty!"

I shake my head. There was a time knowing Jackie purchases Christmas gifts in June would bug me. The way I see things now, I figure that's just the way my new friend is built. She can't help it if her molecular makeup demands that all her blouses hang color-coded in her closet. That's just who she is.

Besides, since the Andersons have dropped off our friendship map, there's simply little need to find a new couple to hang with. Not when the Hohmans navigated into our lives, like this whole thing was planned. Okay, I'm not that into their churchy stuff like Steve is, but Paul and Jackie are nice people. They've been here for us when we've needed them most.

One of the traits I most appreciate about Jackie, for example, is how she understands my grief. She doesn't push me to be happy when I feel dark and want to just stay in bed. She sees the emptiness I feel inside, and how much I miss my daughter. She lets me talk about Pearl. Something no one else seems to feel comfortable with—even when I barely mention her name.

And she gets why there are times I just need to be alone for a little while, when the pain sneaks out of nowhere and stabs my heart yet again.

After the final balloon floats overhead, I mention I'd like to check out those quilts. I don't invite anyone to go with me. Jackie's eyes meet with mine, and a look of understanding passes between us.

Steve, on the other hand, looks confused. He suggests I take Aaron with me. My son also picks up on my need for some time away from everyone, and says "Naw, I hate quilts."

Instead, he accepts Paul's offer and they go off in search of the perfect caramel apple, leaving Jackie to calm my husband's fuss with her homemade brownies.

The River Festival attracts tourists from several states and this year, every square inch of land is filled with a booth or a body. A bit of an exaggeration, but not entirely.

I wander past a woman offering samples of beef jerky and try one of the teriyaki flavored strips. I smile and tell the woman I like the flavor before moving on to a display of beautifully matted nature photos taken at Redfish Lake, one of my favorite areas in all of Idaho.

I continue bumping my way along the flow of people to a booth selling matching leash and hat sets for dogs when a voice calls my name from somewhere behind where I stand.

"Mrs. Graeber?" A man steps forward. A guy I immediately recognize, even though his hair is cut much shorter than the last time I saw him. He wears jeans and a white button-down shirt. And a smile.

"What do you want?" I ask, turning as if ready to move on. The last thing I need today is to be hounded by a reporter.

The guy reaches out and lightly grabs my arm, his touch sending a strange feeling up toward my shoulder. I scowl. "Excuse me?"

He looks sheepish as he pulls his hand back, instead extending his palm as if he believes I will engage in a handshake. "Let me start over. My name is Chad Nelson."

"Yes, I know. We've met." I let the tone in my voice convey my annoyance. "A couple of times, I believe."

He nods and lets his empty hand drop. "Look, I just need to talk to you." He runs his hand through his now short hair. His tanned face breaks into a timid smile. "It'll only take a minute. I promise."

Against my better judgment, I look around, buying time to weigh my options. I know what Mother would say. She'd warn me to steer clear of any reporters. I can hear her often spoken quote, "Never trust the media." Never mind she worked even the most seasoned reporters to her benefit during every election.

"It's about Michael Warren."

The mention of the coach's name gets my attention. "What about him?"

"Look, can we talk somewhere a little more . . . private?" He motions toward a large tree several yards past where the crowds mingle.

My eyes follow where he points, curiosity getting the better of me. "I don't have much time."

The reporter assures me what he has to say won't take long. He leads me away from the throng of people and together we sit in the shade of the tree. I make no effort to hide my impatience. "Okay, what's this about?"

Chad Nelson slides his backpack to the ground. He unzips the blue bag and pulls a thick manila envelop from inside. "Here, this will explain."

I take the package. My hands unclasp the flap and I slide the contents to my lap, never letting my gaze leave Chad's face. Finally, I look down. With shaking hands, I lift a news article off the top and raise it to a level where I can read the headline.

What I see leaves me stunned.

30

SEATTLE TIMES

Popular Football Coach Resigns in Sex Scandal

Following allegations of sexual misconduct leveled against him by a minor, Michael Warren, 32, has resigned from his post as high school football coach. "We're sorry to lose such a talented member of our coaching staff," an anonymous school authority said. "But these are serious accusations, and the board would have no choice but to place Warren on leave pending the outcome of a full investigation. Given the circumstances, I understand his decision." Prosecuting attorney, Jack Knutt, declined to comment about whether charges would be filed against Mr. Warren.

MY EYES quickly scan the remainder of the article. Finished, I let my arms drop, feeling my insides draining away, emptying. "So, he's done this before."

Chad Nelson nods. "I'm an investigative reporter for KING News Network. I've been working to develop an expose of sorts.

Following Warren is a key component of my story." He picks at a blade of grass.

"How long have you had this information?"

"I've been following rumors for a while. But I just got my hands on this concrete evidence recently," he answers, his tone solemn. "You see, what I'm discovering is only about a third of suspected cases like this get reported by school administrators."

"Ridiculous. How can that be true?"

"There's no way to prove it." Chad's eyes are piercing blue, and they are fixed on mine. "I strongly suspect it's much easier to pass the problem along, rather than deal with the consequences of reporting."

I get indignant. "But that's wrong. We're all taught to report. Failure to follow the legal mandate could result in serious charges brought against us as educators."

A couple of middle-school-aged girls wander near. We stop talking, letting them pass. One girl whispers loud enough for us to hear. "He's cute. He looks just like Matthew McConaughey." The other girl nods and giggles.

Indignant, I gather the stack of articles and shove them back in the envelope. "Coach Warren is the adult. He's supposed to maintain proper boundaries. Sawtooth High School wouldn't hire a coach with this background."

Chad Nelson sends a silent message, loud and clear.

"But . . . they wouldn't." My heart pounds. "Surely knowing this—" I offer the envelope back to Chad. "Our school board wouldn't hire Warren just to win some football games." Even as the words leave my mouth, I know the truth.

I stand, brushing off my pants. "They can't get away with this. Somebody's got to stop this insanity."

Chad lifts from the grass. He tucks the envelope inside his backpack, says nothing. I watch him rake his hand through his hair, notice the thin black leather strip tied at his wrist. Then it hits, me. What Chad Nelson has not explained.

"Why are you telling all this to *me*?" I struggle to put my thoughts together. "And why did you show up at our house after Pearl died?"

In the background, I hear an announcer's voice broadcast from across the river. I see a bluebird flutter across my line of vision, landing on a clump of day lilies. The breeze catches a gum wrapper, sending the tiny piece of paper fluttering across the grass only a few yards away.

I focus on all these details, instead of acknowledging the answer already dawning in the back of my mind. I fight to keep the idea from fully entering my conscience, knowing my mind can't accept one more painful, heart-rending bit of information. Over the course of the last six months, I've been through hell. The heat singed my soul.

Chad lightly places his fingers on my forearm. His eyes connect with my own. "I understand Warren thought a lot of your daughter," he says quietly.

I step back, shaking my head. "You think my Pearl . . .?" I stop mid-sentence. Surely this reporter from Seattle will intercept the notion forming in my head. These suspicions could not be true. I watch his face, waiting.

The possibility that my own daughter had crossed the line with the high school coach stings my emotions with such intensity, any sense of inner security vanishes like smoke on a windy day. I navigate this new possibility by shutting off my mind. There is simply no way. "No, you're wrong."

Then I remember. A voice inside my head murmurs . . .*The cell phone call—the last number she dialed that night.*

Could that have been Lisa Warren's voice? Is that why she showed up at our house, completely blotted?

At this moment, I wish I were a religious woman. Maybe faith would be an antidote to a world that crumbles beneath your feet. "Pearl would never do that," I state with as much force as I can muster. Sadly, my voice sounds weak and not very convincing.

My mind pans through the litany of events, choices we never suspected our daughter would make. As much as I want to scream at this man, tell him that Pearl would never in a million years be with Michael Warren—the deepest part of me fears he may be dead center on this one and I begin to tremble.

"Mom?" Aaron bounds across the grass, heading our way. "Dad sent me looking for you. He says to tell you we're about ready to pack up and head over to the Buffett concert."

Shaken, I take a deep breath, trying to compose myself. "Look, I've got to go.

Chad Nelson nods.

I take Aaron by the shoulder, and together we head back in the direction of the Hohman's motorhome. "Hey, isn't that the news guy that came to our house?" he says.

I don't answer. Instead, my head turns and I glance over my shoulder briefly. The man who has just rocked my world yet again stands, watching me walk away.

I don't care what he thinks he knows. My little girl would never get involved with Michael Warren.

But even as I say it, I know it's a lie. And Chad Nelson knows it, too.

31

On my sixth birthday, Daddy surprised me with a dollhouse I'd seen in Mother's Sears catalog. The gift was my greatest treasure. I arranged the tiny plastic furniture and made up conversations between my perfect little play family for weeks, guarding the miniature structure with my life. I shared my prized possession with no one—not even my best friend.

One fateful day, Mother called me into lunch and I made a quick decision to leave my dollhouse set up on the front door step. Eating my tuna sandwich would only take a minute, and I'd be right back.

I didn't count on Mother making me peel hardboiled eggs for her potato salad she needed for bridge club and by the time I returned, that bratty Danny Marcum from next door had snuck over and scattered the furniture pieces all over the yard. I found Mr. Nelson's dog chewing on the sofa and the little table.

Now, finding myself unable to sleep, I stare into the darkness of our bedroom, thinking even in grown-up dollhouses, there always seems to be a Danny Marcum in the wings.

I glance at the clock on my bedside table. Steve's been slumbering sound for hours, but I can't seem to slow my racing mind.

It strikes me now, as I listen to Steve softly snoring, that maybe I shouldn't have put off telling my husband about the conversation with Chad Nelson. In my mind on the way home from the River Festival, I'd tried to come up with the words, attempted to formulate just the right way to break this new idea to a man that cherished his little girl. No matter he'd adopted her, Pearl was flesh of his flesh in every sense of the word and something like this possibility will destroy him.

Even if Pearl and the Coach had been intimate, and the thought is inconceivable, how will any of us survive yet another blow? Still, I have to know for sure.

My feet slip to the floor and I wrap my robe over my shoulders, quietly making my way out of our bedroom and down the hall, careful not to disturb Steve and Aaron.

For weeks, I've left the door to Pearl's room closed. At first, being near her things brought comfort. But lately, the bed she'll never sleep in, the clothes hanging in her closet she'll never wear, the dresser mirror that will never again reflect that beautiful face—all of it haunts me.

Tonight, when I turn the knob and pad across her carpet in my bare feet, the thing I notice most is that her smell is fading. I breathe deeply, trying to capture the essence of my baby girl, but she's gone . . . in one more way, she's left me.

At the back of Pearl's closet, I rummage on the top shelf for the yellow bag. The one with her clothes from that night. When my hand lands on the slick plastic, I pull it down and to my chest.

Steve wanted the contents destroyed. Said the reminder was too painful, and hanging on to the clothes she wore that night was morbid. But I could no more toss these things than I could pitch her baby blanket in the garbage. Some items are too sacred to a mom's heart, even if the articles make that heart ache.

Inside, I feel for her cell phone. I'd listened to her greeting so many times in those early weeks, I thought I'd wear the battery down. My thumb presses the power button.

Nothing.

As quietly as possible, I make my way downstairs and retrieve my charger and the Sawtooth High staff directory. Back in the dark of her room, I plug in her phone—and I wait. Thirty minutes maybe, trying not to think. Instead, I hum a lullaby I used to sing whenever my little blonde toddler wouldn't settle down and go to sleep.

Finally, I reach and turn Pearl's phone on. Within seconds, the face lights up revealing rows of tiny apps.

My forefinger slides over the surface until her call history emerges. One particular number appears several times, the one no longer in service. I flip through the directory to the last page, and slide my trembling forefinger down the page to the listing for Michael Warren.

In that moment, knowing replaces all doubt. I fight to breathe, tears clawing at the back of my throat. In vain, I try to quiet the jackhammering inside my chest wall. Is it possible for an anguished heart to explode?

Why Pearl? Why would you do such a thing?

There's no way to know how long I've sat on the floor of my daughter's closet, tears flowing down my face, when Steve pokes his head inside, his dark hair frumpled. "Barrie? What are you doing?"

I look up into the face of the man I love, the guy who scooped me and my four-year-old little girl into his life all those years ago. I stand and move against him. My lips go to his and I kiss him, softly and filled with the hope this tender connection will somehow ebb the impact of what I am about to tell him.

"YOU'RE CRAZY!"

"Honey, listen to me." I shove Pearl's phone into the palm of his hand. "There's proof. She called him over and over that night. And in many days before that."

Steve's eyes go steely, like flint. Only his voice conveys more hardness. "You listen to me, Barrie." He points his finger in my face. "There is no way—NO way—an ounce of truth rests in what you're saying. You hear me?"

The ferocity of his tone causes me to step back and take another approach. "Shhh—you'll wake Aaron."

As if on cue, our son wanders into the room, balled fists rubbing at his sleepy eyes.

A dark storm passes over Steve's face. "Let's get you back to bed, Scoot." He pushes Pearl's phone back into my hand, then he places his hand on Aaron's shoulder, and guides the half-asleep boy out the door and back to his own room. I shove the phone in my robe pocket, and follow.

With Aaron tucked back under his covers, Steve turns to me. In his eyes, I see a swirling soup of hurt and anger. He brushes past and heads for our bedroom.

In a vain attempt, I try to broach the subject again as Steve plants himself on the edge of our bed. "Steve, you have to consider this very real possibility."

With a terse whisper, Steve tells me there is no way under God's heaven his little girl had sex with a married man nearly fifteen years older. "No pickin' way," he says. He warns me he's had enough drama to last a lifetime. "I mean it, Barrie. I'm done. I don't want to hear anything like that again, understand? It's nothing but nonsense, and I can't take any more," he says, his voice breaking.

"But if I'm right, that means—"

"No more." Steve grabs his pillow and heads for the door. "I'll be on the sofa."

I let myself drop to the bed. Those cell phone calls are all the proof I need to know what Michael Warren did to my little girl. And I know one more thing.

He'll do it again, if I don't stop him.

In a burst of fury, I pull Pearl's cell from my robe pocket. With the directory on the bed, I brush my finger over the face and tap out the second number the directory lists for the coach, his home number. Within seconds, I hear a dialing sound.

Brrring . . . brrring . . . brrring.

My heart pounds. Click.

"Hello?" A man's voice, heavy with sleep, answers.

"Michael?"

"Uh-huh? Yeah?"

I pause. "This is Barrie Graeber."

"Barrie?"

I imagine him sitting with the phone perched at his ear. "I know what you did to my daughter."

32

I'm not entirely sure when I make the decision to take matters into my own hands.

Maybe it's over the Fourth of July, after old man Stafford wins the greased pig race down Main Street for the sixth consecutive year. I see Coach Warren heading into Murphy's Drug, his hand placed casually on his trophy wife's back. He sees me too, and keeps his distance. The sight leaves anger broiling in my gut.

Or perhaps, my mind can't take any more when he judges the football throw sponsored by the Rotary Club in their effort to raise funds at the county fair for our local teen pregnancy hotline. Does he believe the benevolent deed makes him less guilty?

Then just like that, he shows up on television with a sports reporter asking how he plans to pull off a winning season next fall. Coach Warren's calm reply says it all. "Like everything I do," he says. "With ease."

Even Mr. Voorhees tells me his office will not be able to prosecute, that neither the incident with Callie or the cell phone calls on Pearl's phone provide sufficient proof for his office to proceed with a criminal action.

I beg off doing the dishes right after dinner, instead telling Steve and Aaron I need to pick up a few things at the local Albertson's.

"Can't that wait until tomorrow?" Steve asks.

"No, I forgot I wanted to take brownies over to Edith Bensen. She just had hip surgery. I won't have time tomorrow."

"I'll do the dishes for you, Mom." Aaron slides Omelette off his lap and moves from the sofa. "I don't mind. Really."

"Thanks, Pumpkin."

He sighs. "Mom, I'm going into the fifth grade this year. Could you quit calling me that?"

I apologize for the mommy faux pas, grab my purse and head for the car. Minutes later, I'm carting a grocery basket with a bottle of vegetable oil, a carton of eggs and two boxes of Betty Crocker brownie mix toward the check-out counter when I hear voices drifting from one aisle over.

"Did you hear Callie Pratt got arrested for driving under the influence last night?"

I don't stop to listen to the details. The news hits me hard. Even after what Callie did to Pearl, my heart aches when I hear of her continued poor choices.

I step into the store's parking lot, noticing a slight chill in the night air—a sure sign summer is drawing to a close and a change of seasons is not far off. Despite the bushes filled with roses, and the bright purple cone flowers surrounding the monument sign, it won't be long before the leaves covering the burning bushes will turn the shade of aged cabernet and the oaks lining the street will burst with fall color.

For some unknown reason, I decide to take a different route home. I consider stopping at the Rolly's Ice Cream Boat on the way. Rolly's is a favorite of Aaron's, where teens in pink and white striped paper caps serve up scoops from over fifty flavor selections into little plastic canoe-like containers with spoons in the shape of oars.

Tonight, I want to surprise Aaron with one of their specialty cakes layered thick with French vanilla and mocha chocolate. Grandma Tess isn't the only one who knows how to spoil my son.

I whip my Acura into a parking spot directly in front of the ice cream shop. It's then I see the sign on a nearby building sandwiched next to the river. I've notice the office many times, but never really seen it, if you know what I mean. Tonight, I take the sighting as a signal.

Throughout the summer, I'd waited. After weeks of complying with Steve's edict to lay low on the whole Michael Warren thing, biding my time until I can make my move—without any doubt, I realize the time has arrived.

I perch my purse on top of my car, dig inside and pull out paper and pen. Quickly, I scrawl a name and phone number. When I finish, my hand shoves the note back into my bag. A smile plays at my lips when I consider the call I'm going to make first thing in the morning.

Several minutes later, I'm on my way again. My foot punches the gas pedal and I lean back into the seat, focusing on the car's acceleration instead of my jangled nerves. A part of me is relieved the wait is nearly over. But, in spite of knowing what's ahead, I'm also keenly aware things are about to get worse before they get better.

~

"MRS. GRAEBER?"

I look up and my hand automatically straightens my hair. "Yes?"

"Ms. Crane should be wrapping up her conference call any

time." The older woman looks over her reading glasses. "Can I get you something to drink?"

"Uh, no—thanks." I give the woman a weak smile. "I apologize for being so early. Traffic wasn't as bad as I'd expected."

"No problem, dear." She moves her attention back to the files on her desk, leaving me to continue flipping through last month's issue of Trial Lawyer magazine while waiting to see Madeline Crane.

"Most people call me Maddy," she'd told me on the phone. "With the exception of a few attorneys who have had the misfortune of facing me in the courtroom. They call me Mad Dog. Behind my back, of course," she said, laughing.

I toss the magazine on the table, then nervously lean over and straighten the mess I'd created. With the volumes all neatly back in place, I turn and look at the clock on the wall next to the receptionist.

Although it seems much longer, it's only been less than a half hour since I'd parked and wandered through the front doors of Crane Law Offices, a small building tucked nearly out of sight on the banks of the Boise River.

You can tell the office belongs to a woman. The waiting area looks like something out of a Georgian mansion, with its sweeping draperies and claw-footed furnishings. Not exactly my taste, and certainly a departure from what you see in most law offices.

I stand and wander to the wall opposite the windows. Ornate frames in various sizes encase press releases and newspaper clippings. Letting my eyes drift, I examine a news article with the headline: *Wrongful Death Lawsuit Nets Record Damage Award.*

I remember then, seeing a news segment featuring a bereaved couple who'd told how no amount of money could recompense them for the loss of their baby. Prescription error, if I recall correctly.

"Ms. Crane can see you now."

The receptionist's voice startles me. I thank her, gather my jacket and purse, then follow the gray-haired woman down a hall lined with more ornate frames. The internet research I'd done was right on. Michael Warren might be a winning coach, but this lady has quarterbacked more than a few victories herself.

Madeline Crane looks very little like the photo on her website. I recognize the attractive blonde woman, but she's considerably more petite than depicted in the snapshots. Unlike what I picture in my head when I imagine a strong-minded successful woman attorney, the lady in front of me wears a flowing black skirt topped with a ruffled light pink blouse and stiletto heels decorated with tiny bows. Frankly, this forty-something gal looks like she just stepped off the set of a Designing Women episode.

As soon as we're introduced, she extends her hand. Her shake is surprisingly firm.

"Thank you for seeing me on such short notice, Ms. Crane."

"Please, call me Maddy." She leads me to a white sofa against the opposite wall, sitting next to me like we'd been life long friends. "Alice, get us some tea, would you dear? Oh, and some of those little chocolate éclairs I brought back from Seattle."

The receptionist complies, bringing in a large floral tray filled with dainty cups on saucers and a basket draped with a linen napkin. Maddy reaches for an éclair and offers the basket to me. "So, tell me what this visit is all about."

I tell her the whole story. She listens patiently, sipping her tea and occasionally nodding. When I finish, she sets her cup down and takes my hands in hers. "Barrie, I'm going to be honest. I can make a good case, based on the facts as I understand them."

She stands and retrieves a file from her desk. "After you

contacted me, I took the liberty of doing a little research. That's why I kept you waiting. I have an excellent paralegal investigator I often work with and she did some preliminary work, finding Warren never stays in one place long."

She grabs a pair of reading glasses and slides them on her nose. "She tells me the longest he's ever remained in one school district is three years." She looks over her glasses at me. "Now, astute legal counsel could argue he made each of these moves predicated by decisions intended to accelerate his career—each time moving to larger, more prominent teams." She pauses.

I lean forward. "But—"

"But, my money is on the probability Coach Warren's reputation keeps catching up with him. You see, legal counsel often recommends to school administrators not to borrow trouble, advising the cleanest way for them to move forward is to allow these predators to quietly resign. Instead of facing the music, the perpetrators simply move to another district, taking the school's headache and potential legal problems with them."

I slowly nod. "So, you believe that's what's happened here?"

Maddy cups her chin with her hand. "Let's find out."

She moves behind her desk, taps on her computer keyboard and studies her monitor. Grinning, she presses a button on her phone set. When the phone rings on the speaker, she places her finger to her mouth, signaling me to stay quiet.

On the third ring, a voice intercepts. "Good afternoon, Kavik and Preston Law Office."

Maddy winks at me. "Madeline Crane for Jake Preston."

"Mr. Preston is unavailable at the moment. I'd be happy to take a message if you'll tell me what this is regarding." "Tell Mr. Preston this relates to the paternity suit."

"Uh--whose paternity suit would that be, ma'am?"

"His."

The woman on the other ends clears her throat. "Please hold." Click.

Several seconds pass before a booming voice interrupts the silence. “Maddy Crane, how are you?”

Maddy’s face breaks into a wide grin. “Why, Jake. I’m just fine, thank you.” She winks. “Look, I don’t have a lot of time to chat, but I wanted to extend a professional courtesy and tell you that by the end of the week I’ll be filing a civil lawsuit naming Michael Warren as defendant.” She pauses, adding drama to the moment. “We’ll be forced to include the school district and Sharon Manicke, the principal, as well.”

The mention of Sharon’s name twists my gut. I never expected to include her, despite my frustration over her lack of reaction to the situation.

“Noted,” Jake responds. His voice takes on an edgy tone. “What are the allegations?”

Maddy’s jaw sets and her blue eyes turn steel gray. “My client is Barrie Graeber.”

“I see.”

My mind races. What does *that* mean? It’s as if he knows full well who I am and what all this is about. Like he’s been expecting a call of this nature. I tighten my grip on the arms of the chair, trying to take in all I’m hearing.

In a chess-like verbal joust, the attorney on the other end of the line warns Maddy, “You know the rules. Judges tend to toss frivolous complaints.”

Maddy slides a paper clip around on her desk with her manicured nail. “Hmmn, I suppose you’ve got to know the rules, before you know which ones you can break. And Jake, darlin’?”

“Yes?”

“Ole’ Mad Dog’s going to prove the district broke them all.”

33

You did what?" Steve drops his coffee mug down on the breakfast table. Coffee sloshes out, creating a tiny brown puddle next to his plate of eggs and toast.

I take a deep breath, resigned to the argument I know is coming. "Look, Steve, I don't want to fight about this. Let's just talk."

He looks at me, eyes wide. "Did you listen to a word I said? Does anything I think or feel matter to you anymore, Barrie?" He stands and gives his chair a shove. "And what about Aaron? Did you stop and think how filing a lawsuit over all this would impact our son? Or our daughter's reputation? For pity sakes, let our little girl rest in peace."

"Steve, please. Calm down. Just listen to me a minute—"

"No," he barks. "I'm done listening. I'm done—" My husband storms to the coat closet, grabs his work jacket and heads for the door.

Surprised by the level of his fury, I hurry to stop him. I've got to make him listen to reason. "Honey, wait. You don't understand."

With his hand on the door knob, he looks back at me with

disdain. "I understand plenty." The door slams behind him, rattling the frames on the wall.

"But, if we can just talk—" my voice trails off. Tears pool in my eyes as I consider our heated exchange.

My eyes drift to our family portrait on the wall to the right of the door, the one we had taken the summer before Pearl's accident. We looked so happy, despite the tension created when I forced everyone to wear matching red shirts.

My hands reach and I straighten the frame, knocked lopsided from the slamming door. I swipe my tear-filled eyes. Given time, Steve will settle down. Eventually, he'll understand. Somehow.

"Did you and Dad have another fight?"

I turn to find Aaron eying me suspiciously.

"No," I avert my gaze, not wanting him to see the lie in my eyes. "We're just working through some things we don't agree on. That's all." I place my hand on my son's back and lead him into the kitchen. "You're going to have to hurry and eat, or we'll be late."

After dropping Aaron at the bus stop, I head off to school. I don't know which I dread more, seeing the coach, or finding myself face-to-face with Sharon Manicke.

Technically, the lawsuit won't be filed until Friday morning, but I know myself. I'll never be able to look her in the eyes, knowing what I'm planning.

Luckily, I never meet up with Michael Warren. But near the end of the day, I hear someone tap at my door. I look up to see Sharon standing there, her features looking like she'd swallowed a nasty piece of spoiled fish.

"Barrie, can I have a moment?"

The business-like tone in her voice sends a ripple of tension down my back and causes my gut to clench. *She knows.*

I try to make my voice sound light. "Of course, what do you need?"

"The district's counsel has alerted us of your allegations regarding Coach Warren and your daughter—and of your legal plans."

"Oh—" I lean back in my chair and steeple my hands, pausing to collect my composure before trying to explain. "Sharon, I have to do what's right here. She was my little girl. You know?"

She weighs her words carefully. "I know since Pearl died you've been under considerable pressure, but—"

"And I don't want to name you. But, I have no choice."

"You're—you're naming me as well? Naming me personally?"

I swallow quickly, trying to calm the sinking feeling in my stomach. I let my hands drop, hoping she won't see my trembling fingers. "Like I said—I have no other option."

She lifts her chin. "Barrie, you know I have great respect for you as a counselor. But more than that, I considered you my friend."

The past tense she uses does not slip my notice. "Likewise, Sharon. But there is simply too much at stake in this situation. I can't let my personal feelings distract me from what has to be done."

"But, Barrie—"

I hold up my open palm. "My daughter is no statistic in a news article somewhere. She was a beautiful, bright girl with a whole lifetime ahead of her."

I look my principal in the eyes. "This school board should be ashamed as educators. All of you have looked the other way, pretending none of this is going on in our school." To emphasize my point, I add, "What price is too high for that football championship, Sharon? Should a trophy cost a young girl's self-worth? Or my daughter's life?"

I huff in disgust. "Every year when the janitor dusts off that shiny prize, will he remember Sawtooth High School sold out and failed to protect our young women in order to call ourselves winners?"

Sharon's eyes grow dark. "Don't be ridiculous, Barrie. Do you really think these girls will finally be safe if you take Coach Warren out of the picture? Oh, sure, he won't be enticing another naïve student into his bed. But let me clue you in on something. Do you think Coach Warren's file is the only one in my locked cabinet?"

Her lip quivers. "I've been in school administration for nearly twenty-five years. This problem is at epidemic levels in our schools. There are individuals like me out there in every high school in America. We want to stop these teachers who cross the line."

My heart thuds painfully. I sit motionless, listening.

"But take a look around. As a society, we need to pull our heads out of the sand. We've robbed teachers of any ability to discipline, and tied the hands of administrators when we try to terminate poor-performing instructors. We're not permitted to have the Pledge of Allegiance and prayer in our classrooms. And after seeing the movies and television programming coming out of Hollywood these days, are we really that surprised when respect and morals get blurred in our schools?" She lets out a defeated sigh. "So, go ahead, Barrie. Name me as a defendant, if you must." She turns to leave, then hesitates. "But when you do, ask yourself what role *you* played as a parent. Do you think you and Steve have no responsibility in what happened to Pearl?"

The verbal slap makes it difficult to draw air. Reeling, I consider the woman standing in my doorway. The only thing I can do is recite what Madeline Crane told me yesterday when I'd timidly admitted I wondered the same thing.

"Mothers can't protect their daughters from getting bit, when schools won't keep the snakes off the football fields and out of their classrooms."

34

Feeling somewhat shaken from the events of the day, I decide to swing by and pick up Aaron from school. He's taken the brunt of a lot of the tension at home, and it'll be a treat not to have to ride the bus. Besides, missing his last period study hall won't hurt, just this once.

Less than a half hour later, I enter the school office to check out my son.

"Can I help you, Mrs. Graeber?"

I greet the young lady behind the counter, one of my former students. "I'm here to pick up, Aaron."

She looks puzzled. "I'm sorry Mrs. Graeber. He's not here."

"What do you mean he's not here?"

"Well, his dad dropped by just after lunchtime and checked Aaron out of class. Said he wouldn't be back for a few weeks and asked us to collect his assignments, so Aaron wouldn't fall behind."

I stare in disbelief. *Gone? For a few weeks?*

Trying to keep panic from my voice, I thank her for the information and mumble something about forgetting who was to pick Aaron up.

I rush home, dropping my purse on the floor the minute I enter the front door. "Steve?" I holler. "Aaron?" An eerie silence greets me.

I race up the stairs, stopping first by Aaron's room. Throwing the door open, I call out again, even though my mind tells me no one is inside. "Aaron, are you there sweetie?"

Omelette sits on the floor by my son's bed. He whimpers as I move past him to Aaron's chest of drawers. The underwear drawer is open. With my hip, I slide it shut.

My hand goes to my mouth, as the lunch I'd eaten a few hours earlier threatens to come up again.

I hurry into our room. There, on the pillow, I see an envelope leaning against the white pillow case. My name printed across the front in bold letters.

With trembling fingers, I lift the envelope and tear open the end. Inside, I discover a single sheet of white paper. I open the letter carefully and hold my breath as I read Steve's message.

Cabo? He took Aaron and they went to Cabo?

Tears burn at the back of my eyes. I blink hard, letting the moisture run down my cheeks. I slump to the bed.

Without me?

My hand crumples the paper, letting it drop to the floor. I shake my head miserably. My fingers slide my staff badge from around my neck. I place it slowly on my dresser.

After kicking off my shoes, I pull the bed covers back and crawl beneath the sheets. Under the darkness of the blankets, my mind grapples with the notion I've always seen myself as strong and brave, willing to do the right thing no matter the cost.

In truth, it's just the opposite.

Barrie Graeber–wife, mother and high school counselor extraordinaire—is really just a lonely, scared woman unable to conquer her vast weakness, no matter how hard she tries to hide that reality.

I draw my knees up and let out a deep moan.

How could Steve do this to me?

Hours pass before my tears finally subside. Exhausted, I pull the blanket free and kick at the crumpled sheets.

Knowing what I must do, I lift myself from the bed and pad across the darkened room. Omelette follows closely on my heels as I move down the stairs, to the front door. Bending, I lift my purse and dig for my cell phone.

Madeline Crane is the fourteenth person in my contact list. When her name appears, I press the call send button and wait. She answers her personal cell phone on the second ring.

"Madeline Crane here. What can I do for you, darlin'?" I release a heavy sigh.

"We need to talk."

~

AFTER SPILLING my guts to Madeline Crane, I feel so ashamed my eyes fill with tears. "So, there you have it, Ms. Crane. He left yesterday, and I don't know when he'll be back."

She hands me a tissue. "Darlin', don't you worry none about that man of yours. I've had four husbands, sweet men each and every one. Trust me, they come around. And the ones who don't—" she shrugs. "Well, then you learn to move on."

She sees my raised eyebrows and quickly adds, "Oh, don't look at me like that. I truly adored each and every one of the men I married." She leans close. "Especially the rich ones."

Her humor hits the mark. My face breaks into a grin. Maddy returns the sentiment with her own warm, pink-lipped smile, and she pats my leg. "Well, let's get down to business. We have a lot to discuss."

She stands, brushes lint from the front of her black silky trousers, then moves behind her massive white marble desk. "First, I want you to take a leave of absence once we actually file. We need to limit any contact you have with our plaintiffs without me present. Next, it's important we issue a press release before the news hounds get wind of any of this. If they haven't already."

She lifts a file from her desk, then reaches for her reading glasses. "I'm not going to kid you, darlin'. Lawsuits have been won, and they've been lost based on public sentiment."

"But, you know this town," I meet her look, trying not to flinch. "I'm going to get roasted, toasted and hung from the goal posts."

Maddy's face lights up. "Oh, but there's more than one way to peel a pigskin. You just leave everything to Maddy Crane, sweet thing.

In the parking lot, I check my phone for messages. Three from Mother, one from Jackie. My heart sinks. Nothing from Steve.

I tuck my cell phone in my purse.

It hits me I might not be up for this, no matter how encouraging my attorney tries to be. Everything I hold dear is at risk. My job. My marriage. Pearl's reputation.

But, how can I possibly live with myself if I don't stop Michael Warren?

Jackie said Pearl admired my courage. If she's really up there somewhere, looking down on me—I want her to see her mother was unwilling to fold to pressure. Pearl needs me to prove her death counted for something.

Steps from my car, I stop dead in my tracks. A familiar black town car pulls up and rolls to a stop. The darkened back window slowly opens.

"Barrie, I need to talk with you." Mother looks at her driver. "Could you give us a few moments, Charlie?"

I climb in, feeling like I'm ten years old again. Her driver steps out of the car. He moves several paces away from the door, standing with his white-gloved hands folded in front of him.

"Mother, you amaze me. How did you know I'd be here?"

She lets out a heavy sigh. "Barrie, must I constantly remind you how people talk?" She fiddles with the black leather gloves in her lap. "So, you are going to ignore every piece of advice I provide and move forward with a lawsuit? Despite what that means?"

I sink back into the plush leather seat, closing my eyes. "Please, not now."

"You've been crying." She says this not as a question, but a statement.

I turn and look out the window, noticing a few rust colored leaves have begun to fall from the poplars, even this early in the year. "So, I guess you've also heard about Steve and Aaron?" I say, not bothering to face her.

Mother doesn't respond right away. Instead, she weighs her words like a chef measures out the ingredients for a prize hollandaise, knowing if the proper balance of lemon and butter are off even a little, the sauce might curdle. "My banker saw them at the airport."

In an uncharacteristic move, she reaches for my hand. "He'll be back."

The unexpected tenderness catches me off guard. Hot tears burn at my eyes. I try to blink them away, but it's too late. Built-up emotion, coupled with lack of sleep, leaves me defenseless to ward off the need for release.

I bury my face in my hands. Through muffled cries, I tell her how scared I am. "What if Steve doesn't come back? I think he's done with me."

"Nonsense. Steve lacks many things, but he's not a stupid man."

She opens her handbag and pulls out a handkerchief, placing it in the palm of my hand. "C'mon now. Dry your tears."

A tiny rap on the window causes us both a startle. When I glance up, Maddy Crane's smiling face looks back.

I quickly collect myself, and roll the window down. "Darlin', I hope you don't mind. I sent your driver inside for a glass of sweet tea." She fans herself with a pair of white gloves. "It's a might bit warm out here."

Embarrassed, I open the car door.

Maddy peeks around me, her hand extended. "You must be Elaine Taylor."

"I'm pleased to meet you." Mother points to the seat opposite us. "Won't you join us?"

"Why, thank you." Maddy bends and lifts first one heeled shoe inside, then the other. Once situated, she adds, "Elaine, *yuh* husband was one of the kindest men I've ever had the pleasure of knowin'." She rests her diamond-laden hands in her lap. "We served together on the St. Luke's Auxiliary. Through his leadership, we raised ample funds to complete the children's oncology wing. Wasn't a person who could say no to his charm."

Mother beams at the compliment. I smile, knowing Madeline Crane has made a friend. A feat few accomplish with as much ease.

Maddy leans forward. "Of course, I often find men rarely succeed without a strong woman's support. You have a stellar reputation in the community as well."

Oh, she's good. Really good.

Over the next minutes, I listen as the two women chat like they've known each other for years. Finally, my attorney glances at her sapphire-encrusted watch. "Oh, look at the time," she says with a pout. "I have to scoot off to a mediation. Another big-wiggy up in Sun Valley couldn't keep his General Lee from marching when his wife went out of town." Her hand goes for the door. "I don't do a lot of divorce work, but on occasion, us women have to stick together. Speaking of—" she looks at me. "I'll be filing your complaint first thing in the morning. Then we're off to the races."

Mother clears her throat. "Ms. Crane—"

My attorney smiles. "Please, call me Maddy."

The look in Mother's eyes softens. "Maddy it is, then. Tell me," she pauses. "Michael Warren appears to have a history of this sort of activity."

Maddy nods. "He fits the profile. A man who blurs the lines between himself and his students, trying desperately to be liked. A narcissist who takes unbelievable risks, ignoring the possibility he might get caught."

"So, you believe Michael Warren will do this awful thing again, if not stopped?"

Madeline Crane stares Mother directly in the eyes. "Elaine, there is no doubt in my mind."

Mother reaches for Maddy's arm. "Then just promise me one thing."

"What's that, Elaine?"

"No matter what, I want you to take that Warren man down."

The petite woman with a southern drawl steps from the car, grinning. She peers back, looking like a pit bull wrapped in ruffles. "Oh, Michael Warren is going down. Question is, darlin'—who else are we going to take with him?"

35

Steve finally calls the next day while I'm at Jackie's house. When I see his name appear on the face of my cell phone, my immediate relief quickly turns to anger. "Nice of you to finally make time to check in with your wife."

Steve sighs from his end. "Look Barrie—I know what I did was a bit mean—"

"A bit?" I swallow hard, and a flush heats my cheeks. "That's an understatement, don't you think?"

Fury swirling in my gut builds into my throat, leaving a bitter taste. Even a second swallow fails to erase betrayal's rusty flavor. "Snatching Aaron out of school and whisking him off for a little vacation in Mexico, leaving me behind with only a note on the pillow goes way beyond mean, don't you think?"

In a show of solidarity, Jackie places her hand at her heart and gives me a sad smile. She politely scoots into the other room, leaving me to wrestle my marriage demons in private.

Even though I'm now alone in the room, my voice drops to a whisper. "Steve, how could you do this to me?" Hot tears burn at my eyelids.

I use my shirt sleeve and wipe at my eyes, waiting for his

response. Instead of the apology I hope for, he says nothing. Sometimes silence can be the loudest way to win an argument.

Hating that my voice sounds more like a whimpering puppy, I close my eyes and approach his softer side. "I need you, Steve."

"Paul tells me news of the lawsuit hit the newspaper and television this morning."

"You talked to Paul?"

"We need to shelter Aaron from all this. I think it's better if we stay down here with Mom for awhile."

"But what about the business?"

Steve's sarcastic laugh crackles across the airwaves. "Oh, now you think about the business? Do you have any idea, Barrie, what the future holds? Both of the restaurant tenants that were going to build on the corner lots already backed out, and that was just this morning."

The realization of what my husband is telling me makes my mouth go dry. Never did I stop to think what going after the coach when this town thinks the school has a shot at the state title this year could do to Steve and Paul—or, to our ability to pay back our line-of-credit if things really go sour.

"Steve—"

"Look, Barrie. I'll call you in a week or so."

"Steve, don't do this. Don't wreck . . . us."

"Funny you should say that," Steve replies, his voice like steel. "Just a few days ago, I believe I tried to convey that same message to you."

"But—"

"I'll call you."

The phone goes silent. I slump into Jackie's plush sofa, my whole body trembling. Dazed, I stare at the Hohman's family portrait hung above Jackie's fireplace, the happy-faced image blurs as tears pool. How had my own life become such a mess?

The door opens and Troy Hohman saunters through, his backpack slung over one shoulder.

"Hey, Mrs. Graeber."

"Hi, Troy." I quickly swipe at my tears.

The young man tosses his pack on a chair. "Where's Mom?"

"Uh, in the kitchen I think." I stand, slip the phone in my jeans pocket. "So, your mom told you about the lawsuit? That you would probably have to give a deposition?"

"Yeah, that's cool." Troy brushes his slate black hair back from his eye. "Anything I can do to help out."

I look at this kid, with his scary exterior, yet sweet interior and I can't help but think how my daughter was lucky to have him as a friend. I suppose the old adage you can't judge a book by its cover is true. Especially when the book he carries most often is the Bible.

"Barrie, you okay?" Jackie moves into the room, wiping her hands on a towel. "Oh, Troy. Honey, you're home early."

Jackie tells her son there is a plate of warm cookies waiting on the counter. After kissing his mother's cheek, he heads in that direction, saying he's starving.

No matter how close we become, I can't help but compare myself to this queen of domesticity. The only thing waiting for Aaron when he gets home from school is a box of Twinkies. If I haven't already eaten them all.

But, none of that matters now. My entire family is in shambles.

As if reading my thoughts, the look on Jackie's face softens. "Barrie, God can heal that broken heart of yours."

She sees me roll my eyes. With a tone that's soft and gentle, she adds, "But you need to give him all the pieces."

I ponder her remark while driving home. How can I hand my heart over to the The Big Guy Upstairs when he keeps ripping my guts out and stomping on them?

Self-pity wells up inside my heart and I let my mind wander

to all the cruel losses I've been forced to endure—first my precious Pearl. And now, perhaps, even Steve.

Instead of heading straight to my empty house, I navigate toward MacMillan and Eagle Road. It's been months since I've driven past the accident site, but today I long for some connection to my daughter. As morbid as it sounds, this is the place where she exited this earth.

In those early days, people built a memorial of sorts at the edge of the road, made of flowers and helium balloons tied to stuffed toy animals. As I pull off the road, I see a few scattered vases, the only visible sign left of the tribute.

After climbing out of the car, my feet carefully step over a small irrigation ditch. The field looks nothing like it did back in January with acres of frozen dirt, scattered with occasional skiffs of snow. Corn stalks now cover the field, their long leaves wilted and yellowed, waiting to be cut and made into pig feed.

Gone are the deep grooves that used to mark where the Jeep Pearl was driving skidded off the road, before catapulting end-over-end, throwing her body out like a discarded gum wrapper.

The early evening air feels warm against my face and smells faintly of the dairy farm a few miles away. I take in the color of the sky, a blue unlike the bright color of the morning hours, but a muted gray-blue slightly shadowed with the looming sunset.

A v-shaped line of geese flies overhead in the direction of the river. They flap their wings heading for some far off destiny, their honking a plaintive call to those below.

I don't really know why I came here. But standing in this place feels a bit sacred.

As a mother, you push fear aside and cling to the hope your children are immune to the evil in this world. That when the time comes to face decisions that have the potential to alter their lives, they will come to you for direction.

It doesn't always work out that way.

I want to believe what the Hohmans claim, that this field was not the end. That my sweet Pearl still exists in a place where no one like Michael Warren can get to her. I hope she's in heaven, wherever that is, and I want her happy.

A single tear rolls down my cheek.

More than that, I want to know for sure that someday . . . I'll see her again.

~

I TURN ONTO OUR STREET. Lights are already on in several of the neighbor's windows. Our own porch light is on a timer, a fact I'm grateful for as I approach our driveway.

I think, why didn't I grab something to eat before I drove home, when suddenly I notice a car parked in front of my house, blocking my entrance. A police car.

With my heart thumping wildly, I pull to the curb and cut the engine. Two officers stand in my front yard. One holds a clipboard and is making notes. The other wields a flashlight and is directing the beam against my house.

As I approach, the first officer stops writing. "Are you the homeowner?"

"Yes," I confirm. "What's going on?"

Then I see.

The entire front of my house has been vandalized with eggs and toilet paper streams from the branches of the maple in our front yard.

"Your neighbor down the street, Robert Emberly, called the report in. Says a pickup loaded with four individuals drove up and unloaded on your house." He shakes his head. "Probably kids."

I explain about the lawsuit, and he takes copious notes. The second officer joins us. "Well, ma'am. Doesn't look like anything more than a prank. No windows broken."

The first officer rips a paper from his clipboard and hands me the light yellow slip with faded lettering. "We'll file a report, but we're not likely to catch the perpetrators. Like I stated, probably a bunch of kids making a little trouble in support of the coach."

I thank both of them and watch as they pull out of the driveway. As I move my car into the garage, I see Mrs. Otis peering out her window next door. I wave, and she drops the curtains.

Inside, I click on the lights and toss my purse and keys on the counter before grabbing Omelette's bowl. I start for the bag of chow, then on second thought open the refrigerator door. Ducking my head, I rummage the shelves until I find the remains of a steak.

The hungry dog chomps her meal, gulping down the treat in mere seconds. Finished, she returns to the door leading to the garage where she sits, waiting.

"What's the matter? You miss the boys?"

I grab the bucket from under the sink, knowing I can't let that egg remain on the outside of the house or the paint will be ruined.

Omelette drops to the floor, her head resting against her crossed paws. The poor thing looks lost without Aaron and Steve.

I know exactly how she feels.

36

In a preliminary hearing, Maddy Crane convinces an administrative judge this case warrants the fast track, allowing for a limited discovery period and a faster trial date. No doubt motivated by his client's desire to get back to the football season as quickly as possible, Michael Warren's attorney consents.

Normally, a matter of this magnitude could take up to two years before the parties are ready for trial. But in less than six weeks, here I sit in my attorney's office listening while she tells me what to expect.

"We're the plaintiffs, so we'll put on our case first. After we pick a jury, and give opening statements, I'll call you to the stand."

I slide my pizza across the conference room table, no longer hungry. "Are you sure I have to go first?"

Maddy dabs her mouth with a linen napkin. "Yes. I want you to tell the story. The jury will need to know Pearl, who she was, her dreams and aspirations. You'll need to explain what this loss did to your family." She pulls a file from a stack to her right. "This is our biggest opportunity to create empathy. I'm going to do everything I can to seat lots of mothers on that panel, and it's your job to connect and make each of them feel like your loss is their own."

I look around the conference room filled with boxes, at the table piled high with deposition transcripts. "And Steve?"

Maddy gives me an encouraging smile. "He understands how critical it is to show solidarity between the two of you. Remember, it took a while, but he finally consented to letting us name him as a plaintiff. Besides darlin', it'll work in our favor if I play this right. What juror can't relate to your need to protect Aaron from all that is going on? Shows what solid parents you both are." She pats my hand. "I told Steve I'd call him to the stand last, and he promised he'd be here."

I let out a sigh of relief. It's a rare person Madeline Crane can't win over.

Maddy presses the intercom button on the console in the center of the table. "Joanne, darlin'—why don't you come on in and join us?"

"Barrie," Maddy says gently. "I want to show you our photo blow-ups now, so when you see them during the course of the trial, you won't get too rattled." She leans back in the plump leather armchair. "Emotion is good, but it won't help if you fall apart." She looks me in the eye. "You with me?"

I nod, as Maddy's paralegal enters carrying several unwieldy foam core boards, wrapped in plastic. Her eyes are framed with dark circles, likely from too many late nights in a row. "The blow-ups turned out great."

"What's that?" I ask, curious.

Joanne sets the boards against the wall, next to several large leather bags packed and ready for trial. "We'll leave the computerized presentation to the big boys. Our team will display demonstrative evidence the good old-fashioned way, right, Maddy?"

My attorney's eyes sparkle. "Studies prove using high-falootin' technology in the courtroom often gives the impression there's a lot of money backing the effort. We'll leave that to the other side. In their subconscious, we want those jurors believing the defendants have pockets that run deep."

Her remark reminds me what's really at stake. Early on, I explained to Maddy our family wasn't taking this action to get rich, that all I wanted was to send a message our education system must do better.

Frankly, I want to punish school board members who callously put the interests of the football team over and above protecting young girls from sexual exploitation. Sure, in reality, the insurance company will write the check. But, I want a record made of these inexcusable actions. I want it known that what they did was wrong. If school officials hadn't looked the other way in order to win football games, Pearl would never have come in contact with Michael Warren, never would have slipped into a dangerous relationship that ultimately cost her everything. My little girl paid a high price for their irresponsibility.

That's what a courageous mom does. She stamps out evil any way possible. If that takes a legal judgment that hits their pocketbooks hard, so be it.

Maddy shows me the photos. After several shots of Pearl and our family, a scene of mangled metal appears. My gut tightens. I clasp my hands tightly in my lap, to keep them from shaking.

During the remainder of the evening, Maddy goes over my testimony. When opposing counsel cross-examines me, I'm told to listen to the entire question before responding, to think carefully before answering. I don't need to feel pressured to answer before I'm ready. And, she reminds me, only answer what is asked. Nothing more.

She runs me through a litany of potential questions defense

counsel might pose. After several hours of this, I'm relieved when she finally asks if I have the time.

I look at my watch. "It's seven-thirty."

"No," she scolds. "I asked if you had the time. That's a yes or no question."

I bury my head in my hands. "Ugh, sorry."

She clicks her pen closed and slaps the file shut, grinning. "I pull that stunt so you'll remember to listen carefully and only answer the question posed when you're on the stand." She rubs at the back of her neck. "You're ready, Barrie. Now it's time to get some sleep. Tomorrow's going to be a big day."

FROM THE MOMENT I turn onto our street, I notice lights on at our house. My heart hammers with fear, until I see Aaron in the front yard, playing with Omelette.

I rush to park and scramble from the car with outstretched arms. "Aaron!"

My son, who's grown at least two inches in the weeks he's been away, charges at me, wrapping his arms around my waist with enough force to knock me off kilter. "I've missed you, Mom."

I step back, grinning. "Let me have a good look at you." I ruffle his hair. "You need a haircut."

The door opens and Steve steps out onto the front porch. He's wearing jeans and a faded Boise State t-shirt—and a deep tan. I find myself wanting to rush up to him, wrap my arms around his neck and take in the smell of that spicy deodorant he wears.

Instead, I hold back, feeling strangely timid.

"Hey," he says.

I recite the obvious. "I didn't know you'd be home."

"Yeah," he lifts his chin, ever so slightly. "I should have called, I suppose."

I don't know what to say, so I wrap my arm around my son's shoulder and lead him inside. "You hungry, buddy?"

"Nah, Dad ordered pizza."

Steve brushes my cheek with a kiss as I near, then steps back so I can pass through the door. In the kitchen, he tells me Tess and Anthony send their love. Apparently, they married while Steve and Aaron were there. Made things right with the Lord, Steve claims.

Funny how I feel more lonely than when the house was empty. Distance isn't always calculated in miles.

Aaron chatters non-stop. I learn you have to use fifty pound test line to catch a marlin, that palm trees and cactus are now his favorite plants of all time, and there's nothing more beautiful in all the world than a sunset over the ocean. "Wish you could have seen it, Mom."

"Oh, listen to this. *Que pasa, Madre?*" He puffs up, looking proud.

"What?"

Aaron grins. "It means *how are you, Mother?* That's Spanish." He gives Omelette a pat on the head. "You miss me, girl?"

I sense the nearness of my husband. He stands only an arms-length from me, and I can feel his heat. It takes everything in me not to turn and bury my face against his chest. Instead, I lift my chin. "Trial starts in the morning."

"Yes, I know."

I nod, slowly. "Thanks for coming back."

Steve's hand grasps my elbow. He pulls me aside. "Look," he says with a lowered voice. "We need to tell Aaron what's going on. Before he hears from someone else."

I look up in shock. "You didn't tell him?"

"What was I supposed to say? Besides, the whole point of

the trip to Mexico was to keep him in the dark on all this. I was hoping—" His voice fades.

"Hoping I'd change my mind and drop the lawsuit?"

A deep weariness crosses his face. "No—I knew better."

I watch his eyes, for some sign. Any small flicker that might reassure anger has not erased the love I always counted on.

He sees the pain on my face, and his expression softens. "How are you?" he says.

Do I see a glimmer of need in his eyes as well?

"I'm . . . I'm glad you're home." Taking a risk, I let my fingers drift to his arm. When we touch, he quickly moves away. "Look, we need to talk to Aaron before it gets much later."

Feeling like someone just kicked me in the diaphragm, I let my arm drop. The old me would have confronted this situation head-on. Demanded we talk things through and get to the bottom of this conflict, before the dissension festers even more. I know how unresolved anger can bleed a relationship dry. No doubt, our marriage is in desperate need of a transfusion.

But, I can't go there. Not tonight. Not with the trial starting tomorrow.

Instead, I let out a resigned sigh and focus on my son.

A sadness moves inside me. What words can we possibly choose to lessen the blow? From the conflicted look on Steve's face, he's thinking the same. Like me, he fears nothing we say will keep our little guy innocent of the evil that has been perpetrated upon our family.

What is fear when you're a parent?

A year ago, my answer would be different.

I'd have told you I feared Aaron wouldn't look before crossing the street. Oh, yes, I know he's nearly twelve. But Aaron gets distracted and forgets things like that sometimes. Especially if he's tossing a football in the air.

I'd have said I feared Pearl wouldn't get an A on her biology exam. She never was strong in science. Or I feared she would choose the wrong major. Or perhaps, if I got really honest, I'd say I feared she might not listen to me and get herself in an awkward position with some guy. . . . okay, with Craig. I worried she'd cross the line with Craig before she was ready.

Ha! Never, ever in a million years did I ever conceive—or let my head wander to the notion any of *this* was possible.

How could I anticipate the resigned and profound despair that follows the realization that when it comes to protecting your children from the really big things, you are totally impotent?

Huh? Tell me, how?

I watch my son's face crumple as Steve explains what we've learned, knowing each word nicks his innocence, until my little boy's heart is completely exposed to things better left to late night television.

A tear rolls down my cheek. I wonder—not for the first time —why? No eleven-year-old should know this ugliness.

When the trial is over, and those responsible have been made to pay, our family will heal. We'll move past this painful season in our lives, and be normal again. Despite the mocking voice at the back of my mind saying otherwise, I try hard to believe it.

37

Fitful sleep finally fades into slumber only hours before the alarm, leaving me feeling like I never went to bed at all. The reason I toss and turn all night is anyone's guess.

The most obvious is the impending legal proceedings. But in all honesty, a small part of me wonders how the spot next to me in bed can be filled after weeks of vacancy and still leave such a void.

Downstairs, Steve sits at the kitchen counter, a cup of coffee in his hand. The television is on. Before I can say good morning, an image of Troy's mangled Jeep flashes on the screen, and I hear the reporter say, " . . . trial begins today on civil claims brought against Coach Michael Warren and the Sawtooth School District."

Steve points the remote and clicks the program off.

I open my mouth to protest, but change my mind feeling too tired to argue. I drag my slippered feet across the kitchen floor and pour a cup of much-needed coffee, while reminding Steve that Jackie will drop Aaron off for school.

He nods, his eyes reflecting the same angst I feel inside. "You told me already. Twice."

I hold back a barbed response. "Perhaps you should get in the shower first," I suggest, in a tone as measured as the emotional distance still between us.

Less than an hour later, we head for the car. My husband slips behind the steering wheel, looking a bit uncomfortable in the gray chinos he wears in place of his typical jeans. He clears his throat. "You look nice."

I plant a weak smile on my face and nod. "Thanks." After shuffling in my closet for nearly a half-hour, I finally settled on a simple black skirt, white blouse and heels. There are no fashion magazines telling me what to wear to the trial for the man who mutilated my trust by sleeping with my child.

We meet up with Maddy and Mother near the courthouse entrance. As we make our way to the large double-glass doors, waiting news reporters shove microphones at us. A man with headphones draped over his jet-black hair steps forward. "Can you tell us what you expect will happen in the courtroom today?" A woman's voice shouts from the crowd, "Would you care to make a statement?"

Amidst flashing cameras, Maddy steps forward holding a bright red leather briefcase that matches her shoes—and her lips—perfectly. She stands erect, her hair swept up into a chignon making her slight frame appear taller.

She pulls one of those charming looks across her features and tells the media she's confident justice will prevail. "Ladies and gentlemen, I've participated in more than a few trials throughout my years." Coyly, she adds, "Although a lady never reveals just how many years that might be." She pauses, letting her audience appreciate the humor, before continuing. "Jurors are intelligent, thoughtful people, and I have no doubt this jury will find their way to the truth."

A harried-looking young woman with a press badge steps

next to me, notebook in hand. "You work with Coach Warren at Sawtooth High, isn't that correct?"

Maddy places a protective hand on my back. "I'm afraid that's all for now." She pastes a wide smile and winks at the crowd. "If you'll excuse us, my clients have a trial to win." She turns and guides us through the tangle of bodies, cameras and microphones, toward the courthouse door.

Inside, we make our way through security. I ask the lady waving a wand down my torso if she knows where I could find a restroom.

"At the end of this main corridor, take a left. Directly across from Judge Canton's courtroom."

"Thank you."

Benches line the hallway, mostly empty but for one where I see an elderly woman leaning against an older man's shoulder, her tears creating a noticeable damp spot on his blue cardigan sweater. He takes a handkerchief and gently blots her eyes. I glance over at Steve. He sees them, too.

Down the hall, a different scene plays out. A young man in an orange jumpsuit trudges behind a uniformed officer, hands clasped in handcuffs, his face sullen and angry looking.

The nervous feeling in the pit of my stomach magnifies. I turn to Steve. "Do I still have time to go to the restroom?"

He checks his watch. "If you hurry."

Minutes later, after washing my hands, I turn off the water and grab for a paper towel. The mirror above the sink reflects a washed-out face mapped with worry. I ruffle through my bag to find the powder blush I'd slipped inside earlier. A heavy dose to the cheeks, and I'll be good to go. No one will suspect I'm powering through this day on less than two hours sleep.

I hear a click and the door to the stall farthest down the row opens. At first, I fail to recognize the striking woman with nutmeg-colored hair, but as she draws closer, my breath catches.

Lisa Warren—the coach's wife.

She sees me about the same time. We both freeze.

I toss the compact into my purse and fling it over my shoulder, wanting desperately to ignore this unexpected encounter.

Tears spring to her eyes. "Barrie—I, uh . . ."

Her words falter, and it hits me. I'm not the only one who's been victimized by that scoundrel husband of hers. I know I should say something, make this easier for her. But something deep inside won't let me. Instead, I flee the room without a word.

Steve is powering down his Blackberry when I approach. "There you are. What took you so long?" He nods at the deputy standing at the door. "Your mother and Maddy are already inside."

The courtroom looks like what you'd see in the movies. Despite the fact this building is not yet ten years old, great care was taken to replicate the courtroom interiors of the former courthouse located next to the State Capitol Building, a grand old structure now listed on the historical register and used to host special events.

I remember thinking, when I saw the article in the newspaper all those years back, the expenditure was a huge waste of tax dollars, but I have to admit the austere marble columns and carved wood creates a reverence for the legal system and the power the judge yields. Something I only now fully appreciate.

Over the hushed whispers floating in the room, I ask Steve how he's doing. He shrugs and says, "Never better." Sarcasm is my husband's tool of choice when he wants to cover his true emotions.

Thankfully, the media is excluded from the actual proceedings. Although I have to admit, a tiny part of me would love to see the Warren's face splashed on the news showing his reaction the moment the judge reads the jury's verdict.

A familiar voice drifts from somewhere behind me—Michael Warren's voice.

I fight the urge to turn and look, to stare him in the face with a silent demand asking why? How can he show up at this proceeding and try to justify what he did with my daughter?

Steve hears his voice too. Surprisingly, his arm goes around my shoulders, and he gives a slight squeeze. I lean against his strength, before moving to my designated spot next to Maddy at counsel's table. Steve sits with Mother in the pew behind the railing.

The notion doesn't slip by that Steve and I have been in a courtroom together only one other time—at Pearl's adoption proceeding.

At the defense table, a man with a precise haircut slightly grayed at the temples unloads a large black bag. I watch as he lines up three very expensive looking pens on the table next to a leather folder with gold lettering.

As if on cue, a much younger woman sitting to his right lifts the water pitcher and fills first his glass, then her own. Finished, she buries her attention in an iPad.

My eyes follow a tangle of cords leading to two guys camped behind a wall of computer monitors. Their blue polo shirts coordinate with boxes lined against the wall, printed with big blue letters *Kavik & Preston Law Offices.* In the gallery on their side of the room, suits nearly two rows deep sit with pens poised on legal pads.

There is an electric feel in the courtroom, a palpating anticipation of sorts, the kind that causes a tingle in your belly when a stage curtain parts and the lights dim.

Maddy gives me a reassuring smile.

"All rise."

In sweeps a tall woman with a striking resemblance to former First Lady Laura Bush. She adjusts her robe, while her courtroom deputy announces, "Now is the time for the trial in the matter of *Graeber vs. Warren, et al.*, Honorable Judge Jane Canton presiding."

From her perch beneath the large gold seal of the State of Idaho, Judge Canton's voice echoes off the walls. "You may be seated." She directs her attention at our table. "Counsel?"

"Yes, Your Honor. Good morning. Madeline Crane for the plaintiffs."

Michael Warren's attorney stands. "Jake Preston, Judge. I'm here on behalf of defendants." He motions toward the woman to his right. "This is Alexa Dean, my co-counsel."

I let my eyes drift past to where Lisa Warren sits. Her face looks ashen, and she stares straight ahead, hands clasped tightly in her lap.

For a brief moment, I try to conjure compassion for this woman. I too have felt the sting of infidelity. The difference is, I kicked Pearl's birth dad to the curb.

Judge Canton scans the complaint. "As I see it, plaintiffs cite multiple counts against Michael Warren—primarily a wrongful death claim, but also plaintiffs allege negligence and reckless and wanton conduct." She looks over the top of her reading glasses. "All these claims extend to the school district and to the principal of Sawtooth High School. Am I correct, Ms. Crane?"

"Yes, Your Honor. We plan to prove Michael Warren had sexual relations with a minor, my client's daughter, Pearl Graeber. Subsequent to those acts, Pearl became pregnant and in a desperate foolish decision, she snuck out of her parents' home in the middle of the night. She borrowed a friend's vehicle and was on her way to meet Michael Warren when she got in a terrible accident, which took her life. Cell phone records will show she was on the phone with Michael Warren at, or near, the time of the accident."

Mr. Preston stands. "If I may, Your Honor?" She nods.

"The defense's position is, and has always been, that the cell phone records prove nothing more than telephone conversations took place. There is no evidence my client, Michael Warren, had sexual relations with Pearl Graeber."

The judge steeples her fingers, scowling. "Well, unless there are motions in limine you need me to hear, let's get started." She turns to the bailiff. "Go ahead and bring in the potential jurors and we'll begin *voir dire.*"

Nearly the entire morning is taken up with picking a jury—a rather arduous process that you don't often see in courtroom dramas on television.

Thanks to Mother's checkbook, Maddy hired the services of a highly respected and extremely expensive jury consultant from Los Angeles, a woman who came up with a profile of our perfect juror—someone with at least a high school education, who has a strong sense of moral justice with a household income considered middle-class. Preferably, a mom. But even more important, a person who can put themselves in my shoes and empathize with what our family has been through.

The attorneys delve into the personal lives of nearly forty individuals. We break for lunch after seating seven women and five men, not counting the alternates. Among the selected candidates is a mortgage banker, a diesel mechanic (which is completely different from small engine mechanics, he explained), the mother of four small children who runs a church daycare, and a retired nurse who is also a grandmother. The nurse made eye contact with me several times during *voir dire.*

Maddy says that's a good sign.

After a quick lunch where my nerves cause me to eat my club sandwich and half of Steve's, we hurry back. We're already seated when Jake Preston makes his way down the aisle, followed by his entourage. He nods as he passes our table, leaving a scent that reminds me of the men's fragrance counter at Macy's.

Minutes later the bailiff leads in the jury. They take their seats, a mixture of hesitation and anticipation evident in their eyes.

Openings are next, and Maddy goes first.

"Ladies and gentlemen, over the next several days, you're going to be learning about Pearl Graeber, and what happened to rob this young woman of her future.

"Pearl was exceptional. By all accounts, she was a bright, thoughtful girl who enjoyed dance team, being on stage and with her friends. She excelled in academics, and was looking forward to graduating high school and attending college. Over the course of this trial, you will hear from witnesses who will tell you Pearl was beautiful, smart, and funny . . . every parent's dream child. On January sixth of this year, that dream turned into a nightmare."

Every juror drills their attention on my attorney as she clips back to our table and picks up her notes. After quickly scanning the pages, she tosses the papers back to the table, and shakes her head for effect.

"Michael Warren's record is equally impressive. During his coaching career, this man racked up ten district championships, seven regional championships, and a state title. There is little doubt why the school officials sitting in this courtroom wanted to bring someone like him on board. Everybody loves a winner.

"That explains why they looked the other way when the plaintiff, Barrie Graeber, reported seeing a student in a vehicle with Coach Warren late at night, noticed him tuck her hair behind her ear, and then caress her cheek in a manner suggesting inappropriate intimacy."

Maddy pans those sitting in the jury box with her eyes. "Can you even imagine how these parents felt when they later learned their own daughter had been victimized by this man?" She points in the coach's direction. "Oh, he denies the relationship, just like he denies all the others." She pauses letting her words sink in. "Yes, there were others.

"You're going to hear these are not the first allegations of this nature brought against Michael Warren. You'll listen to experts who will testify the coaching profession has among the highest rates of sexual-misconduct complaints and that if the district had looked closely at this particular coach's employment record, they'd have learned dire information."

Maddy stops in front of the mechanic. "Some of you know how the failure to identify a problem can have catastrophic consequences—how if you miss something, the results can be destructive with little opportunity for repair. Knowledge of this man's misconduct was available to anyone who looked, and certainly before Pearl Graeber died."

Maddy's red stilettos clack against the polished marble floor as she marches away from the jury box. She points back at Preston's table. "The defense claims Michael Warren is not responsible for Pearl's death. They will try to tell you this young girl had bad morals and lack of judgment. But evidence will show the defendant failed to respect appropriate boundaries and ignored his ethical obligation to this student, acts that ultimately were the proximate cause of that seventeen-year-old girl's death. Further, we'll prove the school authorities failed to do the necessary background checks when they hired the coach, providing ample gateway into this young lady's life, setting her up to be victimized."

She shakes her head. "Ladies and gentlemen— something is terribly broken in a system where winning football games trumps the safety of young girls."

Maddy speaks directly to the church daycare lady. "If this man prays inside the school, he'd likely be fired. But when he *preys* on young women outside the locker room—" She gives her shoulders a shrug. "—this school board awards him Coach-of-the-Year."

After giving a satisfied nod at the jury, Maddy returns to our table. Her hand covers my own, and she squeezes.

Clap, clap, clap.

Jake Preston stands, slowly applauding. "Excellent performance, Ms. Crane. Oscar-worthy entertainment." His eyes narrow. "But let's look at facts, shall we?

"Fact—anyone can make an allegation. These prior incidents alluded to? There is no evidence my client, Michael Warren, was ever *convicted* of a crime. None.

"Fact—when Mrs. Graeber brought her concerns to the school board, the members did investigate. There was simply nothing to substantiate the claim Mr. Warren had acted in an inappropriate manner with any student, minor or otherwise. Would you expect the district to fire one of their employees with no proof?

"Fact—when the district hired this coach, he came highly recommended. True, his performance spoke volumes about what sort of ability this man had to maneuver a football team into the winning circle. But isn't that what is expected?" He laughs. "I mean, how long would my client last in the coaching profession if he constantly lost?"

"Fact—Pearl Graeber might have been every parent's dream. But the plaintiffs were every struggling child's nightmare. Witnesses will testify she had no one to turn to as life became difficult. When she struggled, she couldn't confide in her mother, who expected only perfection. And her father was busy with his new business venture, and too often unavailable."

Michael Warren's attorney saunters over to the jury box. He lifts his chin and clears his throat. "Pearl confided in Coach Warren, just like many young people who look up to him. He's a good coach for a reason. He's gifted at motivating a person to turn their weakness into their greatest strength."

The jurors' eyes are riveted on Mr. Preston. He knows it, and continues, his voice louder and more emphatic. "The facts, ladies and gentlemen, are not as sinister as the plaintiffs want you to believe. Michael Warren was simply this girl's mentor . . . not her killer."

He walks back to the defense table, places his hand on his client's shoulder. "Your school district was lucky to have a man of this caliber on their staff, and they knew it. And more, this guy will make a great parent. Just two days ago, he learned he is going to be a father. Congratulations are in order to both Mr. and Mrs. Warren."

The revelation causes me to audibly gasp. I blink several times and stare straight ahead, trying to maintain my composure, despite the rancid irony.

Jake Preston straightens his tie and smiles. "Members of the jury, it's people like you our system counts on. Level-headed, thoughtful individuals who won't react out of emotion, but will listen carefully to the testimony provided and determine the only outcome that makes any sense in this situation—you will find the defendants not culpable."

38

Jackie greets us at our door, dish towel in hand. "How'd things go?"

I say, "fine," and Steve says, "awful," at the same time. We follow her inside, recounting all that happened in court today. I tell her about the jurors, and how gifted Madeline Crane is at wooing them to our side, even in these early stages. She gasps as well when I disclose Mrs. Warren is expecting.

When I start to tell her about Jake Preston and the accusations he made against us as parents, Steve heads to his office, his expression dark as the storm clouds that often roll over the Owyhees in the heat of summer. I sigh, and add, "I think the first day went as well as it could've . . . considering."

Jackie gives me a sympathetic smile and tells me a baked ziti casserole waits in the oven. "And there's a salad in the refrigerator." She unties her apron and warns me Aaron is in his room. "I think he had a bad day, Barrie. I tried to get him to talk to me, but didn't have any luck." She gives me a hug.

"Jackie, thank you." I whisper, squeezing extra hard. "I don't know what I'd do without your help."

She pats my back. "You'd do the same."

I'd like to think what she claims is true. But unlike my own natural instincts, Jackie somehow meets needs we don't even know we lack—a quality Pearl was the first to recognize in Jackie.

After my friend leaves, I change into more comfortable clothes and head back to the kitchen where I holler at the guys to come down for dinner. I pull the steaming casserole from the oven, bump the door shut with my hip and move to the dining room.

"I'm starving." Steve grabs his napkin. Aaron sits, but says nothing.

I head into the kitchen for the rolls and pitcher of lemonade. Wanting to keep the conversation on a topic other than the trial, I call back over my shoulder. "I ran into Joey's mom at the store the other night."

"Yeah?" Steve cautions Aaron the pasta is hot and not to spill.

After placing the rolls on the table, I move to pour lemonade in our glasses. "She tells me Aaron isn't registered for the basketball team. Shouldn't we get on that?"

My son remains silent.

"Where are the registration papers, honey? I didn't see them."

"Let's bless the food." Steve bows his head.

After Steve finishes praying, I look up to find Aaron staring at his plate with tear-pooled eyes. "Son?"

Steve sets his fork down. "Scoot. What is it?"

Aaron drops his fork with such force, the plate rattles. "I just don't wanna play, okay?"

Steve places his hand on our son's shoulder. "All right, Scoot. You'd better tell us what's going on."

"The guys don't want me on the team."

"What?" Out of the corner of my eye, I notice Omelette

nudge her head into Aaron's lap. "Oh, son, who told you that? Maybe you misunderstood."

Aaron's eyes narrow. "I didn't misunderstand. Jason Knight emailed everybody and said my sister was a skank."

I feel the air whoosh from my lungs. How could anyone, especially a young boy, say such a thing?

"I texted back and told him to shut up. Then all the guys on the team joined in and took Jason's side." He looks up, a strange mixture of anger and misery in his eyes. "The only kid who stood up for me was Tyler, but today at the mall he told me his dad said Pearl is bringing down the whole Cougar football team because she didn't have any morals." He shoves his plate back. "Can I be excused, please?"

Anger flashes across Steve's face. I know him well enough to understand he's swallowing what he wants to say. Instead, he carefully chooses his words. "There seems to be a lot of folks ready to make judgment over what happened with Pearl." He takes a deep breath. "And some of the things people say hurt our feelings and make us mad, too. But look, Scoot. This is the deal. What Pearl did was wrong. But she isn't the only one who made dreadful choices in that situation. Sis is not responsible for the consequences Coach Warren suffers for what he did wrong. And no matter what people think, or say, we are Pearl's family. We know her. And a person isn't defined by her mistakes."

I push my plate back as well, my appetite gone. "Baby, all of us have to learn to close our ears to the horrible things people can say."

Steve grasps Aaron's chin and lifts his face. "We love you, son. Your mother and I will support whatever decision you make regarding being on the team." He glances at me for confirmation, before continuing. "But one of the best ways to deal with these things and get past them is to place the situation in God's hands and go on about your business with your head held high."

Steve's right. This family has no reason to feel ashamed. The only person who deserves to hang his head in humiliation is Michael Warren.

"I hope you'll consider what Daddy says, Aaron. You love sports, especially basketball. Why let people with really bad manners steal something away you enjoy so much?"

He nods. "Okay, maybe I'll play." He wipes his eyes with the back of his arm. "Besides, I think Sis would want me to stand up to them."

His comment fills me with a wide sense of relief. Aaron will weather this storm. But, unlike Steve, I for one don't entirely trust God will do his job. Which is why I hired Madeline Crane.

As an added measure, I make a mental note to take care of things my own way when that Knight kid gets to high school. When the time comes, the mama bear in me will make sure the boy who hurt my son's feelings will get all the strictest teachers available.

I grab my fork. Suddenly, my appetite is back.

39

Judge Canton looks down from her seat behind the bench. "Good morning, everyone. I presume, Ms. Crane, you're ready with your first witness?"

"Yes, Your Honor. Plaintiffs call Barrie Graeber."

Despite my attorney's continued reassurances up until this moment, I lift from my seat and make my way to the witness box feeling a bit weak in the knees.

Every eye watches as I get settled and fold my hands in my lap. I take a deep breath, remembering my attorney's instructions. *Just relax and answer my questions. Our story is compelling and your job is to make the jurors feel your loss.*

"Please state your name for the record." "Barrie Eileen Graeber."

I look out and see Mother. She gives an encouraging smile. Steve, too, though he's not as enthusiastic.

The early questions are easy. I give my education background and my work history, highlighting the fact I've worked almost ten years as a high school counselor.

Next, she asks me about Pearl. I recite my practiced responses, telling the jurors what a delightful baby she was, about how close she and Steve were. I mention that at age six, she wanted a hammer and nails from Santa so she could be just like her daddy. And I help them know all that she had planned for a bright and promising future.

"Thank you, Mrs. Graeber. Now I'd like you to tell us about the morning of January twenty-sixth."

My heart pounds, and I hear a slight ringing in my ears. "Uh, all right."

Maddy nods. "Tell the jurors what that day was like for you."

I remember to look at them before answering. "That was the morning we learned Pearl had been killed—the worst moment of my life."

Over the following hour and a half, I delineate for the jury what those early hours were like after we learned she'd been killed. I try to describe the debilitating grief and loss our family has experienced, how none of us will ever be the same without her.

Maddy gives me a reassuring nod. "Tell us what you discovered shortly after she died."

I pause. How can I make these strangers understand how scared she must have been, how unlike Pearl to hide anything from us, that she grappled with her mistakes alone because she was too ashamed to confide in us and let her parents help?

My voice drops to just above a whisper. "We learned my daughter was pregnant."

"Did you suspect Coach Warren was responsible?"

"Not then, no."

Maddy's questions turned to the incident with Callie, what I'd seen and later reported to Sharon Manicke.

I answer each of her questions, telling them how I'd followed them in my car. That I'd ended up in the hospital after pulling out in front of a pick-up truck, causing an accident.

My attorney looks shocked. "But you were okay?"

"Yes. My injuries were minor. Mostly bruising and sore muscles."

"What did you do next?"

"I scheduled a meeting with my principal and told her what I'd seen. Each year, the staff is reminded to notify authorities of these kinds of things. As a school counselor, I am especially aware of our reporting responsibilities, and the ethical obligations we have to protect students."

"And what did Ms. Manicke, your principal, tell you?"

"She promised a thorough investigation and initially agreed that he should be fired. Sadly, she later reported both Michael Warren and Callie Pratt denied the incident—and that the board had decided not to discipline Mr. Warren."

"I see." Maddy cups her chin. "And did you accept their decision?"

"I had no choice. I went to work every day and tried my best to avoid running into that man, while trying to move on in my own life. Despite the fact my heart remained broken, I focused on being a good wife and mother, and on serving my students to the best of my ability, given the circumstances."

I take a deep breath, trying to calm my nerves. So far, we are right on script. I sneak a peek at Jake Preston and Michael Warren.

Michael will not look at me. Mr. Preston, on the other hand, analyzes my every move. Occasionally, he picks up on of those expensive pens and jots a note in that leather folder.

"What changed?"

I recite how Chad Nelson showed me his file, how I'd learned of Michael Warren's history and that there had been multiple incidents in former schools. The information had made my blood boil and confirmed my suspicions that the Sawtooth High School coach had no problem crossing boundaries of what was appropriate."

Jake Preston jumps to his feet. "Objection. Speculation."

"Sustained."

I glance at the Judge, and she nods for me to proceed. Maddy saunters to the jury box. "Help our jurors understand what you heard on Pearl's cell phone."

Following her lead, I reveal there were dozens of calls to a certain number in the weeks prior to the accident.

"And do you know who that number belongs to?"

"Yes," I say. "The number belongs to Michael Warren."

Maddy turns and faces me. "Why do you believe that to be true, Mrs. Graeber?"

I take a deep breath. "The number was listed as Mr. Warren's in our staff directory."

We recess for a short break, and then it'll be my turn to be cross-examined. Maddy leads us down the hall, where our discussion can be private.

"Jake Preston will try to get you rattled, just like we rehearsed." Maddy warns. "Remember what I said, focus on his questions. Listen carefully before answering. Given the chance, he'll twist what you say."

Steve scowls. "But isn't it your job to stop him if he tries?"

Mother fingers the front of her neck. "Steve, let Maddy do her job."

Like a chastised little boy, my husband's mouth drops shut. He looks too worried to argue. Instead he pulls out his Blackberry and checks for messages.

I lower my voice to a terse whisper. "Steve, didn't you see the signs? You're supposed to turn that off."

Ignoring the exchange, Maddy places a hand on my shoulder. "You'll do fine, sweet thing."

Mother sniffs and brushes at her sleeve. She lifts her chin, and says to no one in particular, "Your father and Judge Canton's father used to be in Elks together."

Maddy peeks at her watch. "Showtime, everyone."

The sound Mother's shoes make on the shiny tiled floor grates on my nerves as we parade down the hall back in the direction of Judge Canton's courtroom. As usual, she's dressed impeccably, wearing black heels with yellow buckles, which compliment the trim on her Hermes suit—the one she wore the night Daddy was elected. She claims the garment brings good luck.

Minutes later, I'm back in the witness box. Jake Preston approaches, and the coffee I'd drank earlier boils like acid in the back of my throat.

"Good morning, Mrs. Graeber."

My hands go clammy in my lap. "Good morning."

"When did you discover your minor daughter was sexually active?"

My head jerks up. "What?"

"Let me rephrase." He looks at the church lady in the juror box. "When did you and Mr. Graeber discover this young girl was unmarried and pregnant?"

"Uh, we learned from the prosecuting attorney's office."

Mr. Preston slowly nods. "Yes, that's right—after they discovered the Planned Parenthood slip in her car. Did you know she planned an abortion?"

Maddy stands. "Objection. Outside the scope of direct. And, assuming facts not in evidence."

Mr. Preston pulls at his starched cuffs. "If Ms. Crane wants, the defense is prepared to call witnesses from the prosecuting attorney's office and from Planned Parenthood who will testify that Pearl Graeber made an appointment to terminate the pregnancy."

"And we have a witness who will testify she changed her mind," Maddy counters. "Yuh Honor, I believe the defendants' counsel is trying to manipulate this jury. My client's daughter is not the one on trial here. Surely the Court will direct Mr. Preston to refrain from assassinating the character of this young girl in order to divert attention off the reprehensible behavior of his own client."

Judge Canton holds up her hand. "Counsel, please." She turns to Mr. Preston. "I'm going to sustain the objection. And as you proceed, please have a point here beyond the obvious."

Mr. Preston nods. "Never mind, Your Honor. I'll retract."

He moves back to the defense table and scans his notes before walking toward the witness box. He approaches, smiling like a shark. "Now, Mrs. Graeber, you maintain you and your daughter had a close relationship, isn't that right?"

I set my jaw and look him directly in the eye. "My daughter and I were extremely close."

"Yet, she didn't tell you she was pregnant." He says this more as a statement than a question.

I take a deep breath and provide my rehearsed answer. "It's my belief she chose not to tell me she was pregnant because she didn't want to hurt me."

"Hurt you? Or, disappoint you?"

"Both," I admit before turning to face the jurors. "My daughter always understood how much I wanted only the best for her. She knew there was nothing she could ever do that would shake my love for her." I turn back to Mr. Preston. "Nothing."

Maddy smiles, and I can almost hear her say, "Well done, darlin'."

Mr. Preston's eyes narrow. "Did your daughter have a drinking problem?"

"Of course not."

He lifts his hand and shakes a paper he holds. "I'd like to offer the accident report as defense exhibit one."

He waits for the courtroom deputy to place a sticker on the

corner of the paper, before he shifts it into my hands. "Could you take a look about half way down?" He points to a line on the report. "There—where it indicates your daughter's blood alcohol level at the time of her accident. Did you know your daughter was drunk when she catapulted her vehicle into that field?"

"I—I don't think this low level means she was drunk."

Maddy gives me a warning look, and I swallow. "I mean, no. No, she wasn't drunk."

Mr. Preston grins at the jurors. "Oh, I guess she was what —pickled?"

Maddy's voice rings out. "Objection."

Judge Crane looks over her reading glasses. "Sustained."

Maddy scribbles notes on the pad in front of her.

I swallow against the dryness forming in my throat. My hand reaches for the glass of water on the sideboard.

"Mrs. Graeber, I'd like you to take a look at this image and tell me what you see?" Mr. Preston gives a nod at the computer geeks and the lights dim in the courtroom. A large screen descends from the ceiling and suddenly, a projector broadcasts an image.

I gasp.

It's my Pearl. Obviously at a party, with a fifth of what looks like tequila tipped high in her hand. She's drinking directly from the bottle.

I can't help myself. My hands cover my mouth and I shut my eyes. The water I'd swallowed only moments before reappears in my throat.

Mr. Preston's voice is strong, sure. His eyes go steely gray, like a hawk going in for the kill. "What *exactly* were you and Mr. Graeber doing to deal with your daughter's drinking problem?" He pauses, smiles. "Or was this bottle filled with punch?"

~

I FEEL Steve's hand on my back, vaguely aware he's moving me out the courtroom doors and into the hall. In the recesses of my mind, I hear Maddy remind us not to say a word until we get outside.

Several feet ahead, I see the piece of vermin hug his wife. Fighting to maintain control, I remind myself to breath.

Inhale. Exhale. Inhale. Exhale.

We plow toward the front entrance, past security and out the doors. Near the parking lot, Jake Preston steps up to a bank of microphones. In the distance, I see Michael Warren help his wife into their car.

I brush the wrinkles from my skirt with shaking fingers and keep my attention on Maddy.

"Look, I told you Mr. Preston would try to take the focus off Coach Warren. It's the only thing he can do really, when his client is clearly a predator." She grabs my hands. "The worst is over, darlin'. Remember, we have evidence. Michael Warren won't fare well when he takes the stand."

A guy with short brown hair and khakis leans against a news truck, his arms folded. He smiles and waves.

"Who's that?" Steve asks.

"Chad Nelson, the news guy from Seattle." I wave back and glance around. "Where's Mother?"

Steve shakes his head. "She said she'd meet us out front." After several minutes, we're still waiting. Steve suggests I go look for her, even though I tell him she's probably hung up talking to someone she knows.

Maddy says she thinks she last saw her head for the ladies' room, and reminds me to talk to no one when I say I'm going to go find her.

I suffer another security check and clip my way back down the hall to the restroom across from Judge Canton's courtroom. I yank the heavy door open. Inside, the room appears empty, until I hear muffled sobs.

At first, I hesitate. The person deserves privacy. But curiosity wins, and I bend and peek under the stall doors. What I find fills my heart with a strange mixture of surprise and sadness.

A pair of black shoes, with bright yellow buckles.

40

The following morning, Maddy calls Steve to the stand.

He climbs into the witness box, looking like he'd rather hammer his thumb. He raises his right hand while the courtroom deputy administers the oath, then sits and gives the jury a nervous smile.

Maddy walks forward. "Please state your name for the record."

"Steven Edward Graeber."

"And you're one of the plaintiffs in this action?"

"Yes, ma'am."

She gives him an encouraging nod. "Tell us what you do for living."

Steve shifts in his chair. "I co-own Hohman Graeber—a commercial real estate development company with a primary focus on retail shopping centers. Our most recent project is located on the corner of Eagle and Chinden, anchored by the Albertson's grocery store with a dozen or so in-lines and four outparcels.

"And you started this venture—?"

"Approximately a year ago."

Oh, Steve. Listen to her entire question before responding.

"Mr. Graeber, I'm not asking you to disclose proprietary or personal financial information, but I'd like you to briefly describe for the jurors the effect bringing this action has had on meeting your business plan."

"This lawsuit ticked off more than a few folks in town. Consequently, we've had tenants back out of their plans to build with us."

Maddy raises her eyebrows. "Bet that makes it hard to sustain a cash flow."

Steve lifts his chin. I see a look of defiance in his eyes as he answers. "It could've. Fortunately, we had other options available to us."

Maddy moves to the witness box. "Are you acquainted with Joe Anderson?"

Steve draws a deep breath. "Yes, I've known Joe for years. We played college football together up at Moscow. "

"And you've remained friends?"

"Up until recently, yes." Steve grabs for his water and takes a large sip.

I glance over at Joe. Dressed in a suit and tie, his appearance is considerably different than what you'd see on game days. Connie sits beside him. She looks miserable . . . and angry.

"Would you say Joe Anderson is a football fan?" Steve snorts. "Yeah. Yeah, I'd say he's a football fan."

"In your opinion, do you think Joe Anderson's devotion to the Sawtooth High School football program clouded his judgment when it came to Coach Warren?"

I don't know what surprises me more. Steve's answer or the vulnerability in his eyes. "There was a time when, if anything happened to me, I wanted Joe to step in and take care of my family." He gives his former buddy a pained look. "Now I wouldn't trust him to take care of my dog. No matter how much skin wraps them bones—there's not much character on the inside."

Maddy reaches and pats my husband's arm. She turns to Jake Preston. "Your witness."

The coach's attorney slowly stands. He rubs his chin as he approaches the witness box. "So I take it character means a great deal to you?"

"Yes, sir. In my view, character is the measure of a man." Mr. Preston clasps his hands behind his back and looks at the ceiling, as if deep in thought.

Finally, he pulls his attention back to Steve. "How long have you and Mrs. Graeber been married?"

The question is unexpected, and I feel myself brace for the worst.

Steve looks at me, smiles nervously. "I'm gonna get this one wrong." He pauses, as if mentally calculating. "I guess we've been married just under fourteen years. Something like that."

Mr. Preston gives a slight chuckle. "Safe answer."

The jury laughs. Maddy says Mr. Preston's attack style is off-putting to the jurors, particularly the women. But I'm not so sure. He's building a rapport, if you ask me. You don't get to be senior partner in one of the largest firms in Idaho without learning how to romance a jury.

My hands absently move to Pearl's bracelet on my wrist. Somehow the smooth gold band gives me strength. Bringing this lawsuit has been difficult, but my baby girl deserves all this effort and more. By the end of this trial, everyone will know what that man did to her—and Michael Warren and the others will be made to pay. More than that, winning this case will stop him from having access to female students and doing anything like this again.

"Would you say you and Mrs. Graeber are good parents?"

Oh, be careful Steve. He's setting you up.

My husband shrugs. "Yeah. Sure. There are no perfect parents, but we're good ones."

"And yet neither you or Mrs. Graeber were aware your daughter was not in her bed the morning of January twenty-sixth. In fact, you didn't really know whose bed she was in."

I see the mortgage banker wince.

Maddy taps her pen on the table. "Judge, is there a question in there somewhere? Or does Mr. Preston want to take the stand so he can continue to testify?"

Disregarding the interruption, Mr. Preston continues. "Mr. Graeber, approximately how many hours per week would you estimate you spent getting your company started and the development off the ground?"

Maddy sighs. "Time frame, Mr. Preston?"

"In the six months prior to January twenty-sixth."

Steve shifts in his chair. "Look, there's no doubt I spent considerable time focused on my business efforts during that time period." He turns to the jurors. "My family means everything to me. I'd go to the moon and back to provide for them, to pay for college and . . . weddings." He swallows, his eyes glistening.

"If you want to know if I have regrets, sure I do. With the power to wind the clock back, I'd scoop that girl into my arms and keep her safe." Steve looks at Michael Warren. "I'd do a better job of warning her about the dangers that lurk." He pauses.

"And . . . I'd hug her more."

"PLAINTIFFS' call Joe Anderson to the stand."

Joe lifts himself from the hard wooden bench. Connie gives his hand a squeeze, and he moves to the witness box, where he takes the oath. Next, he maneuvers his linebacker-sized frame into the chair.

"Mr. Anderson, please state your name for the record." He leans toward the microphone. "Joe Anderson."

"No middle name?"

"Nope. Just Joe."

"And you are married to Connie Anderson?"

"Yes, ma'am." He smiles at his wife.

"Together you own Jaycee Jewelers?"

Joe nods. "Yes. A little twist of my first initial and Connie's."

Maddy shakes her head. "I see. Clever."

His mouth draws into a grin. "Yeah, we thought so."

"And from the records Mr. Preston produced in discovery, I determined you were elected to the school board three years ago. Is that correct?"

He nods.

The judge reminds him that the court reporter needs an audible response.

"Oh, sorry," he says. "Yes, that's correct."

"And, shortly after that, the district hired Michael Warren as head football coach at Sawtooth High School." She flips the pages of her file. "Were you involved in that hiring decision?"

Joe lifts his chin and adjusts his collar. "Yes. I sure was."

Maddy closes the file and places it on the table next to me. She moves toward the witness box. "Would you say you love football . . . Joe?" She flutters her lashes and gives him a sly smile. "You're a big fan, isn't that right?"

"Yeah . . . yeah, I am." Joe grins and runs his hand across his shaved head. "Some say football is a matter of life and death—but it's more important than that.'"

The diesel mechanic laughs.

Joe is a great salesman. He could peddle a truckload of shoulder pads to a bed-ridden eighty-three year old in a nursing home.

Maddy steps to our table and lifts a stapled stack of papers. She hands them to the courtroom deputy and asks they be marked Plaintiffs' Exhibit 2. With the sticker in place, Maddy provides the documents to Joe. "Prior to hiring Coach Warren, were you aware of these prior incidents?"

"Allegations," Mr. Preston corrects.

Maddy nods. "Allegations." She adjusts her reading glasses before scanning the exhibit. She looks up at Joe. "Were you aware there were so *many* allegations?"

Joe swallows. "Coach Warren came to us with high recommendations."

"Please answer my question. Were you aware that more than a dozen girls had accused Michael Warren of inappropriate conduct?"

Joe shifts in his chair. "It's not our job to find what doesn't appear in a candidate's official employment record."

Maddy's eyes narrow. "Because football is more important than life or death."

Jake Preston springs to his feet. Before he voices his objection, Maddy smiles. "I'll retract."

She hands the exhibit to the courtroom deputy. "Now, let's turn to Mrs. Graeber's report." She rubs her chin. "You were aware of *that* incident, correct?"

Joe nods.

The judge raises her eyebrows at him, and Joe gives an audible response. "Yes."

"Could you tell the jurors what the school board did to investigate Mrs. Graeber's claim that she'd seen Michael Warren with an underage student, acting inappropriately?"

"The board conducted a full investigation." He gives an indignant huff. "We questioned both the student and Mr. Warren. Both vehemently denied what Mrs. Graeber *claimed* she saw."

"Did you call the student's mother to see when the girl returned home that evening?"

Joe's eyebrows knit. "No."

"Did you question Lisa Warren to see if her husband was at home that evening?"

"Didn't need to."

"But you conducted a thorough investigation?"

Joe leans back in the chair. "That's my testimony."

"No further questions."

Judge Canton checks the clock. "How long do you expect cross to take, Mr. Preston?"

"We'll be brief, Your Honor."

She nods. "Fine. Proceed."

Mr. Preston stands. The light from the overhead catches briefly on his diamond ring. "Mr. Anderson, the defense has only a few questions. Did you, or any of the other board members, ever have actual knowledge that Michael Warren acted inappropriately, or was involved sexually, with a minor?"

"No, sir."

"Did you, or any of the board members, ever have actual knowledge that Michael Warren acted inappropriately, or was involved sexually, with Pearl Graeber?"

"No, sir."

"Were you aware in the six months prior to Pearl Graeber's death that Steve Graeber was struggling financially?"

"Yes. He couldn't get a loan until he partnered up with Paul Hohman. And the development project took up a lot of his energy. Never had time for Rotary Club meetings. Showed up at games late. Even missed his daughter's dance team performances."

Mr. Preston looks up at Judge Canton. "No further questions."

"Fine, we'll recess for today. Court will reconvene at nine o'clock a.m."

AFTER THE LONG day in court, I'm entirely too exhausted to cook. Jackie left our freezer filled with enough food to last the trial and well beyond, but after this stress-filled day, I'm even too tired for clean up. So take-out and paper plates, it is.

"Aaron, honey. What kind of pizza do you want?"

"Pepperoni," he tells me, never taking his eyes off his television program.

"Keep him away from the news." I whisper to Steve, as I rifle through the coupons I'd stuffed by the telephone.

Steve nods. "Hey, Scoot. I need some help outside."

Aaron sighs. "Ah, can't it wait until later?"

I make my way to the garage, with Steve's voice in the background telling our son he'll give him ten minutes, and then chores have to be done.

I smile. What a softy.

Twenty minutes later, I'm sitting in a booth at Take Me Bake Me Pizza. The local joint is located less than a mile from home and in addition to the best take-out pizza, the restaurant tucked against the foothills serves frosty mugs of root beer, just like the old Arctic Circle drive-in Daddy took me to when I was a kid.

I'm sipping on a large-sized mug when the news flashes on the television mounted against the wall. I see Michael Warren's face appear on the screen. "Could you turn that up?" I shout at the little gal behind the counter.

A voice-over begins as the screen turns to an angry crowd in front of the courthouse. Many hold picket-like signs. "As you can see, this trial has impassioned many of the residents in this community." The reporter holds a microphone in front of a man in his twenties holding a sign lettered with MICHAEL WARREN over a red heart. "What would you like to say?"

The man looks around at the crowd for support. "We're all

out here in support of Coach Warren. No way did he do any monkey-business with young girls."

Another man, older and with a bigger belly, steps forward. "These little cheerleaders wear dresses that barely cover their private parts, and yeah—us older dudes look. Who wouldn't? And why is the man always to blame? Takes two to bed bump, know what I mean?" He grins, and pops his chest with one fist.

My heart sinks. "Sorry. You can turn it down now."

The gal shrugs and grabs the remote. She presses a button and the sound mutes.

"Goats behinds."

Startled, I look up. Chad Nelson stands with a beer, grinning. I offer him a seat, and he slides in the bench across from the table.

I lean back against the vinyl seat. "You following me?"

Chad shakes his head. "Nah. Called your house and your husband told me you'd be here."

"Well, my attorney has asked me not to talk to any reporters." I scrape my finger down the side of my frost-covered mug. "Even you."

"Yeah, I get that. But that doesn't stop me from talking to you."

I take a deep breath. "Yeah?" Despite my calm exterior, my insides are shaking. I've seen this look on his face before.

"Word has it Warren's attorney has some tricks up his sleeve. He's lined up a bunch of football players who will testify they slept with your daughter in the month before she died."

The news hits me with the force of a half-back's helmet ramming into my gut. "How—how do you know?"

Chad shakes his head. "Never mind the source. Do you know Dennis Cutler?"

I curse under my breath. "Yeah," I answer, and nod miserably.

"Craig Ellison?"

My voice dims to a whisper. "Pearl's former boyfriend. But it's not true. I can't believe he's willing to perjure himself."

Chad downs the last of his beer. "Craig Ellison and the others think they have a shot at the state title—but not without Coach Warren."

This new reality sinks in. I cup my hands over my mouth and fight back tears. If these boys march in and tell those jurors they had sex with Pearl, that not only puts Michael Warren's paternity in question, but in their minds my daughter will become a slut. And we'll come off looking like parents trying to cash in.

How could I have so miscalculated Craig's character and let him date Pearl in the first place?

Chad hands me a napkin. I dab at my tear-filled eyes, before anyone in the restaurant can notice I've lost control of my emotions. No telling what might get back to Jake Preston and the defense team. "What am I going to do?" I whisper, barely able to keep despair from my voice.

Chad's eyes fill with kindness. "That one's for your attorney to figure out." He cups my hand with his own. "In the meantime, if you need anything call me."

I swipe my eyes. Before Chad leaves, I reach and touch his arm. "Thank you."

His face breaks into a wide grin. "No problem."

I pay for the pizzas and head for the car, wondering what I'm going to feed Steve first. Pepperoni—or this new information.

Both are going to give him heartburn.

41

When I call Maddy and report what Chad Nelson told me, she calls an emergency meeting at her office, even though it's after nine o'clock.

Maddy meets us at the door and escorts Steve and I into her conference room, where Mother stands next to the window, peering out at the dark. She turns when we enter, but says nothing.

I take a seat at one end of the large granite table. Steve sits across the table from me, letting his head drop into his hands. When I finish reiterating what opposing counsel has planned, he lifts and says, "This is exactly what I warned would happen."

I look at him miserably.

What can I say really? He's right. As much as I wanted to hold Michael Warren and the others accountable by going forward with this trial, I've placed our family—and Pearl's reputation in grave danger.

After this, we'll have no choice but to pick up and move. Maybe to Alaska, a place where the ice and year-round darkness prohibits high school football.

My mind turns to Aaron. I can just hear his so-called buddies now, taunting my sweet boy with this new revelation that Pearl slept around, however unfounded.

And Steve will never forgive me. We'll grow into another of those couples who sit across from each other at dinner in an elegant restaurant, with nothing to say to one another. The kind that scoop buried resentment and drink it like soup.

Worse, I've let Pearl down. No matter how courageous she thought her mother was, all the courage in the world isn't going to pull this one from the toilet.

Maddy plants her fists on her hips. "Frankly, this doesn't surprise me all that much. Jake Preston is a lot like the Georgia poison ivy I avoided as a child. The leaves seem pretty, but one touch and you'll be nursing blisters for a good long while." She sits and plants the heels of her bubblegum pink ostrich boots on the table.

Her hand punches out a number on her cell phone. "Joanne? Hey darlin', sorry to call so late but we have a problem and I need some information." She gives her paralegal the names of the football players on the list in her file. "Start with the Cutler kid and Craig Ellison. Find out everything you can." She pauses, listening. "Yup, sweet thing, I need it by morning."

She clicks the phone closed. "Well, that's all we can do for tonight. Tomorrow, the experts will testify and then I'll put Warren on the stand." She gives us a look of reassurance. "Even poison ivy has an antidote. We'll have a plan well before Preston puts on his case."

Mother turns. "It goes without saying, I suppose. I don't want my daughter hurt further." She looks at Maddy for emphasis. "I don't care what it costs."

A string of experts are next to testify.

First, the county coroner takes the stand and states the alcohol content in Pearl's body was over the legal limit, but barely. Pearl was not wearing a seatbelt at the time she was thrown from the car, which the coroner admits contributed to her demise.

Maddy calls a brief recess, allowing me and Steve to wait in the hall while photographs of the accident and Pearl's body are shown to the jury. We agreed that even though there was some value to letting the jury see our emotions, no one would benefit if I completely broke down. I don't want those images in my head when I think of my daughter.

Mother, on the other hand, chooses to stay.

When we're allowed back in the courtroom, the jury's empathy is hard to mistake. Neither is the streak of mascara smeared across Mother's Elizabeth Arden face.

Maddy claims Dr. Nancy Lukas is our big gun. A licensed psychologist, she has a dual Ph.D and an Ed.D. from Stanford University, is multi-published in the field of sexual abuse prevention in the education system, and appears regularly on radio and television. She's consulted on over eighty cases and has testified in thirty-two of them. No one knows more about the growing phenomenon of coaches sexually exploiting students than Dr. Lukas.

"Dr. Lukas," Maddy begins, once she's got her admitted as an expert. "Describe if you will, what educators are required to do, in terms of investigating a potential hire."

Dr. Lukas straightens in her chair. "In this state, fingerprint-based FBI and state criminal background and sex offender registry checks are required of all certified teachers, and public school employees with unsupervised contact with minors. However," she adds. "Education administrators across the country are well aware of the potential for these kinds of problems. There is considerable information distributed cautioning school boards to go much further.

"For example, I often cite from two reports. The U.S. Department of Education published a study in 2004 and more recently, the U.S. Government Accountability Office collected data and published findings. Both clearly warn of potential dire consequences when there is inadequate investigation prior to hire."

"I see." Maddy taps her pencil against her cheek. "Are situations in which coaches cross the boundaries into improper sexual contact with students prevalent?"

Dr. Lukas nods enthusiastically. "Oh, yes. The number of incidents is staggering, and rising all the time. As a profession, coaching has among the highest rates of sexual misconduct complaints." She turns to the jurors. "A growing number of these sad events are occurring with every passing year. Many of us are well aware of the increased incidents reported on television and other news outlets. Especially after the advent of social media and access to students in off hours."

"Given these reports, what should this school board have done prior to hiring Michael Warren?"

"Well, it's my opinion a district is required to do whatever it takes until the hiring authorities possess sufficient information to believe an employee is of good moral character and has never committed an act of unprofessional conduct with a minor. At a minimum, a district must follow the elements required by the state. But in addition, I find that often a few telephone calls to prior districts where the candidate worked is helpful. Despite the reluctance to offer details, administrators will answer honestly if asked directly. There are, of course, exceptions."

"Exceptions?" Maddy scowls. "What would motivate an administrator to withhold such critical information?"

Dr. Lukas sighs. "That is where the situation gets complicated. You see, I've discovered districts routinely keep investigations into these matters secret by failing to document them or by signing agreements with accused coaches promising not to tell. Far too often problem teachers and coaches are passed on to new school districts after being disciplined, pushed out or fired for sexual misconduct. This approach eliminates the cost of paid leave pending the investigation process and holds off potential lawsuits. The old adage, sweep the problem under the rug and let someone else deal with it."

Maddy looks shocked. "But then how would a district know not to hire a problem coach?"

"There are usually red flags."

"What red flags might an administrator see?"

Dr. Lukas' face grows solemn. "Well, in this particular instance, on Coach Warren's employment application, he failed to respond to the question asking whether he'd ever been disciplined. And he failed to check any box next to the question about whether he'd ever been convicted of a crime."

Maddy waves a stapled document. "On this employment application?" She marches forward and shows it to Dr. Lukas, who nods her head in the affirmative.

"Plaintiffs would like this marked." She hands the application off to the courtroom deputy, and continues. "Dr. Lukas, in light of their failure to follow up on the missing responses, is it your professional opinion that *this* district failed in their responsibilities in *this* situation?"

"I'm afraid so, yes."

"Thank you, Dr. Lukas. Nothing further."

Jake Preston approaches. "Good afternoon, Dr. Lukas."

"Good afternoon."

"Let me see if I understand your testimony. You believe that education administrators should call all former employers of each and every candidate prior to hire?" He raises his eyebrows and chuckles. "Sawtooth High School alone has more than two hundred employees, and that's not the entire district. Many have years of experience. Can you even imagine the time that would take? Let alone the cost to the taxpayers?" He raises his hands, palms up. "Is that really realistic?"

Dr. Lukas responds with a steady voice. "It's my opinion that this approach is not only realistic, it's mandatory for the safety of students."

"And what if a coach's earlier record is simply unavailable?"

"Well, in this particular case, I understand Michael Warren's history of allegations were uncovered by a reporter who simply checked the internet."

For the first time, I see several jurors write furiously in their notebooks. Dr. Lukas charges an exorbitant hourly rate, which Mother is footing. But I've got to say, she seems to be worth every penny.

Jake Preston notices the jurors' reactions, too.

He looks at the ceiling, his forefinger at his lips. When he directs his attention back to Dr. Lukas, his face takes on the look of a bowler lining up for a strike. "Obviously, you've reviewed the records in this case extensively. Did you find anything in the documents that brought you to the conclusion that Michael Warren engaged in any conduct that was sexually out-of-bounds with Pearl Graeber?"

"I can tell you that Pearl Graeber fits the victim profile. Most people believe the students most vulnerable are those from single-parent homes or who have addictions in their families. Interestingly, research proves that to be true for younger victims.

"But with teenagers, another scenario is just as true. Girls who are achievement-oriented and often overly responsible are just as much at risk. Their maturity draws them to older males." She looks directly at Michael Warren. "It's up to adult men to maintain the proper boundaries. Too often the perpetrators in these situations act like they are one of the kids, and the lines get blurred. They socialize with the students, hang out with them, if you will. And the lines of communication go well beyond school related activities.

"For example, in this case, I believe I read Michael Warren interacted with female students via Facebook."

Mr. Preston sighs. "Thank you for enlightening the court, but please answer the question I posed. Did you find *anything* that linked Michael Warren with Pearl Graeber?"

"No," Dr. Lukas admits. "No, I did not."

I watch Mr. Preston retreat back to the defense table, a smug look pasted across his face. He may not have scored a strike, but unfortunately, he managed to pick off a few pins.

42

In a last minute decision, Maddy calls Troy Hohman to testify as a character witness.

Given Chad Nelson's warning, she feels the jury needs to connect with Pearl and who she was. He can also deflect the abortion allegation made by Jake Preston early in the trial.

When Troy enters the courtroom, I barely believe he's the same boy I've known. Jackie told me earlier on the phone that he'd declined her request to attend with him, saying he'd feel nervous with her watching.

His black hair is cut short and he wears dress slacks and a shirt and tie. His tattoos are hidden and he's removed all the hardware from his piercings. Frankly, he looks like he stepped off the cover of a GQ magazine.

I shake my head in amazement. Ham-man has turned handsome. I realize then that he wants to make a good impression. For Pearl.

The thought moves me, and I want to stand and hug him. Instead, I listen as he gets sworn in.

"State your name, please."

"Troy Paul Hohman."

Maddy rewards him with a smile. "I understand you and Pearl Graeber were friends."

"Yes, ma'am. I met her when our dads became business partners."

"How well did you know one another?"

"Not really well, at first. We kinda ran in different crowds. She was on the dance team and dated the team's quarterback. I'm not too into football."

Maddy nods. "How did you get to know one another better?"

"I was hanging out at a friend's house and some guys came over. One of them said he heard there was a big party at a house south of town. I didn't pay too much attention until I overhead Pearl's name mentioned."

"Pearl Graeber?"

"Yeah, someone said she was at the party and not doing so well. They said she seemed upset and was drinking and stuff. So, I figured I'd go check things out. Even though I didn't know her well, I knew her dad, and he was always talking about her. So, the way I figured, she didn't usually do things like that."

Maddy glances at Steve before asking the next question. "What did you find when you arrived at the party?"

"Pearl had obviously been drinking, and I knew she couldn't drive like that, so I offered to take her home. She got sick a couple of times on the way to her house and started crying." A sad look crosses Troy's face. "I told her everything was going to be okay."

I see the nurse on the jury give Troy an encouraging smile.

"And after that?" Maddy asks.

"The next morning, I called to see how she was. We talked, like for about an hour. She said she was going through some things—that she'd caught Craig, that was her boyfriend, with her best friend, Callie. She felt pretty betrayed." He shrugs. "We just became really good friends after that. I liked hanging with her."

Troy's lip quivers slightly and he fights for control.

It dawns on me Troy considered Pearl more than just a friend. I lock my eyes with his and a new understanding passes between us.

Maddy's voice softens. "Mr. Hohman, I understand how close you and Pearl were and that friends keep certain confidences. But I want to remind you of your oath here today. Despite any promises to the contrary, you are legally obligated to answer my questions truthfully.

"I understand."

She nods. "Now, were you aware Pearl was pregnant before she died?"

Troy focuses on Steve. He swallows. "Yes."

"I'm sorry, could you speak up?"

He looks at Maddy and nods. "Uh . . . sorry. Yes, I knew."

"When did you learn she was pregnant?"

Troy adjusts in his seat. "She told me two days before she died. Pearl told me, but made me promise not to tell anyone." He looks at me before adding, "She wanted a way out. That's why she made that appointment. But we talked, and she knew she couldn't go through with it. She was going to tell her parents. But first, she wanted to tell the baby's father."

Maddy slows nods. "And you let her borrow your Jeep that night?"

Troy's head drops. "Yes, ma'am. I did." "Do you know who the father was?"

The question hangs in the air like a bad smell. Every one of the jurors leans forward, anticipating his answer. The answer I already know.

Finally, Troy looks up. "No. She would never say."

Maddy smiles at him. "And the abortion?"

Troy blinks back emotion. "I want everyone to know I was

with her when she called and cancelled that appointment. She used my phone."

"Thank you, sweet thing." Maddy glances at her notes. "Mr. Hohman, one more thing. Where was the party? The one where you drove Pearl home?"

Troy looks across the courtroom. "At the coach's house."

A FLURRY of activity descends on the defendants' side of the courtroom as several suits stand and scurry out. They barely hit the door before lifting cell phones to their ears. Mr. Preston's associate, Alexa somebody, sits with a stunned expression. She looks to Mr. Preston, who remains perfectly still.

Michael Warren also fails to noticeably react. His hand holds tight to his wife's. She drills her attention to the floor.

It's obvious the defense has just taken a major hit.

Forgetting Maddy's admonition not to react to any testimony inside the courtroom, I turn and wink at Steve. Mother's lips crinkle into a slight smile. Like me, she relishes our attorney's surprising maneuver.

Judge Canton's voice rings out, breaking my mental revelry. "Mr. Preston, do you care to cross?"

The question seems silly, given the testimony bomb that exploded only moments before.

Jake Preston broadcasts a wide grin, in stark contradiction to the black in his eyes. "We would, Your Honor." He scribbles a note and passes it to the woman sitting next to him. She nods, stands and approaches the witness stand.

She smiles. "Good morning, Mr. Hohman. I'm Alexa Dean and I'd like to ask you a few quick questions."

Troy scowls. "Okay."

"Mr. Hohman, you testified you lent Pearl your vehicle on the night of her fatal accident, isn't that right?"

"Yes, ma'am. I did."

"Yet the Graebers have not sued you for contributing to the death of their daughter?"

"Objection," Maddy shouts. "Irrelevant."

"Sustained."

Ms. Dean regroups, never letting the smile drift from her face. "Withdrawn."

She moves closer to Troy, still smiling and looking like one of those models for a teeth brightening product. "Mr. Hohman, have you at any time, and especially during the six months prior to Pearl Graeber's death, relapsed?"

Troy takes a deep breath, and looks away, resigned. "No, ma'am. I haven't."

Confused, I turn and glance at Steve. His expression tells me this line of testimony has caught him off guard as well. I feel Maddy's hand pat my leg. I know she wants me refrain from reacting to what I'm hearing, but that's easier said than done in this instance. How could I have known Jackie all this time, and she not confide in me?

"Isn't it true, Mr. Hohman, that you spent nine months in a rehab facility a few years ago," she rubs the side of her head as if trying to remember something. "For . . . oh, yes, for meth addiction?"

Why, that little—

I watch helplessly as Michael Warren's attorney skewers Troy and holds him over the sacrificial flame. Seems this legal team will roast anyone to save their client's hide.

I lean and whisper to Maddy. "Can't you do something?" She shakes her head in an almost unnoticeable fashion.

There is a second where I see her jaw twitch and I know she's not happy, but her face doesn't reflect it.

Anyone in this courtroom with any sense knows defense counsel is anxious to deflect the impact of Troy's testimony about the party. But how could they believe ripping at this young man's character could accomplish that goal?

I guess if the school board members are willing to sacrifice young girls to win a football championship, they'll lose little sleep over crushing a young guy's reputation and self-esteem to save writing a big check for damages.

My eyes pan the jury, trying to assess their reaction. Frankly, I can't tell what any of them think. Reading what goes on inside a juror's head is a lot like guessing what's inside a can with a missing label.

Troy straightens in his seat. "I escaped an addiction to methadone by attending a rehabilitation program three years ago. I've remained clean ever since." He turns and faces the jury. "It's not like I would choose that route again. But going through all that stuff created an awareness of my deep need for God." Troy's face slowly breaks into a grin. "The scripture is true—He turns all things to good for dudes willing to seek Him."

Alexa Dean clears her throat. She looks to Mr. Preston for guidance. Getting none, she declares she has no further questions and returns to her seat at the defense table.

"PLAINTIFFS CALL Michael Warren to the stand."

A hush falls over the courtroom as the coach stands. He leans over and cups his wife's chin, mouths he loves her, and makes his way to the witness box.

Before taking his seat, he smiles at the female court reporter, then at Judge Canton. Despite the fact he's climbing into the hot seat, Michael Warren looks relaxed—almost confident. Unlike every other witness, he accepts the offer of a lapel microphone and expertly clips it in place. Then he nods and lets an easy grin fall over his face. "I'm ready."

Maddy steps from behind our table and moves forward. "Good morning, Mr. Warren."

He awards her with an even wider smile. "Good morning."

"For the record, could you state your name?"

"Michael Edward Warren."

"And how old are you, Mr. Warren?"

"On my last birthday, I turned thirty-four."

I listen to Maddy walk him through his education background and early employment history. The exchange is a little like watching a tennis game, with the jurors' heads moving back and forth as Maddy serves up a question and the coach volleys back an answer.

"Mr. Warren, what drew you to coaching football?" Unlike what her nickname implies, Mad Dog's questioning comes off like she's chatting with the coach at Starbucks.

The coach leans back in his chair. "My father was an Army colonel. We moved around a lot when I was a kid. The way I made friends was playing football."

He looks over at the jurors. "Guess I was pretty good, because everybody wanted me on their team. I ended up playing for UCLA, where for a number of years, I held the record for the most touchdown passes in a single season." He turns back to Maddy and shrugs. "Football is my life. The game molded me, provided the leadership skills I employ today. Life skills I want to pass on. It's why I coach."

Maddy lifts her file in the air. "Those leadership skills have served you well. Your coaching career is impressive."

Michael nods. "I'm proud to have been a part of some really great teams. I'd like to think my influence molded the character of hundred of students. A lot of people think football is all about winning. But really this sport creates men who are trained to tackle life using the same skills needed in approaching an opponent on the field."

Maddy smiles and shakes her head. "And what kind of

influence and life skills did you provide when you hosted a drinking party for minors in your home?" she says, throwing the chat aside.

Michael Warren's eyes narrow. "Let me clarify a few things that I think have been misrepresented here." He sighs. "First, I did not host a drinking party. In reality, my home is always open to students. My team knows my wife often prepares pots of spaghetti or taco fixins, and we'll feed anyone who wants to drop over.

"In this particular instance, some students showed up at the house already intoxicated. It would have been irresponsible for me to send them on their way, and to let them drive in that condition. So I gathered keys and made them hang out until they sobered up."

"So your home is a bit of a sanctuary of sorts? For kids who shouldn't be driving?"

"Yes, ma'am." Michael Warren thinks for a minute, then looks directly at me. "You'd be surprised at the number of students who cross the boundaries of safe behavior and drive when they shouldn't."

The truck mechanic pulls his pen from his shirt pocket and scribbles something on his notepad. Finished, he looks up and our eyes meet. He quickly averts his gaze back to the coach.

"When did you first meet Pearl Graeber?"

"Well," he says. "I can't give you an exact date, if that's what you're looking for. But I'm sure I met her at school. She was a student at Sawtooth High, and her mother and I were on staff."

"Were you ever alone with Pearl Graeber?"

Michael Warren scratches at the back of his right ear. "Well, not in the sense you're implying. I think everyone here heard the Hohman kid's testimony about the night he drove Pearl home from my house." His eyebrows draw into a stubborn angle. "I don't want to speak ill of the dead, but that girl was completely blotted that night. She showed up looking like she'd been crying, and I could smell alcohol on her breath."

"Was she alone when she arrived?"

"You know, I'm not really sure. All I know is it was pretty fair knowledge that Craig had dumped the gal for somebody else, and she wasn't happy about it."

My heart pounds and I have to remind myself to breathe. Night after night following Pearl's accident, I'd played an imaginary scene in my head, trying to recreate what might have happened the night Troy drove her home from that party. Maybe for the first time, I'll know what really occurred.

Maddy's eyebrows lift. "Craig?"

"Ellison. He was the quarterback last year, and they had a thing going for a while. Rumor had it she was heading out of state to some fancy school, and he wanted to accept an offer to play for Boise State." The coach shrugs. "Things happen when you're that young. Different dreams and such."

"Go on," Maddy prompts.

Jake Preston coughs . . . twice.

Despite the obvious signal from his counsel, Michael Warren continues. "Anyway, when Ellison showed up with some gal nuzzling on his shoulder, the Graeber girl shut herself in the bathroom. I coaxed her into unlocking the door, and we were alone for a few minutes."

He sits forward. "That's when she broke down and confided in me. Told me no one understood what it was like for her. I did my best to calm her down. The Hohman kid showed up not long after, and he took her home. End of story." The coach's smile turns almost imperceptibly forced.

"And your wife? Where was she?"

Michael Warren draws a deep breath. "Lisa was with her family in Philadelphia that week, going through a fertility procedure that would correct problems my wife was having that prevented her from getting pregnant." He winks at his wife from the stand, then turns to the jury. "Treatment that worked, I might add."

"Yes. Your counsel told us." Maddy marches to our table and picks up another file, opens it, and turns back in the direction of the witness box. "Mr. Warren, six years ago, on October 9, did you fondle a sixteen-year-old student's breast?"

"No, I did not. I—"

"And later that spring, did you allow a female student to spend the night in your home with no one present but you and her?"

"Of course not. In that instance—"

"And the year before you accepted a position at Sawtooth High School, did you have sexual relations with a seventeen-year-old, a student at the school where you coached?"

"No, I did not." Michael Warren's lips draw into a tight line. "Can I say something—?"

Maddy fires back, "No, Mr. Warren. You may not. This is not a media interview. This is an examination under oath in a court of law."

Her words may as well have been a shot fired from a cannon. From the look on the coach's face, the battle is on.

I sit perfectly still, relishing the change in Maddy's approach. I've waited a long time for someone to nail Michael Warren and make him pay for what he's done. My moment is here.

Maddy moves closer to the witness box. "And in May of this year, were you in a vehicle alone with Callie Pratt?"

The coach lifts his chin. "I didn't tuck her hair. I simply handed the girl my handkerchief to wipe her tears. Her mom brought another puke home, and they had a huge argument, and Callie took off. I discovered her crying in her car parked out by the football field.

What would you have me do? Leave her there, crying?" He

drums his fingers on the sideboard. “I did not do anything inappropriate with that girl.”

Jake Preston stands. “Your Honor, perhaps this is a good time to break for lunch?”

Judge Canton pulls her attention from Michael Warren and glances at the wall clock. She nods. “Yes, given it’s now twelve-thirty, we’ll break and reconvene back in an hour.”

Michael Warren climbs down and joins his attorneys. From the look on Jake Preston’s face, the coach is going to get taken to the wood shed during the lunch hour.

We’re to meet Jackie and Paul at the Basque restaurant a few blocks from the courthouse. Maddy elects to stay back to prepare for this afternoon. Before we part, I give her a quick hug. “Thanks, Maddy. I appreciate all you are doing.”

She smiles back. “No problem, darlin’.”

Steve asks if we can bring her something to eat. She grins. “Nope. I plan on having Michael Warren for lunch.”

We step through the courthouse doors into unexpected warmth, the kind that comes from the delicious Indian summer days in southern Idaho. For the first time in while, I feel free to fling my head back and enjoy what the sun has to offer. That is, until a reporter calls out my name.

Steve’s hand grabs my elbow, and we scoot to the curb where Paul’s car waits. As soon as we’re settled inside, Jackie tells us she talked the restaurant’s chef into making us a to-go package. She lifts the bag like she’s snagged some fabulous deal at Nordstrom’s. “Hungry?”

Paul checks his rear-view mirror to make sure we haven’t been followed. Convinced we’ve left the press behind, he jigs and jags through traffic and points us in the direction of Julia Davis Park.

Jackie adjusts the air-conditioning vent. “I thought Elaine was joining us.”

"Mother said she had some calls to make. She'll meet back up with us in court."

Paul glances in the rear view mirror. "How'd the morning go after Troy took the stand?"

Steve thumbs through text messages on his phone. "Madeline Crane is knocking Warren into tomorrow."

Jackie huffs. "Good. Couldn't happen to a more deserving guy."

Minutes later, I'm helping her lay out the blanket on the grass. When we're out of earshot of the guys, I lower my voice and ask, "Why didn't you tell me?"

She shrugs. "It's Troy's story to tell. Not mine."

I smile and nod. Another reason to like Jackie Hohman. She's loyal to the bone.

Steve chugs from a bottle of water. Finished, he shakes his head. "I just don't know how all this works. That scum is never going to admit what he did. And what proof do we have?"

Jackie hands him a chorizo on a crusty bun. "Well, from what Barrie tells me, that snappy attorney of yours will figure something out." She gives Steve's arm a squeeze.

Across the grass from us, a young girl laughs. The gal gazes up into the sky, her blonde head tucked into the lap of a denim-clad guy. I quickly look away, amazed how the pain of losing Pearl never truly subsides.

I've never been one of those who believe life is random. Even though I barely admit it, even to myself, I've always considered when bad things happen to a person, they must deserve it somehow.

I watch Jackie pass out brownies. Surely there doesn't exist a nicer person, a woman who loves like there's no tomorrow.

No one will ever convince me she deserved what happened with her son and the pain that must have caused.

And maybe I don't deserve what happened with Pearl either.

Troy's words from the stand drift back into my mind—the way God turns things to good. Pearl may no longer be in my arms, but I'm starting to believe she's safely tucked in his and that someday I will see her again. The thought brings me incredible comfort.

Maybe, just maybe—feeling pain is not how all this ends. For the first time since Pearl's accident, I let myself hope, even if only a little . . . and I mentally send up my first timid prayer.

43

Word of Maddy nailing the coach on the stand must've leaked out during the lunch break. The mob of press outside makes passage back into the courthouse nearly impossible.

Maddy's paralegal meets us just inside the door. She quickly explains the situation to one of the security clerks who thankfully pulls us to the front of the line.

We get seated minutes before Judge Canton enters the courtroom and reconvenes. "Mr. Warren, I'd like to remind you that you're still under oath."

The coach nods as he takes the stand. "I understand."

Maddy takes a deep breath, and approaches. "Now, before the lunch break, your testimony to this court is that you did not act inappropriately in any of those . . . what, four incidents?"

"I did not."

"You have never fondled, or had an inappropriate relationship with a minor? Is that your testimony?"

"Yes, that is my testimony."

Maddy flicks something from the jacket sleeve of her black suit. "And you testified that you've served as a mentor of sorts, for the young men you coach—" She pauses. "—and on occasion, for a couple of heartbroken young girls?"

"Objection," Jake Preston bellows. "Mischaracterizes my client's prior testimony."

Maddy awards opposing counsel a shrewd grin. "I'll retract."

She then saunters across the courtroom floor, her face painted with contemplation. "Mr. Warren, I couldn't help but notice the tender relationship you seem to have with your wife." She gestures toward Lisa Warren.

Michael Warren straightens in his chair. "We've been married ten years, next June. I love my wife very much."

"And I suppose at times you send your wife flowers? Or maybe buy her jewelry?"

The coach's expression turns wary. "Sometimes."

"To mark special occasions and such, I would imagine. Tell me, did you do anything like that to celebrate when you recently discovered you were going to be parents?"

Michael Warren glances at Jake Preston. "Yes. I sent her a dozen red roses."

"Mr. Warren, let's cut to the chase, shall we?" Maddy's voice slices through the tension in the room. "Did you have sexual relations with Pearl Graeber?"

My breath catches. I watch Jake Preston lift from his seat. "Objection. Asked and answered."

Maddy looks at opposing counsel in the same manner she would a naughty child. "Not so. Earlier, I asked if he was ever alone with Pearl." She squares herself directly in front of Michael Warren. "Now, I'm asking you if you ever had sexual relations with Pearl Graeber."

The coach's cheeks go taut. "No. No, I did not."

"Did you make Pearl Graeber pregnant?"

"No," he thunders. "Absolutely not." His voice booms off the granite pillars.

"Did you place or receive calls on your cell phone from Pearl Graeber a total of twenty-two times over the course of the four months prior to Pearl Graeber's death?"

"I—I talked to her on the phone. I don't know how many times." He rubs his cheek. "Not that many."

Maddy points her finger at him. "Were you on the phone with my clients' daughter on the morning of January twenty-six at approximately five o'clock a.m., when the vehicle she was driving careened into a field, tossing her out, and breaking her neck? An event that ultimately caused her demise?"

"That doesn't prove I had any kind of romantic involvement with the girl."

Maddy whips around and marches to our table. She slides a small piece of paper from a file and walks forward. "Do you recognize this, Mr. Warren?"

He takes the paper from her hand. His brows knit as his eyes quickly scan the document.

"Do you recognize that receipt, Mr. Warren?"

The coach's face drains of color. "So? It's a receipt for some jewelry."

"Can you tell us who issued that receipt?"

Several seconds tick by before he responds. "Jaycee Jewelers."

"And, darlin', can you remind this court who owns Jaycee Jewelers?"

A rumble of disturbance ripples through the courtroom. Out of the corner of my eye, I see Lisa Warren stand and walk out the door.

Jake Preston leans back in his chair, his fingers steepled. Next to him, Alexa Dean directs a blank stare at the witness stand.

I hold my breath, waiting for Maddy's next question.

"Mr. Warren? A response please?"

"Joe and Connie Anderson."

"Who?" she asks.

"The Andersons," he repeats.

"For the jury's benefit," Maddy says, "Joe Anderson—the school board member who testified earlier in this proceeding?"

Michael Warren nods.

"We need an answer for the court reporter, please," Judge Canton reminds him.

He clears his throat. "Yes. That Joe Anderson."

I sneak a glance back at Steve. Mother's lips slide into a sly smile.

"Does the receipt you now hold in your hand reflect a purchase you made last December?"

"Uh—I'm not sure."

Maddy's eyebrows lift. "You're not sure? Isn't that your credit card number?"

"Yes," he admits. "I purchased a bracelet."

Maddy walks over to me. She whispers and asks me to give her the bracelet off my arm. I comply and she holds the gold trinket high for all to see. "This bracelet? The one you paid to have engraved *FOREVER YOURS*?"

Michael Warren nods and says in a voice barely audible, "Yes."

Jake Preston stands and buttons his suit jacket. "Your Honor. The defense would like a recess at this time."

Judge Canton looks over her glasses. "Yes, I bet you do."

MADDY SWEEPS into her conference room. She claps her hands together. "We have an offer."

Steve pounds the table. "Yes. I knew it." His face breaks into a wide smile. "That's great."

"Let's not celebrate just yet," Mother cautions. "What is their offer?"

Maddy slides into a thick leather chair at the head of the table. "Several times more than anything I expect the jury would have awarded—especially given what little actual evidence we had available and the character assassination we expected the defense to pull."

Steve shakes his head. "Elaine, I've got to give it to you. How in the world did you find out about that bracelet?"

Mother tucks a stray hair back in place. "Sending Christmas chocolates to the girl who cleans my rings each year turned out to be quite valuable." She looks in my direction. "Barrie dear, we won. You're supposed to be happy."

"What's the catch?" I ask.

Maddy leans back and clasps her hands across her chest. "What do you mean, sweet thing?"

"I mean, so the insurance company ponies up a pile of money. What consequences will Michael Warren and Joe Anderson suffer?"

Steve gives me one of his looks. "Now Barrie, don't you think we've gone far—"

"We? I didn't drag my feet on all this and spend weeks in Cabo."

Mother reaches across the table and clasps my hand with her own. "Let it go, sweetheart."

I'm confused. Who is this woman? Did someone kidnap my mother and whisk her off to a foreign country, leaving this stranger who looks just like her?

"Honey, let it go," she repeats. "I've watched over the years, and this man has always been there for you. Take some advice. Don't let anger and resentment build. It'll wreck what you've got."

I don't know what surprises me more, the fact my mother called me sweetheart or that she's actually defending Steve. Regardless, I squeeze her hand and step into my own foreign territory. "I love you, Mom."

Her eyes glisten. “I love you too, baby.”

I turn to Maddy. “Just tell me Michael Warren will never be allowed to teach or coach in settings where he has access to young girls ever again.”

Maddy assures me she’ll handle that part of the negotiation to my satisfaction. We give each other a quick hug. The door opens and Maddy’s receptionist enters carrying a tray of champagne flutes filled with bubbly.

We each take a glass and prepare to toast when Maddy gets a telephone call.

“Excuse me,” she says. “I’ll be right back.”

Minutes later, she returns. “That was Mr. Voorhees. The prosecutor’s office believes they have enough evidence to proceed with criminal charges against Michael Warren. But don’t worry, there won’t likely be another trial. Voorhees says Jake Preston has already contacted him about a plea deal.”

She grabs her glass of champagne.

We clink and take a celebratory sip.

I know I should feel elated, but strangely I don’t. Even after all this, I sit here without my daughter. And now, there will be a little child raised without a father.

In situations like these, no one really wins.

44

I glance out over the nearly filled auditorium from the wings of the stage.

In the front row sits Mother, her handbag tucked neatly in her lap. Next to her, Aaron watches with anticipation. To his right, Tess spots me. She leans across her husband and waves wildly.

I wiggle my fingers back as inconspicuously as possible.

"Are you ready for this, sweetheart?" Steve rubs my shoulders.

I nod as a man steps to the microphone. The lights dim slightly and he clears his throat. "Good evening, everyone. I'd like to thank all of you for making time out of your busy schedules to travel all the way to Philadelphia for the Tenth Annual National Symposium of High School Counselors. My name is Leonard Aldridge and we have a special night dedicated to a very important topic—educator sexual abuse of underage students.

"You might recognize our keynote speaker from her appearances on the popular Seattle talk show *Let's Talk About It.* Barrie

Graeber is not only a respected high school counselor in her state, but a mother who has experienced this tragedy first hand.

"Because of her courageous candor, much needed light has been shed on the epidemic of teachers and coaches who cross the line of appropriate behavior. She tirelessly promotes awareness and serves on an adjunct basis with lawmakers to enact legislation that will hopefully curb the outrageous behavior of those who fail to understand students are off limits. Now please, help me welcome Mrs. Graeber."

Applause echoes through the auditorium, the pulse matching my beating heart.

I swallow and step into the light. At the microphone, I thank everyone for inviting me to speak. Then, I clear my throat. "I'd like to start by telling you about my daughter.

"I named her Pearl.

"From the moment the nurse placed that tiny infant in my arms, I knew no ordinary name would do. I wanted to call her something special. Something unique.

"When a grain of sand enters an oyster shell, the oyster reacts by surrounding the particle with layers of protective coating. The more numerous the layers, the finer the luster, and the more impenetrable the shell—resulting in a thing of rare beauty.

"It fit her, this name.

"The day my precious Pearl entered this world, I said goodbye to my heart. It would not be the last time . . . "

EPILOGUE

Hey, darlin'—Maddy Crane here. Kellie and I hope you enjoyed reading Mother of Pearl.

We're excited to announce I'll be joining y'all once again in Kellie's new **SUN VALLEY SERIES!** All you sweet things are invited to join us in America's premier ski resort for some highly emotional stories with happily-ever-after endings!

Check out these exciting new books at Kellie's website: www.kelliecoatesgilbert.com

Better yet, scoot on over and get your copies NOW!

Download a FREE copy of **SISTERS** (Sun Valley Series, Book 1) at your favorite retailer by clicking here!

Buy **OTHERWISE ENGAGED** (A Love on Vacation book) at your favorite retailer by clicking here!

Sign up for notices of **Kellie's upcoming releases** by clicking here!

Hope to see you soon, sweet thing!

~Maddy "Mad Dog" Crane

A BRIEF NOTE FROM THE AUTHOR

Thank you for reading *Mother of Pearl.* I hope you feel your time was well spent.

A few of you may have experienced tragedy and are living through your own personal grief. I pray God eases your pain. If you've lost a child, I highly recommend the resources of Compassionate Friends. No one should walk this journey alone. www.compassionatefriends.org

If you are a student who has encountered inappropriate behavior from a teacher or coach, tell someone. Right away. Let your parents or a trusted adult know what is going on. These kinds of relationships lead to nowhere good.

In the event you are an adult who has crossed the line, or who is tempted to leap into inappropriate territory—please stop and count the cost. To the minor, to you, and to the families involved.

I want to express gratitude for the people who shared their expertise and technical information: Alesha L. Lind, Victim Witness Coordinator, Canyon County Sheriff's Office, Caldwell, Idaho; Vickie DeGeus-Morris, Canyon County Coroner, Caldwell, Idaho; and Sherry B. Bithell, Ed.D., author of Educator

Sexual Abuse, A Guide for Prevention in the Schools, Tudor House Publishing.

Big thanks to Jane Thornton and the teachers, counselors and coaching staff at Cedar Hill High School, Cedar Hill, Texas who allowed me a peek into their world.

Finally, I want to thank a girl named Mekayla, who inspired this story, at least in part. May you rest in peace, sweet girl.

Please check out my other novels and new releases at www.kelliecoatesgilbert.com

~Kellie

DISCUSSION QUESTIONS

1. Who is your favorite character in the book? Why?

2. Barrie claims "mothering is not for cowards." If you're a mother, how have you found that to be true?

3. Barrie's relationship with her own mother is complex, and often tense. Why do you think that is?

4. What do you think contributed to Barrie's mother finally lending her support in the effort to seek justice for Pearl?

5. Jackie Hohman is a constant support to Barrie. What examples did you recognize?

6. How do you think Jackie's faith played into her ability to come alongside Barrie when she really needed a friend? Especially in those times when Barrie wasn't kind in return?

7. Why did Barrie view some people's sympathy as a *pity-party* and their prayers were seen as a *holy distribution center?* Do you think there was any truth to her beliefs?

8. Barrie's mother refuses to acknowledge her husband's alcoholism. Why do you think that is? What effect did that have on Barrie?

9. Grief can have a profound effect on a marriage. Why do

you think Barrie and Steve reacted so differently to their family tragedy?

10. What signs did you recognize that Aaron was silently struggling with his own grief? Why do you think Barrie had a difficult time being there for her son in the aftermath of the tragedy?

11. This book explores an ugly reality we see in the news all too often. What can society do to curb educators from blurring the boundaries with students?

12. In Barrie's shoes, would you have filed a civil law suit? Why, or why not?

13. What impact did Troy's character have on you as a reader?

14. Why do you think Barrie struggled to embrace faith? How did that hinder her emotional healing?

15. In chapter thirty-five, Barrie visits the accident site. The book reads:

A v-shaped line of geese flies overhead in the direction of the river. They flap their wings heading for some far off destiny, their honking a plaintive call to those below.

What is significant about that particular passage?

16. Where do you believe people go after they die? Why?